CHAOS: COLLISION OF REALMS

BOOK I
MONICA RED

MONICA DILLENBURG

TO MY WHOLE WORLD, JOSEPHINE

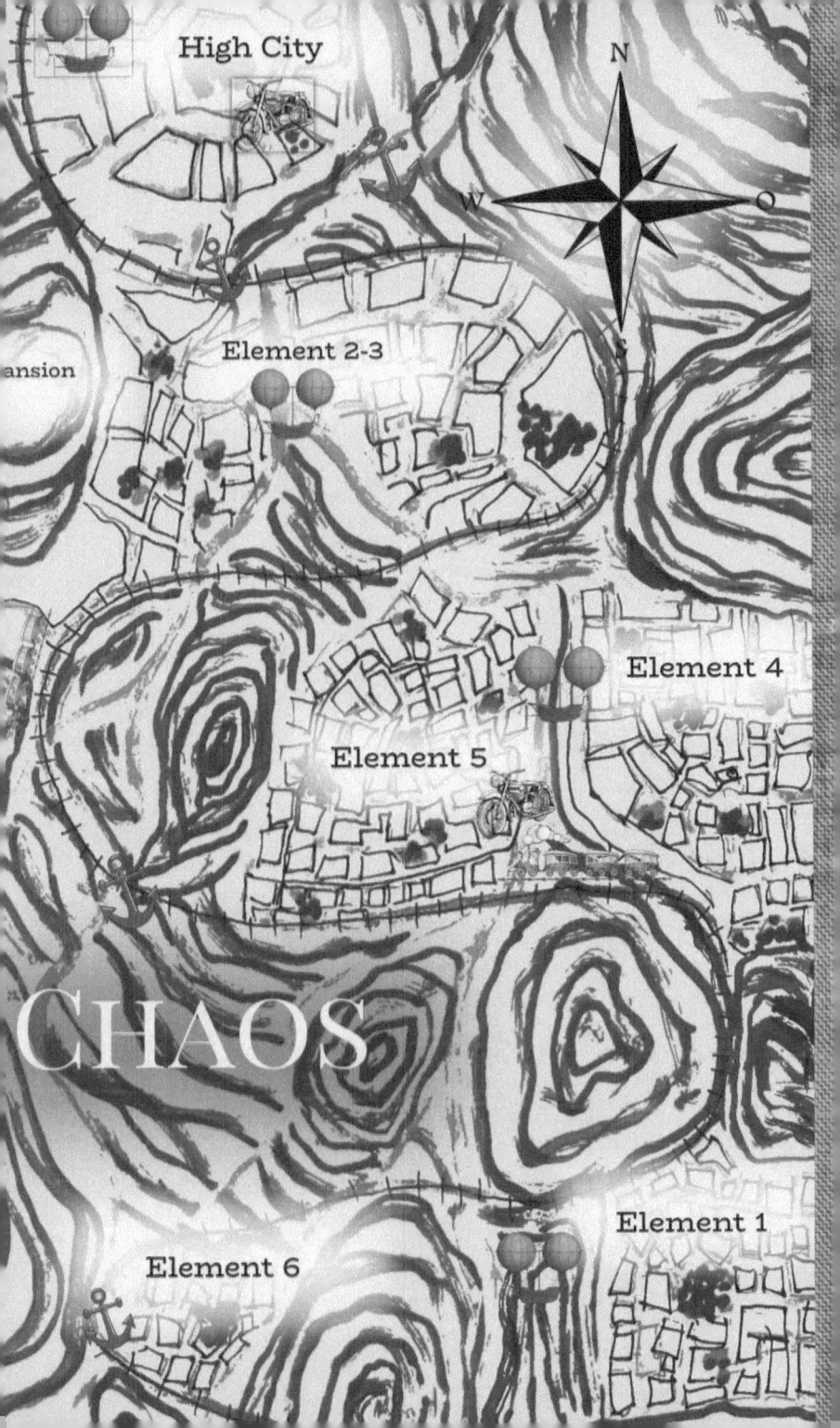

Manifesto

> Chaos happens when the present determines the future, but the approximate present does not approximately determine the future.
>
> Edward Lorenz[1]

Historians have said that our world was once a single realm. Both known sides once existed together, living in a certain level of harmony. A cosmic event created the Barrier that separated our world into two realms: Axiom and Chaos. The division fractured the natural resources of our world and generated an energy wave so powerful that each realm became invisible to the other. Most historians agree that the Barrier holds the balance that allows us to coexist—even when we never meet.

Contrary to this, legend says that in the beginning, chaos ruled everywhere.

Poisonous plants were deadly to humans, and dangerous animals freely roamed the terrain. The high humidity masked the sunlight, and as a result, it rained and snowed frequently. Life was dangerous, and survival was uncertain. According to the believers, the Maker—our creator—grew weary and drew a line through our world. Chaos was punished and forced to live with the monsters it had created. Axiom was rewarded, enjoying the light and warmth of the sun.

Chaos and Axiom are twin realms that coexist thanks to the Barrier containing the energy wave that supposedly passes between them. Without it, both realms would collapse. The great catastrophe of the year 188A22, known as the Disruption, brought dire consequences to both. Our natural resources turned invasive, and parts of our cities collapsed into each other. Peace became a distant dream.

Nevertheless, we kept testing what was left of the Barrier. Resources such as water and food are still trafficked between realms. The powers born from the Disruption continue to destroy everything in their path. The Agency, once our defender, now seeks to control both realms, favoring its own side—Axiom—and hoping to establish a strong regime. Axiom's government wants to conquer and use Chaos as its supplier. The Corrupts, the crime organization, are the only ones helping the victims, though—as expected—their intentions are questionable.

Tom Umbrar-Ment knew all of this. He believed the Big One—his name for the Maker—wouldn't have punished one realm over the other. He also believed that the truth about our world must lie somewhere in between all these versions.

Tom seemed to have found a way. It is only fair to try it.

Jessica Hiem-Sagac
Chaos-Axiom Collision
188A23 Year, Week 19

1. Edward Lorenz, American mathematician and meteorologist best known as the founder of the chaos theory.

Axiom Realm

A year ago: 188A22 Year,
(a year before)

Week 17, Second day, Morning[1]

Tom Umbrar-Ment rolled to his side and turned off his radio. He exhaled, wondering why it bothered him so much when anyone in the news tried to simplify their reality. Another irresponsible authority in Chaos had caused a flood in Axiom's Sector 15.

The government, the broadcast—everyone—loved to pretend Axiom was perfect and Chaos was the problem. Tom sighed. Why couldn't he accept that, too? Why did he care so much? He exhaled again, avoiding the well-known answer. He didn't trust his government or the Agency and hated the entitled behavior of most in Axiom.

With a grunt, he rolled onto his back but stayed in bed. Mornings weren't his favorite time—especially after the long hours of the day before. He would have rather stayed at home, but he had no choice. It was the wedding weekend, and he had a project to finish by the end of the month. He sat up and rubbed his face. The sharpness of the new whiskers made him groan—another reason he hated mornings.

He got up and opened his arms wide, but his muscles sent sharp warnings through his shoulders. There was no point in stretching his legs; that would only make him feel worse. It didn't matter how much he worked every day—installing a new floor was a full workout, and his body loved to remind him of it for days.

As he stood, he remembered his yearly antidote appointment, making him roll his eyes and wish it were already the week after. He needed that ridiculous requirement to build near the Barrier—another way for Axiom to pretend that everything bad came from Chaos, even though everyone knew those nasty, venomous, slippery ophidents [2] lived in both realms.

The events of the day ahead flooded his mind as he walked toward the bathroom, and he hit his head on the stupid hanging plant in his apartment. He should have thrown it away when Charlotte ended everything. Now that pot seemed to exist solely to remind him of his height—and his inability to stay in a relationship.

He pushed the pot to the side, and a new branch poked his eye. That was the third groan of the day, and he hadn't even made it to the shower. At least the mirror in the bathroom confirmed his eyeball was still in its socket.

A deep sigh escaped him when the image of a girl he avoided thinking about came to mind.

"You know, few people have that deep ombré eye color." The memory of Jess's sweet, kind voice was as vivid as the image of her beautiful face illuminated by the sun outside her mother's old house.

He should have taken the compliment—or argued that the way her wavy hair shimmered in the sunlight, almost in different tones, was an even more unique color. Instead, he mocked the comment and ignored his longing to be with her.

"That's dumb. I see a pair all the time," he had replied, not daring to lift his eyes from the bottle in his hand.

He thought he knew better. She was Bill's little sister, and Bill was his best friend. More importantly, he had nothing to offer but trouble. It was best to stay away from her.

He clenched his fist, and even after all these years, the desire to hit the mirror ran through his veins. He'd behaved like a jerk to Jess many times after, and he couldn't even blame teenage immaturity for it.

He rubbed his short hair and continued to the shower. It was going to be a long week. For once, the flooring project seemed more appealing.

Chaos

Second day, Night

J ESS PRESSED HER BACK against the wet wall outside the old store, holding her gun up and ready. The screams from Chaos's people and the gunfire from the Corrupts echoed through the narrow alleyways. The image of the aftermath made her stomach turn as her heartbeat pulsed in her ears.

Hundreds of takuosums[3]—the scavenger creatures from the zone—continued to descend from the trees, preparing for the feast to come. Jess swallowed hard to keep the bile from rising in her throat, knowing how many of those bodies would never be recovered whole.

Something had gone horribly wrong. She knew it the moment her Agency partner, Karen Falc-Axon, walked into her room less than an hour ago—and the problem grew when she had to call for backup. The Agency should have known about any agent extractions, especially those ending an undercover mission involving the Chief of the Corrupts' son, his missing father, and an unavoidable confrontation.

"Put it down, you idiot!" Karen shouted from the other side of the alley, stepping out into the open.

Jess shook her head and swore under her breath. There was no way their reinforcements would arrive in less than four minutes. Karen should have known that, too.

"What the photons?!" a male voice yelled.

A burst of shots followed, drowning out the screams in the alley.

"I told you to put it down," Karen said.

Jess exhaled and peeked around the corner. From her hiding spot, she had a clear view of the Corrupt man in front of Karen. He had to be at least two heads taller and three times her new size. Since her husband's death, Karen had put on weight, and her behavior had grown erratic at times—like right now.

Another barrage of shots exploded, this time closer to Jess. A few takuosums ran around the corner, unaware of her presence. One of them stepped on her foot, its wet nose brushing her knee as its long fur and sharp claws grazed her leg. It vanished as quickly as it had appeared, climbing up the wall and rocks ahead. She was lucky—those things could have killed her within seconds.

Jess took a deep breath and counted down from five as she exhaled.

The man shouted, "Photonic idiot! I'm going to—"

A single shot from Jess's gun struck his forehead, snapping his head back at a strange angle. His body hit the street with a heavy thud that echoed through the alley. For a second, everything went silent—until every bullet from windows, balconies, and doors turned toward her.

Jess opened fire blindly, giving herself a chance to find Karen.

The ground quaked—common in the Chaos Realm—and the sudden movement stopped the attack, sending some of her assailants and several takuosums tumbling to the ground. Large pieces of concrete fell, and the smell of rotten water from the underground filled her nostrils. She ran back a block before finding cover behind a building.

She swore again and reloaded her gun. They knew where she was and could reach her. But her concern wasn't for her own life—it was for the glimpse of Karen's body lying on the ground.

For the next two minutes, Jess took advantage of her remarkable aim and put down several of the Corrupts. Over the years, she had learned not to think about it, but taking a life always left a mark on her—even now, when her need to help her partner outweighed everything else.

The smell of rust and the screech of old hinges filled the air. The Corrupts realized what that sound meant, and although they kept shooting, their running footsteps moved away from Jess. She stepped out just in time to see the familiar light of the opening between realms— portal[4].

As expected, when the Agency arrived in large groups, they landed on the rooftops. It was safer than trusting the realm's unstable ground.

Jess didn't wait for things to calm and dashed toward Karen. The chaos behind her became background noise as she knelt beside her partner. To her horror, Karen's jacket was soaked with a large dark stain on the back. She leaned closer, her eyes filling with tears as she heard Karen's uneven breathing.

"Karen, what were you thinking?" Jess carefully rolled her onto her back with trembling hands. "Where's your vest?"

Blood soaked through her sweater, replacing Karen's usual jasmine perfume with the metallic scent of iron. It shouldn't have happened. Their gear wasn't magical or impenetrable, but the heavy brass would have stopped most of those shots.

"You should've worn your vest."

"Sorry, Jess," Karen whispered, pausing between words to catch her breath. "I thought I could do it, but... not to you. I didn't want to—I just missed him too much."

"Please, Karen, try to—"

"I'm so sorry, Jess. It's my fault..."

Jess sniffled, shaking her head and holding her partner's hand until Karen stopped breathing.

Agents around Jess moved closer. One knelt beside Karen and, passing her hand over her face, closed her eyes. Karen had been a beloved agent, a mentor to many, and her loss was immense.

The rain poured down, white dots nesting in Jess's hair. A chilly breeze picked up the dead essence of the place, and in the distance, the takuosums' screams promised their return.

Peter Nigil-Pax, her captain and old friend, touched her shoulder. "We have to go, Jess. I'm so sorry."

Jess closed her eyes and pressed her nails into her palms. Karen's remains had to stay behind; crossing realms with a dead body was impossible—particles behaved differently with the living.

The Corrupts, being the "good" crime organization they were, wouldn't risk losing their territory. The east end of Chaos was the center of their illegal trafficking operations. A shiver ran down Jess's spine as she tried to erase the image of what those bastards might do to Karen's body. Her only hope was that the takuosums reached her first.

An old prayer came to Jess's mind as she wiped her face. Her father had died when she was fifteen, and her mother had taught her how to ask for peace when loved ones couldn't have a proper funeral.

After Jess completed her training at the Agency's academy, Director Theodore Ven-Larve had appointed Karen as her mentor. Despite being nineteen years older, Karen quickly became a role model. She was the only person who fully supported

Jess's decision to work for the Agency and soon presented her with the chance to become an active agent.

Jess's mother and brother had personal reasons to despise the Agency. They claimed the institution didn't truly work to protect the realm's safety or commerce. Unlike Karen, they had turned their backs on Jess. Losing her mentor made her feel completely alone.

"You know what to do." Peter gave her a faint smile and stepped back.

During training, each agent had to choose an object as their portal key to cross between realms. They kept the choice secret, sharing it only with their partners. After Jess became an active agent, Karen had been assigned as hers. Now that Karen was gone, her key had become a relic[5], and the energy stored from years of travel between realms was too dangerous to leave behind.

Karen's forehead was still warm when Jess kissed it. "I hope you find him on the other side," she whispered. It took all her strength not to fall apart.

Jess placed Karen's key in her pocket, its power leaving a faint electric tingle in her hand. It wasn't surprising—Karen had been an outstanding agent, and her key had absorbed immense energy over the years. In the wrong hands, it could be catastrophic. The only safe way to release its power was to bring it to the Welder—one of the highest positions in the Agency and the only person with access to the energy wave of their world. This was now Jess's responsibility.

With one last look at her mentor, Jess followed the others up the metal ladder. She needed to reach Main City—and soon—for everyone's safety.

Peter stood beside her as he opened the portal to Axiom, her home realm, with an object she couldn't see. Jess bit her lower lip as the bright, almost blinding white light opened before them. It had been too long since she'd laid eyes on it, and she couldn't shake the feeling that the twist in her gut wasn't yearning, but foreboding.

"Something's off, Jess," Peter murmured. "I need to figure it out. In the meantime, these are your orders. You're attending your brother's wedding. On the first day, you'll bring the relic to its final destination."

Jess stared at him, her mind numb as she pieced his words together. Her brother's wedding—something she hadn't even known about until a couple of hours ago, when Karen told her she had declined the invitation in her name—was now part of her mission. Her shoulders grew heavier.

There was a reason she hadn't talked to her brother for years. Bill was bound to throw a tantrum when she showed up after changing her plans at the last second. Now she'd be walking into his special day uninvited. Hopefully, at least their mother would be slightly happy to see her.

1. The assignment of numerical values to the days of the week resulted from numerous intergovernmental discussions among realms on the subject of naming and language use. Rather than employing the term Monday, they make use of "First," and continue this pattern for the remaining days.

2. Ophidents; poisonous creeping reptiles. It inhabits the wooded regions of the Chaos and Axiom meadows, particularly near the Barrier. Poisoning by this creature ranges from severe to fatal. An annual protective antidote is required for those who work or live in these areas. Aggression level: 5 out 5

3. Takuosums; native mammal with extremely strong front limbs and claws, which allow them to burrow quickly with great power. It has a fur coat and a toxic array of spines. Capable of surviving in subterranean areas and a remarkable resilience to high oxygen concentrations but a limited resistance to light. An encounter with these creatures can be deadly due to their behavioral pattern of hunting in large groups, isolating their target and using poison to subdue and finally immobilize it. It is mandatory to report them when found in cities or transportation systems. Aggression level: 4 out 5

4. Portal, an induce opening into the realm's energy that pushes the particles from one realm into the other, allowing a person(s) to cross between realms.

5. Relic, the given name to a portal-key when its owner dies. The power obtained through years of service is retained within the object until it is reintegrated into the energy wave. It is required to release this energy without hesitation, since this power source is open for anyone's use.

3

Axiom Realm

S ummers in Axiom meant plenty of sunshine and high temperatures in the middle of the day, but wonderful evenings when the breeze from the Western Ocean reached every corner of the realm. Axiom's people took pride in this and pitied those in Chaos, who, as far as they knew, lived in an eternal winter.

Tom disliked gossiping about things he didn't understand but agreed that the weather was worth enjoying. Working under the sun had never bothered him.

"Done early?" Frank Ge-Arje asked.

"I am, but you're not," Tom said. "We need to finish by the end of the month. That's what... two weeks from today?"

Frank waved at him and kept walking.

Tom shook his head as he tossed his work gloves into the back of his truck and picked up his toolbox. The house was a critical project for their company, TowerUp. Even though Tom was a co-owner with Bill, his friend had, without consulting him, allowed the client to pay for almost everything in advance and signed a contract with a fixed deadline. Tom feared the harsh consequences if they failed to finish on time.

Not for the first time, he wished Bill had chosen a different month to get married. His best friend was useless on-site—he worked better in marketing and administration. But still, if it weren't for the wedding, Tom would have had another full week to finish the house.

He walked inside, groaning at the missing windows, half-painted walls, bare plywood floors, and the gaping holes for kitchen appliances. The finishes were their company's signature, and everything depended on him. There was too much work left to do. Frank was a good worker, but only when supervised. Tom doubted he'd remember to get the materials for next week's work—another crucial detail.

He pushed his hair back, exhaling. They could lose their company if this contract failed.

"Relax, Tom," Frank said, walking down the stairs with a bucket of paint in each hand. "I got this! It'll be done on time. Then we'll lie to Bill so he can freak out for a change."

"You want to ruin his honeymoon?"

"Hey! That son of the void ruined my weekend and didn't even invite me to his stupid wedding."

"You go! I'll work here."

Frank snorted and shouted from the next room, "You wish!"

Tom grabbed his suit from the closet. He didn't have time to drive home and still beat the traffic to Main City. The plastic bag protecting the suit was speckled with paint and sawdust. Not ideal, but the alternative was leaving it in his truck—a worse option, given what had happened to his now-destroyed hat. Good thing he wasn't a fashionable man, unlike Bill. He just hoped the solvent smell would fade before the wedding. Why couldn't they marry in their own sector?

He liked Arlett when he met her years ago, and until last month, when the wedding planning began, she had seemed perfectly sane. Now, he wasn't so sure.

An hour past his planned departure time, Tom finally drove out of the small settlement. The newscast on his truck's old-fashioned audio stream ended, and a romantic song came on. He tightened his grip on the wheel and shook his head. He knew Bill loved his fiancée, but his commitment had always been questionable. Even Tom's short-lived relationship with Charlotte a few months ago was a love story in comparison. Part of him still debated whether he should warn Arlett.

An incoming call alert appeared on the dashboard. Thankful for the distraction, he picked up the transmitter.

"So, did you finish it?"

"Bill! My day is going great, too. Thanks for asking. I haven't been working my butt off for two weeks—I was just lying in the sun," Tom said.

"Don't be so dramatic! I'm showing you how much I care about our business."

Tom chuckled as he took the ramp to the third level of the freeway. "Sure! I appreciate your interest. After all, you signed the stupid contract with the ridiculous deadline during your freaking wedding week."

"It's a great contract. We get this guy as a client, and we'll secure our—Tom, wait." The sound became muffled, and Tom only caught fragments. "Yes. Here. Tell them... I'm sure... just a minute."

Tom pressed down on the pedal, accelerating his truck, and rested his elbow on the door. Axiom's traffic system reserved the third level of the freeway for non-stop, long-distance trips between sectors—an area with no speed limit. If you could drive fast, you should. It scared most drivers, but he loved it.

"Sorry about that," Bill said.

"Are you at the office?"

"Of course not! Although I wish I was. I'm in the Village. [1] That was more wedding stuff."

Tom laughed—extra loud and longer than necessary.

"You think it's funny? Wait for this. Since I'm stuck here with plate and flower emergencies, I need you to do something for me."

"Plates and what? What emergencies could flowers possibly have?"

"I have little time here, so..." Bill cleared his throat, and a burst of white noise crackled through the speaker. When he spoke again, his voice was clearer and closer. "As expected, we have some family drama. She always wants to be the center of attention."

Tom rolled up his sleeves as his body tensed. "Jess?"

"Photons, yes! I'm talking about Jess. She did it again."

Whatever the issue was, Tom would bet it was Bill's fault. His best friend was a bit of a snob but mostly easygoing—until it came to his younger sister. Then he turned into a jerk.

"So, Mom called yesterday morning. Apparently, Jessica wants to attend the wedding. The fancy agent is lowering herself to accept our invitation. Obviously, I told Mom I didn't want her there, and she burst into tears, which mortified Arlett and—" Bill huffed loudly. "If it weren't for Mom, I'd have sent my stupid sister you-know-where years ago. And get this—Mom told me this morning that I need to pick Jessica up from the airport! What the photons?!"

Tom sighed, shaking his head. His own relationship with Jess was even worse than the one between the Hiem-Sagac siblings. He didn't blame her for hating him—he'd earned that wound himself.

"Well, I'll be arriving at the Village in about two hours. I can handle whatever emergencies there are when I get there."

"Oh no. I need you to pick her up."

"What?" Tom sat forward and stared at the dashboard. "You've lost it, right? Bill, you know how Jess feels about me these days."

"Nonsense. Also, the airport's on your way to Main City."

"It is not! I'd have to cross Main City to get there."

"Really? I have to cross Main City too," Bill said.

Tom rolled his eyes. When he didn't answer, Bill took his silence as agreement.

"Great! Her plane lands in two hours, so you've got plenty of time."

"Two hours? Photons, Bill! I won't make it."

"With how you drive? You'll be waiting for a while."

"I don't think it's a good idea, Bill. Arlett might need me—the best man must have some—"

"Look at you, scared of my little sister. So, be there in two hours. She's coming from Sector 2." Bill snorted. "I guess agents these days enjoy the luxury beaches, huh?"

Bill hung up with a laugh, and the silence in the truck sent a chill down Tom's spine. He hated thinking about the past, and Jess was the definition of it. Was he supposed to ignore everything that had happened between them? Everything they had shared?

Sure, the last time he'd seen her was over a year ago—the night Bill introduced her to Arlett—but that had been another fiasco, courtesy of Bill's stupidity. He hadn't been alone with her since visiting her at the Agency—and that had ended as one of the worst days of his life. How had he gone from seeing her every weekend to not talking for years?

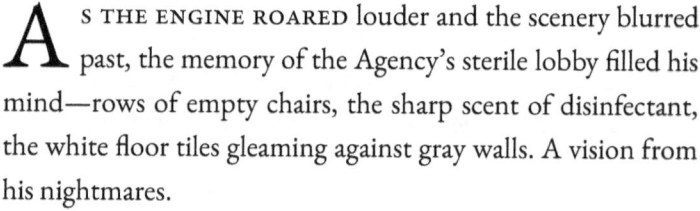

A S THE ENGINE ROARED louder and the scenery blurred past, the memory of the Agency's sterile lobby filled his mind—rows of empty chairs, the sharp scent of disinfectant, the white floor tiles gleaming against gray walls. A vision from his nightmares.

His grandfather had been murdered in one of the most horrific crimes in Sector 8, and the local police had ruled it an accident. Tom was at Agency headquarters because, on the day of the funeral, he'd accused the Agency—and Jess—of his grandfather's death. He'd made things worse by implying that he hated her for working for them and had not-so-politely told her to leave.

A month later, an agent came to his door with new findings about the accident, and Tom ran out of excuses not to apologize.

A day later, he traveled to the Agency in Main City to find her.

"Can I help you?" a man around his age asked from behind a thick pane of glass.

Tom's hands were slick with sweat, and he was afraid to take them out of his pockets. "Is Jess—" He cleared his throat. "Sorry. I'm looking for Agent Jessica Hiem-Sagac."

The agent lifted an eyebrow, stared for a moment, then picked up a receiver and dialed a code.

Tom's heartbeat thudded in his skull, and he couldn't stand still. The man could easily have mistaken him for a suspect. Along with fighting the Corrupts and supposedly protecting interrealm commerce, the Agency also maintained Axiom's internal safety—and that day, Tom's behavior had been erratic.

"Let me see if she's in this zone." The agent pointed at the line of chairs. "Take a seat there."

Tom took a step back, staring at the empty seats.

"Sir?" another agent called, and his legs froze.

"Yes, sorry... I'm looking for—"

"Jessica, I know," she said, "but she doesn't work in this building anymore, Mister...?"

He shook his head, nauseated. "Um... Umbrar-Ment. Tom Umbrar-Ment. What do you mean, she doesn't work here anymore?"

"Let me call again." She smiled before walking away.

He couldn't say whether it was minutes or hours later, but it felt like forever before he heard her voice.

"Tom?"

Jess's voice had always put him at ease, and after years apart, all his feelings for her rushed back. Her delicate frame, her familiar freckled skin, the way her hair shone in different tones—it all made his heartbeat quicken. But her hard expression and Agency uniform turned his smile into a tight line.

"Jess... why are you wearing—can we talk?" he stammered.

She looked past him and waved at the front desk agent, who couldn't hide his stupid grin as he waved back. Tom's mouth tasted bitter.

"Is everybody all right?" Jess asked.

"Yes." Tom stared at her for a second and pushed his hair back. "Yes, sorry. Of course, everything's fine. I just wanted... Don't you work in investigation or something? Do you have to wear that uniform?"

"I'm not in research anymore." Jess exhaled and crossed her arms. "I switched positions a few weeks ago. Listen, I'm about to cross over, so please—what are you doing here?"

Tom's world shifted in that moment. Concern for her safety flooded his mind. Research meant staying in Axiom, safe. Being an active agent meant traveling between realms—and crossing into Chaos meant real danger.

"What? Why? I thought you wanted to improve the resource exchange between realms?"

Jess shook her head. "I thought you believed the Agency was just a criminal organization that killed innocents. Isn't that what you told me I was doing?"

Tom rubbed the back of his neck, glancing around. Nobody cared about their conversation, but he still felt judged.

"Can we talk somewhere else? I want to thank—"

"Thank me for investigating your grandpa's death? No need. I didn't do it."

"Well, maybe you didn't, but I'm sure you're the one who asked for—"

"Hey, H.S., we're leaving," a woman yelled from the entrance.

"I have to go." Jess avoided his gaze, pushing a strand of hair behind her ear.

"Jess, at least let me apologize for my behavior at the funeral."

She shook her head and walked away. When she reached the door, she turned back and said, "I hope the investigation helps a little. For what it's worth, I'm really sorry for your loss."

That day, Jess had opened another void in his heart—one that echoed the loss of his grandfather.

Although Tom thought he wasn't ready to see her again, he found himself driving well above the speed limit on the third level of the highway.

AXIOM

188A22 YEAR, WEEK 17

AFTERNOON

B ILL HAD LIED ABOUT being at the Village—but not about getting to the airport on time. He just prayed he could get back before Tom. Their client had called, asking for a last-minute meeting, and there was no way he could refuse.

"Our plans have changed," the man said from the velvet couch in his office.

"Wait. What? Why?" Bill paced around the room. "The house will be done by the deadline. I talked to my contractor, and he will—"

"Your contractor? I thought he was your partner?"

"Well, yes! That's what I meant." Bill rubbed his face and wished the man's smile would give him some clue about his intentions.

"I'm not worried about the house, Mr. Hiem-Sagac. I'm adding something new to our deal."

Tom would kill him if their client added anything else to the project. Bill pushed his hair back, the acid from his breakfast rising in his throat.

"We could do it, but we may have to extend the timeframe."

"No extensions."

Bill loosened his tie and cleared his throat. "I'm not sure if this—"

"No reason to be concerned. This has nothing to do with the house. Your contractor won't get upset. He won't even hear about it."

Tom's warning about wealthy men came to mind, and Bill shivered. Too bad the warning had arrived too late. Their options closed many months ago, not too long after he got engaged.

"Sit back, Bill. This conversation will test your loyalty."

1. The Village, luxury destination sector within Main City, Axiom. The northern ocean's proximity, as well as the exclusive restaurants, clubs, and casinos, make this a popular destination.

4

AXIOM REALM

A MIX OF SOUNDS—ROLLING trunks, squeaking carts, and incomprehensible voices—filled the airport. The swarm of people coming and going, some smiling, others not so much, made Tom want to leave as quickly as possible.

Directional signs, written and illustrated, hung from the high ceilings and walls. The airport was Main City's primary landing sector, with three tramp lines and five official parking ramps. Tom had to take a trolley for six stops from where he'd parked his truck to the baggage claim section.

He barely made it on time, but unlike his trouble finding the right place, he had no trouble spotting Jess. She was adjusting her beret as she stood by the luggage ramp. He stopped in his tracks and took the chance to watch her from a safe distance.

Unlike him, she didn't seem older—just more beautiful. Her posture had the grace of a ballerina, though her movements were slow and careful. She wore a simple pea coat over a white shirt and travel pants, which somehow lifted a weight from Tom's shoulders. Not wearing a uniform had to be a good sign.

She reached for a suitcase from a cart that had just arrived from the gate behind her and walked to the window marked *Special Items*. Tom took a step toward her but stopped when the assistant handed her a peculiar black box after checking her papers.

Tom pressed his lips together and shoved his hands deep into his pockets as he watched Jess pull out a pistol and check its magazine. His stomach twisted when she turned back and picked up a rifle case. She didn't open it, but knelt to check the padlock. He had nothing against guns—unless someone he cared about needed to carry them for their own safety.

"That's all I have for you, Agent."

She signed a paper. "Thank you. Hope you have a nice day."

"You too—and thanks for your service."

Tom frowned. Why couldn't he just be proud of her, like that stupid airport assistant? Was his hatred for the Agency so strong that it included her?

Jess slipped the pistol case into a sack and slung it over her shoulder. After tightening the strap, she picked up the larger case and rolled her suitcase.

She looked up—and Tom lost his breath when their eyes met.

Something was wrong, though.

He wondered how long it had been since she'd eaten a proper meal, or since sunlight had touched her skin. Strange, considering her flight had come from Sector 2, a region known for its beautiful coastlines. She had dark circles under her eyes, and for a moment, he thought they glistened with tears. But the absence of a spark—or even a hint of a smile—kept him from rushing to hug her.

"Hey, girl. How's it going?"

Jess shook her head and walked toward him. "I told my mother I'd find a ride to the stupid Village."

"Well," Tom cleared his throat, "the airport was on my way."

"Really?" She raised an eyebrow, pressing her lips together. "You're telling me the best man hasn't been to the wedding site yet?"

He chuckled and raised his hands. "Hey, someone has to work."

Jess snorted. "So nothing's changed. Bill still thinks he's the boss."

Tom rubbed his chin and glanced at her bags. "Can I help you with that?" He pointed at the rifle case, which looked heavier.

She followed his gaze but stayed quiet. After a deep breath, she looked back at him. "I wish you could, but it's not allowed."

He shook his head and gestured toward the parking ramp. He should've taken the other bag, but why bother? She wasn't just a girl coming home from a trip. And clearly, she wasn't happy to see him. He should have known better.

He walked quickly, silent, lost in thoughts flashing between their younger days—studying together during intermediate school—and the overtired agent walking beside him now. Only when they reached his truck did he realize he hadn't prepared for company; his passenger seat was a mess.

He rushed ahead of her. "Sorry, it's been a while since I've driven with someone." He opened the passenger door and hurried to clear the seat.

"What about Charlotte? Doesn't she ride with you?"

Tom's muscles tensed.

"Sorry," Jess said softly. "Not my place to ask."

"It'll take me a second... photons!" He swore under his breath. If anyone deserved an explanation—or an apology—for

Charlotte, it was Jess. She'd tolerated Charlotte's insults since Bill introduced them years ago at a school party, long before Tom ever dated her. Why was it so hard to talk to Jess? They'd never had trouble before.

He heard the back door open and braced himself for her to sit there—but instead, after loading her luggage, she closed the door and waited for him. A ridiculous, enormous smile spread across his face as he exhaled, feeling like an idiot. Maybe if he told her how much he still cared, things could change between them.

Tom climbed into the truck as Jess got in the passenger seat and stared out the window.

"So—flying? How'd that go? I'm guessing you didn't check out the panoramic section of the zeppelin, right?"

He knew perfectly well why she'd always taken the three-hour train ride instead of a short flight back from school—it wasn't for studying. It was her fear of heights.

Jess shrugged.

Tom backed up the truck and followed the signs through the maze of the parking ramp. It wasn't until they exited into the sunlight that she broke the silence.

"I don't know. The flight was long. Too many connections. Boring. Crowded." She exhaled and stretched her legs. "I can still smell the egg sandwich from the guy next to me."

"Sounds delightful," he said, though she didn't look at him. "Maybe one day I'll finally take one of those."

"How was your trip? I hope my family didn't force you to—"

"It was good. And like I said, the airport was on my way," Tom interrupted.

She narrowed her eyes. "Sure. Who wouldn't love a leisure-ly stroll through that oversized warren and the joy of driving through the city during peak traffic hours?"

"Some walks are worth the effort, Jess." Tom winked at her as he merged onto the freeway. Even with light traffic, they still had at least another hour ahead.

"Did you know all agents have to keep their receptors on at all times?" she said, yawning and covering her mouth before leaning back in the seat. "My mom called me at least five times while I was on the plane. The announcement lady was just as thrilled as I was to answer. All to make sure I was actually coming to the ceremony. At that point, I wanted to ask for a parachute."

Tom laughed. "Coming from you, that's something! And considering the many connections you mentioned, I'm guessing you weren't staying in Sector 2, so how long was your flight?"

She cleared her throat and leaned forward to adjust the sack at her feet.

"What? You can't even tell me that?"

Jess looked away again.

The old fear that had taken root in Tom's mind years ago twisted his stomach.

"So, did you just jump over—or did you really fly here?"

"Tom, I don't lie. I was on a zeppelin, but I—" Her trembling voice made him glance at her. "I can't discuss anything. I'm an agent. We don't talk about our work—you know that."

His jaw tightened as he turned his focus back to the road. *How can anyone live like that—always in danger, never free to talk about it?*

For a while, Axiom's flat green fields lost their charm. The bright sky above the rolling hills turned dull and gray. The only vivid thing left was Tom's growing fear for Jess's life. He hated the danger her job placed her in—especially since she worked in both realms. He could only imagine the kind of conflicts and crimes she faced.

"Does your mom know?" he asked carefully.

She rubbed her temples and sighed. "She has for a while... I thought you told her—"

"I said nothing, Jessica."

"I'm very aware of that. She had a panic attack when she visited me at the hospital."

Tom's heart raced. He sat straighter, glancing at the road and then at her. "The hospital?"

"Bill didn't tell you?" She slid down in her seat, getting more comfortable. "Well, it doesn't matter. It happened a while ago. I'm fine now."

Tom gripped the steering wheel tightly. The air in the cab felt thick, hard to breathe. Bill should have told him Jess had been hospitalized. He had no right to keep that from him. Maybe Tom was Bill's best friend, and maybe he hadn't spoken to Jess in years—but still, she was *his* friend, and Bill knew it.

"Although," Jess said, bringing his attention back, "knowing you never heard of it explains a lot."

"I would have been there, Jess. I hope you know that."

She smiled faintly, her eyes half closed as she yawned again.

He let the sound of the engine fill the silence, burying the questions that swirled in his mind. She needed to rest, and he owed her at least that. He could wait.

Jess was startled awake by the truck door closing. It took her a second to realize she'd fallen asleep—and that she was inside Tom's truck. She shook her head and rubbed her eyes before looking around.

The sun shone brightly, and vivid flowers decorated several pots at the Village's lobby entrance. As soon as she opened the door, a sweet essence and the aroma of grilled meat hit her. People walked in and out of the building, laughing and sipping drinks with little paper umbrellas. Such a different world from the one she'd been living in only two nights before.

"Sorry, I didn't mean to wake you," Tom said. He stood holding the truck door. The overwhelming need to hold on to him hit her again. She turned away and forced her breathing to slow. At least she wasn't standing this time, wondering if her knees would give out.

"You okay?"

Jess nodded. "Just counting before my mom—"

"Jessica Hiem-Sagac!" her mother's voice echoed from the lobby entrance. "You told me they redirected your flight to Ocean-West!"

Tom looked down, trying to hide his laugh.

"Not funny, Tom."

"No, of course not, Amelia," Tom said. "Shame on you, Jess."

Jess pushed Tom out of the way and, ignoring her mother's complaints, wrapped her in a hug. The familiar scent of her mother's perfume and the softness of her short hair against Jess's cheek carried her back to a time when life was simple—when the biggest comment people made was how much the two of them looked alike. For an instant, the world vanished in the safety of her mother's arms.

A beautiful lie she would have loved to live in—but before anyone could ask what was wrong, Jess let her go.

She walked back to Tom's truck. He had left the door open without touching her luggage and was already pulling his things from the trunk. Genuine offers of help didn't come often in her life. Small gestures like that were something she treasured, even when she had to decline them.

"What is that? I can't believe you brought weapons to your brother's wedding!" her mother exclaimed.

Jess rolled her eyes, grabbed her sack, and walked into the building. The artificially cooled air made her shiver. After living in Chaos for more than a year, she'd learned to enjoy the heat whenever she could.

She was almost at the front desk when the elevator bell rang and her brother, Bill, stepped out. Like every time they'd met since she began her Agency training, her muscles tensed, and smiling became harder.

After their father died, her mother had allowed Bill to rewrite the story of what had happened—after all, he was now the head of the family. Bill claimed he had tried to save their father's life after the car accident. In truth, he hadn't even been there. Jess had been the one riding in the ambulance, watching her nearly unrecognizable father die in the hospital a few hours later.

When the police ran their investigation, the facts didn't line up, and they requested the Agency's assistance. Her mother hadn't been happy when they were called into an Agency office in Sector 4—and she'd hated them after the agents uncovered the truth, especially when her brother broke down crying during questioning.

Shortly afterward, they moved to Sector 8, where no one knew them and Bill could maintain his heroic façade.

Jess had been furious, but there was little she could do. She didn't want to lose her mother, and she was just starting her second year of intermediate school at one of the most prestigious academies in Axiom. Thanks to her perfect scores—and her mother's elitist ideals—Jess managed to stay in the same school, even if it meant living away from her family during the week and traveling home every weekend.

Ironically, the only person she'd ever talked to about her father was Tom. But his grandfather had despised the Agency for reasons unknown—and had passed that belief down to his grandson.

"Hey, you finally made it," Bill said, pulling her back to the present.

Though he still cared about appearances and social norms, he seemed weaker and more uncertain than he had the last time they'd shared dinner. The confident boy who once took charge after their father's death had grown into just another man trying to hold things together. No matter how straight he stood or how much he pretended to understand the world, Jess's experience now far exceeded the three-year gap between them.

"I guess I did."

Bill glanced at the large case in her hand, but instead of mocking or scolding her, he simply pointed toward the desk. "You probably need to leave those there. You know, Village's calmness."

She studied him, trying to see beyond his comment.

"Jess! You're here!" Bill's fiancée said, walking up behind him.

It was strange to think her sister-in-law was almost a stranger to her. But, like all of Bill's previous girlfriends, she fit the same pattern—fashionable clothes, long dark hair, not a single freckle under flawless makeup, and eyelashes so long they cast shadows. At least Arlett had seemed kinder than the others—or maybe that was just because Jess had only met her once, when she learned they were engaged.

"Hello, Arlett," Jess said.

"Bill told me you weren't coming!" Arlett's eyes widened as her hands flew to her cheeks. "Oh no! Bill!"

Her brother's expression shifted instantly. "What is it, Ar?" He wrapped an arm around her shoulders and steered her toward the entrance.

Ar. The nickname made Jess's skin prickle, but she didn't have time to dwell on it.

"Can I help you?" the girl behind the front desk asked with a smile.

Jess turned toward her. "Hello. I believe the Agency called earlier to inform you an agent would be arriving—"

"For the Maker! Yes! You must be Agent H.S. I'm so sorry I didn't recognize you."

"Please, it's fine. No need to apologize."

The girl placed a hand over her heart, her eyes misting. "The Agency saved my father. I couldn't—" Her voice broke, and she burst into tears.

"It's all right," Jess said, and when the girl kept crying, she reached out and patted her hand.

"Thank you for your work, Agent H.S."

Jess nodded, tucking a strand of hair behind her ear, and shifted her gaze toward the entrance.

By the door, her mother stood gesturing wildly while Bill talked into his transmitter, holding Arlett close to his shoulder. Tom leaned against his truck with his arms crossed, watching Jess with the same easy smile he'd given her minutes earlier.

"We have the safety ready for you," the girl said, drawing her attention back. "If you can sign this form, I'll take your weapons."

That familiar emptiness in her stomach returned as she set the large case on a rolling cart and pulled her pistol from her sack. But the smaller box inside caught her eye, dragging her mind back to the events from two days ago.

The screams. The stench of decay. The bitterness in her throat. The image of Karen's body lying on the ground made her hands tremble.

"Everything all right?" the girl asked.

Jess swallowed hard and nodded. "Yes, thank you."

In the background, she could hear her mother yelling at Bill—and by his posture, Jess knew it had something to do with her.

5

AXIOM REALM

188A22 YEAR WEEK 17, LATE
AFTERNOON

T OM OPENED THE DOOR to the room and waited for Jess to step inside.

"You don't have to do this. I can find a place to stay," Jess said.

"So your mom can kill me? No way."

"My family needs to stop troubling you. I'm serious, Tom."

"I have no problem sharing this gigantic... chamber? In fact, it makes me feel better. Plus, I couldn't choose a nicer roommate."

Jess felt a flush creep across her cheeks, and she turned away from Tom. The room was enormous, with a full kitchen that had two ovens. The living room featured a stone fireplace taking up the entire wall from floor to ceiling. Several couches were arranged around it, each overloaded with brightly colored cushions, and the balcony held a dining table that stretched beyond her sight, with six chairs.

"No vestibule?" she asked.

"Vestibule?" Tom chuckled as he set his bags down. "You mean the foyer?"

"What's the difference?" Jess said. "And who cares? It doesn't have one."

"Are you sure? Check the bedrooms."

Jess dismissed his comment with a wave of her hand and stared at the view. Main City was always impressive, but from here, the blue ocean was breathtaking.

"How is Bill paying for this?" She turned to face Tom. "Is he paying for this?"

Tom walked behind the kitchen counter and opened the double-sized cooler box. "He has some savings. Do you want something to drink?"

"Bill? Savings?" She sat on the couch, gazing out at the world beyond the glass. "I'd believe it if we were talking about your savings."

"Not mine, Jess." He closed the cooler and leaned on the counter. "The business is doing great, so..."

She stared at him. His eyes were fixed on the bottle in his hand, and his lips had lost their smile—an expression she knew well. He was hiding something from her.

"Are you sure everything is okay?"

He looked up and winked. "Nothing to worry about, *Sunshine*. The company can afford this. And not everyone has these rooms."

It was hard for Jess to stay serious. He'd stopped using her nickname, sunshine, the day she told him she'd been accepted into the Agency. She had missed it ever since.

He leaned back against the wall and crossed his arms, misreading her silence. "We got a great contract and were paid in advance—"

"You don't have to explain." She cleared her throat. "I just don't trust my brother. Especially if he's taking advantage of you."

Tom snorted and shook his head. "I'm fine. You shouldn't worry."

Jess looked back at the city. She didn't want to argue. He had the biggest heart—and her brother abused it. She shouldn't be the only one to notice.

"Look, if it makes you feel better, we—" Tom's transmitter buzzed, and his expression hardened when he saw the caller ID. "Sorry. I have to take this." He answered the call. "Charlotte, what can I do for you?"

He stepped out of the room, and Jess felt a twinge of loneliness and a dull ache in her chest. Charlotte brought back memories of moments that had gone terribly wrong.

She'd never understood what Tom saw in her. The woman laughed like a hyena, cared only about her clothes, and used her head mainly for holding up that mess of curls. Something must have happened, though—because she wasn't with him now. For Tom's sake, Jess hoped it would stay that way.

The tallest building in the city caught her attention. The gray concrete structure towered over everything else, its long diagonal face so steep it looked impossible to stand. That was the point, though. The Agency was an institution built to face the unbearable.

Only on days like this—when things went wrong and her orders seemed questionable—did Jess start to doubt. She rested her head in her hands and closed her eyes. The thought of going back to her life made her tremble, but staying with her family turned her stomach.

"You should rest," Tom said as he walked back in, "or you'll fall asleep during the rehearsal."

She groaned, which made him laugh—and the sound, though welcome, felt strange. As if fragments of her past were trying to reach her present.

He sat on the couch across from her. "Just lean back and close your eyes. I'll wake you when it's time to go... well, maybe a half hour before, so you can get ready?"

"Don't you have to help Bill or something?"

Tom frowned and pressed a hand to his chest. "Are you already kicking me out?"

She shook her head but didn't have the energy to answer. The sunlight streaming through the window and the gentle quiet of the room made her eyelids heavy. Tom's presence put her at ease—a feeling she hadn't had in months. Her mission in the Chaos Realm had kept her in a red zone where sleep was a luxury greater than any stupid wedding.

Tom flipped open the top of the center table. A typewriter folded out from the cover until he locked it down, transforming it into a small workspace. He turned on the light projector, and the surface became a screen.

Though the image appeared backward from her angle, Jess recognized the blueprints of some kind of installation. Notes and equations filled the margins—written in Tom's peculiar handwriting. It was almost a different language, one she'd learned to translate years ago.

"I have to finish something here, but I'll be quiet." He sat forward, holding a pencil between his lips. "Promise not to bother you."

She closed her eyes, smiling to herself. She knew Tom had struggled with his studies. One of her favorite parts of coming home from boarding school on weekends had been helping him. His mother had died when he was barely three, and talking about his father was taboo in his grandfather's house, where he grew up. For years, she and his grandfather had tried to help him see things differently, but Tom had always been ashamed of his dyslexia—a ridiculous thing, considering how wickedly smart he was.

The memory brought back images of books scattered on the floor and easy laughter. His bedroom, her mother's coffee table—those moments warmed her heart. The scent of licorice from his grandfather's house filled her mind, making her mouth water. A soft breeze brushed her hair, and she didn't care whether it belonged to the present or the past. She let herself drift, lost in better times.

Axiom

188A22 Year, Week 17

Evening

T HE SUN WAS SETTING on the horizon outside the window when Jess opened her eyes. Tom's paperwork, typewriter, and screen were still on the center table, but he wasn't there. Everything seemed to be in the same place, even her sack resting at her side. She sat up and steadied her breathing, trying to calm the mental alarms going off in her head.

One of the doors in the room opened, and Jess's heart sped up. She quickly stood and grabbed the nearest heavy object—a flower vase.

"Just in time," Tom said as he walked in, wearing formal pants and buttoning his perfectly ironed shirt. She set the vase down before he noticed. "I really didn't want to wake you, but what can I say? I fear your mother."

Jess thought he should reconsider who he feared. Unlike her mother, she'd been trained—and had actually killed people.

"Your dress is hanging in the bedroom."

"My what? Did you open my suitcase?"

Tom froze, his hands halfway through fixing his tie. "Ah, no! For the Big Guy, no! Someone from the cleaners brought it up. I guess it's from the wedding party. It matches the stupid napkin for my suit."

"Napkin? You mean handkerchief?"

"Sure." He went back to wrestling with his tie. "Whatever it is, it matches your dress."

Jess grabbed her suitcase and walked toward the bathroom. "It must be a mistake. I'm not part of the party."

"Well..." He winked at her, sending butterflies to her stomach. "I'm just the messenger, all right? Arlett felt so bad that she added you to the formal party."

Jess sat back down. Her shoulders slumped, and she covered her eyes with her hands. To protect everyone, her plan had been to bring Karen's relic with her, even if it meant carrying a ridiculously oversized sack. Karen's relic held too much power. Jess couldn't risk losing it. Now she'd have to argue with her mother again.

"Hey, it's not that bad." Tom crouched in front of her. "I'm part of the wedding party, too."

"I can't do it. I can't pretend to smile for stupid pictures when my mission... I have to protect..." She bit her lower lip, fighting back tears.

"Protect who? Hey, listen. I get it—you can't say much. But if someone's in danger, if you have to leave and jump over to the other realm or something, I can talk to your mom. I was joking about being scared of her."

"What? No, Tom..." She exhaled and looked down at the sack between her feet, wishing she didn't have to keep everything secret. "No one's in immediate danger. The safety of our realm depends on me protecting... something. It's a huge part of my life as an agent. My mission's on hold until the First. Sorry, I can't say more."

Tom rubbed his face, but to her surprise, he didn't argue. Instead, he looked at the bag and nodded. "What was your plan?"

The corner of her mouth lifted. "Pretend it was fashionable to wear a sack?"

He laughed and sat on the armrest of the couch. "How about we hide it? I've built one or two secret compartments before. I'll figure something out."

She shook her head, but Tom's firm grip on her arm stopped her.

"Jess, listen. If this is as dangerous as you say, and someone's looking for it, how suspicious would you look at the wedding carrying a huge purse? If we hide it, we could even leave other clues to mislead anyone."

"Clues?" Jess giggled at the childish idea. "I don't think that would work out, but..."

He had a point—a very good one. She covered her face and sighed. Her mind was failing her; the lack of sleep, anger, and grief made it difficult to think clearly.

Peter had told her the Welder wouldn't be ready until the First day. It was strange, considering the danger, but there was nothing she could do. He'd also said she should attend her brother's wedding.

She needed to accept the loss of her mentor and rest after months of undercover work. More importantly, she had to figure out what had really happened two days ago when they were ambushed. In the short term, removing Karen's relic from its protective case would simplify things. It would fit in her pocket, just like it had when she left Chaos. But the sealed box was there to stop its energy from affecting Axiom. She just wished she had more time to find a better plan.

"How horrible is the dress?" she asked with a small smile.

6

Axiom Realm

188A22 Year Week 17,
Fourth day, Night

The light from the energy wave illuminated the spoon near the matches, blurring the line between right and wrong. When the bastard Marshall Neon-10 the Second set a needle on the table, Peter couldn't help grabbing his left arm, which made the son of the void laugh.

"So easy that it almost annoys me," Marshall said with a stupid grin, showing his perfect white teeth.

Peter looked away, but the big bald man with too many scars holding him down punched him in the face. The small room spun, and the metallic taste of blood filled his mouth, making him gag.

"I can do this faster," Marshall said, adjusting his tie. "It's up to you how much it hurts—or how much it costs."

"Go to the void!"

Marshall picked up a match and took a candle from his pocket. The tip flared, lighting a yellow flame. This time, the sound and scent of burning shook Peter's resolve.

"I already know a lot," Marshall said, looking down at him. "I just need a minor detail—and my sources told me you saw it. When you crossed over? Right before you left Karen's body behind?"

Peter's muscles tensed, his hands shaking with the urge to strike that bastard. Marshall tilted his head, smiling. "Don't look at me like that. I didn't do it... but unlike you, I'll figure it out."

Peter swallowed hard as Marshall set the candle on the table.

"Let's see now," Marshall continued. "As you know, the deal with the Agency broke the second my father went missing. Still, I have a deep interest in Jess's well-being. After all, she accepted the undercover mission and tolerated me for a few months. I'm certain she has that relic. That's too much power in my fake fiancée's hands. Who knows who else might want it? I just want to help her."

He stepped closer and whispered, "You don't have to say much. You see, I even know where Jess is now."

A groan escaped Peter as Marshall pulled him up by the hair. His breath buzzed in Peter's ear, and the stench of garlic and tobacco forced him to swallow bile.

"Tell me, Peter. What does it look like?"

Peter's head snapped back, and he bit his tongue as he fell against the chair. He spat blood and wiped his mouth before looking up at his captor. "Like your photon's mother's face," Peter snarled.

The bald man grabbed Peter by the shoulders and slammed the chair against the table. Peter's breathing quickened. He could take the punches—but his real tormentor sat inside the small bag on the table.

"Don't say I didn't give you an option." Marshall removed his expensive coat, brushed it off, and hung it neatly over the armchair. His cold eyes fixed on Peter as he rolled up his sleeves.

"My sources tell me you've been clean for almost four years. An impressive effort—though useless."

He grabbed Peter's hands and forced them onto the table, locking them in chains.

"You're going to tell me everything you know. That isn't a question." Marshall leaned against the table, smiling as he looked past Peter. "Yttri, how long do you think this agent will last before begging for more?"

7

Axiom Sea Periphery

188A23 Year Week 23, Seventh day, Night

J ESS REMEMBERED WHY SHE was here as she looked up at the dark, towering structure in front of her. Tom.

Her years of training and service as an agent with the Agency had taught her how to steady herself before confronting danger or facing a difficult assignment. This was different, though. The knot in her stomach, her racing heart, and her sweaty palms had nothing to do with the dreadful building ahead—or her mission.

Tom was there, inside the Square. [1]The highest-security prison in Axiom.

It had been almost a year since the horrible accident that caused the Disruption. All those months had only filled Jess's mind with questions—about him, about them, about what he had done and how he had done it. The thought of confronting him was both thrilling and terrifying.

She could have visited before, since their fake civil status gave her that right. However, this wasn't meant to be a social visit—and rumor had it that those in the Square who received visitors didn't live long afterward. The plan had taken too long to prepare, but it was solid now. She just needed to make sure it would work.

"In position," she said into her radio transmitter.

"You are clear to go," a familiar voice replied after a few seconds of static.

Jess inhaled and looked up once more. The next week—the next seven days—would feel longer than the months that had passed since she'd last seen Tom.

Before she stepped forward, her radio clicked again. "Are you sure about this?" the same voice asked.

She stared at the transmitter. Her next step would change her life forever, and there would be no going back.

"It's time to change this madness."

As planned, she dropped the transmitter and smashed it under her boot.

The Disruption had changed both realms so completely that life as it once was could never return. The collision with the Barrier hadn't only destroyed parts of two sectors and unleashed the energy wave—it had taken hundreds of lives.

Nevertheless, what was happening now was even worse. It was time to take their future into their own hands.

1. The Square, a high security prison, was authorized by the
   Parliament of Axiom in 104A22 Year, and it opened the
   year after. The area was proclaimed a danger zone and shut
   off from 110A22 to 115A22 due to the extreme flooding.
   Following a succession of assessments, it was granted permission to reopen in 116A22. Presently, it has a notorious
   reputation for its extreme sentences and is known for its
   dubious

8

Axiom Realm

Tom had to keep counting down from ten after hours of talking about a ceremony that would last less than forty minutes. The wedding traditions in Axiom were overwhelming. The tone of the grass, the color of the flowers, even the birds symbolized crucial omens. Every detail needed to be considered and planned—otherwise, catastrophic consequences could darken the couple's future happiness.

Some wise people ignored most of these absurdities, but Arlett wasn't one of them. So, when the need for an item representing TowerUp came up, Tom ran to get anything that reminded him of their business—or whatever that meant. It also gave him the perfect excuse to yell at his best friend, who had so far done an excellent job of missing all the planning.

The elevator opened on his floor, and Tom thought he heard running footsteps, but he didn't give it much thought until he reached his room. Through the open door, sunlight spilled into the dim corridor.

"What in the hell?" He was sure he'd closed the door before he left.

Tom rushed into the room but froze. Someone could still be there.

He looked around without moving. The only sounds came from outside, and everything appeared to be in place. He inhaled, ready to grab the blueprint from the table and call it good—until it hit him. A flowery essence mixed with something bitter, almost metallic, like old lead water pipes.

He ran into Jess's bedroom, and his heart dropped.

Someone had ripped the closet doors off. One lay on the floor, and the other hung at a strange angle. The bed boards were exposed, and the mattress blocked his way. Jess's dress, along with the rest of her belongings and the bedsheets, had been tossed to the far side of the room, nearly falling off the open balcony.

"Oh no. No, no, no."

He turned and ran toward the window. The sharp corner of the center table slammed into his leg, tearing his pants at the knee. "Photon Maker!" he exclaimed.

He jumped over the oversized couch where he'd slept the night before, as if hurrying would somehow help him find Jess's sack before the intruders.

He felt sick. Whoever had broken in had even ripped open the back of the sofa—pieces of leather and stuffing now littered the floor.

His first thought went to the cooler box in the kitchen, which was still in place.

For a fleeting moment, he thought his years of experience in construction had paid off. No one ever noticed if the cabinets had different depths, and he'd been extremely careful the night before when he'd reinstalled the back panel after hiding Jess's sack.

His heart skipped a beat as he flung open the cabinet door—and froze at the sight of exposed drywall and pipes. The sack was gone.

Tom rubbed his face and looked around. He had to fix this. He was the one who'd chosen the hiding spot. The one who'd suggested leaving it behind, even when Jess hesitated. He had to figure this out.

From the hallway, footsteps approached the room, and when Jess's voice called out, a sudden heaviness settled in his chest.

"Hey, Tom. Sorry to inform you of this, but they need you down—"

She stopped at the entrance. Her cheerful smile vanished as she reached to her side but stopped short. He assumed she was looking for her gun, but following hotel policy, she'd had to leave it at the front desk.

"Are you all right? Did you get hurt?"

Tom shook his head and pushed his hair back. "Jess, I'll find—"

"Did you see who—?"

Bang!

The sound echoed through the corridor long after Jess left the room.

"Jess, wait!" He ran after her. "Where are you going?"

A second shot rang out, and Tom crouched, covering his head.

"It came from Bill's suite!" Jess shouted. "Stay there!"

At the far end of the hall, the elevator doors opened, and Jess's mom stepped out.

"Mom, get down!" Jess yelled.

A window shattered in Bill's room, and Tom rushed over to Amelia, pulling her down.

Jess threw something toward Bill's room, and another shot followed.

"Bill! That came from Bill's room!" Amelia tried to stand, but Tom held her down.

"Tom, stop! Let me go! I need to help him."

"Stay there, Mom," Jess shouted. "Tom, keep her with you."

A soft breeze carried smoke that smelled like burnt steel, leaving an acid taste in the back of Tom's throat.

"Jess, where—" The air thickened, making him cough. "Where are you going? You don't—" He struggled to breathe. "You don't have your gun."

"I know," Jess said. "And I know what I'm doing, Tom."

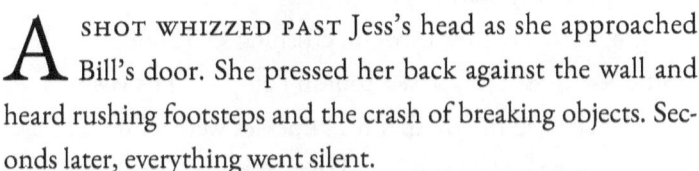

A SHOT WHIZZED PAST Jess's head as she approached Bill's door. She pressed her back against the wall and heard rushing footsteps and the crash of breaking objects. Seconds later, everything went silent.

When she peeked inside, she saw her brother lying on the floor. A dark liquid pooled beneath him. Karen's body flashed through her mind, forcing her to step back.

She inhaled deeply, slowing her heartbeat, and cursed the lost seconds. Her need for recovery didn't matter. In the hallway, her mother was fighting Tom. She had to act before her mother's life followed her brother's fate.

After exhaling, she focused on the other side of the wall.

A curtain brushed against the window frame, creating a rhythmic melody that contrasted with Bill's incoherent mumbling. In front of her, a glass vase on a table held tall flowers. It was spotless, its clear surface reflecting a distorted image of the room. Nothing moved.

She crouched, inching forward. "Bill. Can you hear me?"

"Jess..." His voice was a whisper. "They got her. I have to—"

"Stay down," Jess said. There was a hole in his torso where he'd been shot. "You're bleeding."

"Arlett! They took her!" Bill groaned when she pressed her hand down on the wound. "I need—"

"Don't move, or you'll bleed to death."

"You don't get it. They weren't supposed to take her. They said they wouldn't if—"

"Bill!" Jess's mom ran into the room and knelt beside him. Her hands trembled as she touched his chest, her sobs breaking the air. "Bill! My baby boy!"

Tom stormed into the room, crushing shards of glass under his boots. "Jess, I'm sorry. I couldn't stop—" His jaw was set, fists clenched so tightly that his knuckles were white. His eyes widened as he looked at Bill and then at the window. "Who the hell did this?"

"Tom." Jess's hand was soaked in Bill's blood. "I need you to call—"

"Jess, there's a bright... light gloss downstairs," Tom said.

"Gloss? What?" She froze. That was how some people described portals when they first saw them. "Like a light?"

"Kind of, but not really."

"What color?"

Tom stared at her for a second. He rubbed his face and looked outside again while reaching into his pocket for his transmitter. "Color? White? Light ivory? I don't know. Wait—they have Arlett!"

Jess grabbed her mother's hand and placed it on top of Bill's wound. Her mother's eyes widened, all color draining from her face.

"You can do it, Mom." Jess gave her a quick smile and pressed her mother's hands down to add pressure. "Don't let him move."

Jess reached the window just in time to see the train of a wedding gown being dragged into the portal. Tom was right. The light was pure white—meaning everyone who crossed into Chaos were natives of that realm.

"Jess. Is Arlett gone?" Bill's voice broke.

Rage burned through Jess as she clenched her fists, staring at her brother. "She's in Chaos, Bill. You call her *Ar*, right?" Once she said it aloud, all the pieces clicked into place—even fragments of their first conversation came back to her.

"Someone shot my friend," Tom said beside her, speaking into the transmitter. "We need help."

Bill closed his eyes and let his head fall back. Jess realized it wasn't just pain—it was guilt.

She looked out at the empty yard below, wiping the blood from her hand onto her shirt.

The night she'd first met Arlett came rushing back. Bill had invited her to dinner. After years of barely seeing each other except on holidays, Jess had been nervous, hoping it might be a chance to mend things. Being an active agent—and watching people die, sometimes by her own hand—had changed her view of family. But the moment she arrived, she knew Bill had another agenda.

Bill, Arlett, stupid Charlotte, and Tom sat around a table in a crowded restaurant. As the evening went on, too many things happened for her to process, and her instincts failed her. In the end, the only good thing about that night had been the food—the tender, smoky meat and the sweet, crispy slice of pie.

Now she understood. Bill had just wanted to distract her. Though he hadn't known the full extent of her relationship with Tom, he must have noticed how she'd been avoiding him. And he'd always enjoyed how Charlotte put her on edge. Jess should have realized then that Arlett was from Chaos—and the way Bill had tricked her proved his fiancée couldn't be allowed to live in Axiom.

Tom's hand came to rest on her arm, pulling her back to the present. His eyes, bright as ever, were fixed on her as he tilted his head slightly. He moved less than an inch closer, and the smaller gap sent a warmth through Jess—one only he could awaken, but one she knew she shouldn't trust again.

"Help is on the way," Tom whispered. "I'll be with you."

She shook her head.

He started to hug her, but at that moment, two paramedics burst into the room, and she had to pull her mother away from Bill.

9

Axiom Realm

Tom remembered arriving at the hospital and was certain he'd brought Jess and her mom along, but the hours from midmorning to late evening vanished in a blur of speaker announcements and coffee cups. Guests from the wedding had come to visit and wait for news, but like him, none were allowed to see Bill—not even Dan, Amelia's long-term boyfriend. Most of the day, Amelia and Jess were in the family viewing room, something Tom didn't envy.

Almost six years earlier, his grandfather had been murdered, and from a similar room, he'd watched the endless hours of surgery and medical intervention. He still had nightmares about it. Growing up, he'd always seen his grandpa as a strong, unbreakable man.

That night, he'd said goodbye to an old, pale human with more wrinkles than hair. Tubes and lights surrounded him as nurses and doctors exchanged tools that grew stained with blood under the blanket covering most of his body.

The room had been soundproofed, and as he waited, the silence became unbearable. Some friends had waited outside, but he endured the torment alone because he was the only family member. At least Jess and her mom had each other.

The doors at the end of the hallway opened, and Jess stepped out. She wrapped her arms around herself, but her steps were steady. As she approached the visitors, she wore a smile that Tom recognized as an act.

"The doctors say he'll recover." She looked around the group and gave Dan a quick hug. "Mom and I appreciate you being here, but please, go home and rest. We'll keep you posted."

She spoke to a few others, offering pats on the back and nods of gratitude, calmly ushering everyone out. Her voice never wavered, and her composure never broke. Of course it wouldn't—she was a trained agent, and these situations were part of her daily life. Within ten minutes, even Dan was ready to leave, and Jess stepped outside into the hospital garden.

The fresh air hit Tom's face, clearing his lungs of the heavy scent of disinfectant. Not far away, the smoke from a grill made his stomach growl, and for the first time since breakfast, he thought about food. But Jess's silhouette erased the thought.

She sat on a bench under a streetlight. Her elbows rested on her knees, her hands covering her face. Tom walked over and kneeled in front of her. He didn't need to say anything. She glanced up at him, her eyes glistening and her nose red. She bit her lip before looking skyward.

"I have to call the Agency. They need to know I lost it." She looked down at him and wiped her eyes. "I'm sure I don't have to ask, but please take care of—"

Tom cradled her face in his hands. "No. It's my fault, Jess. I won't let them—"

"It isn't your fault. I was responsible for it. I was the one who left the sack with the relic in the room. You were just trying to help me."

He rubbed her arms and closed his eyes. He couldn't let them take her. One of the reasons he hated the Agency was their unrealistic expectations for their agents—and their idea of punishment. He fixed things. That was his job. He just needed to figure out how to fix this one.

"It's all right, Tom. I should have called the Agency sooner. It'll take them a while to get here, but with Bill and my mom..." She cleared her throat and took a few slow breaths. "My mom was falling apart, waiting...I didn't think she should see me get taken into custody."

"Custody? No, Jess. They can't do that..."

She exhaled, one eyebrow lifting. "There's more than just my family in danger, Tom."

He shook his head, blurting out the first solution that came to mind. "You're here, and you're part of the Agency. They trusted you with that stupid thing. If they're not here yet, why don't we find it instead?"

"We?" Jess's eyes followed him as he sat beside her.

"Yes, *we*."

He rubbed the back of his neck, unable to meet her gaze. His throat was dry, his stomach tight. The chance to save Jess from the Agency—and fix the problem he'd caused—depended on his next words. Words had never been his strength.

"I move fast, and I can lift heavy stuff. I'm good at following orders, and an extra pair of hands is better than none. I'm not very smart, but—"

"Tom! I've told you before—you're brilliant." Jess placed her hand over his. "It's time you realized that." She looked down. "But I can't risk your life."

Although his hand trembled and his heartbeat thundered in his ears, he held her hand, savoring the softness of her skin and the faint coolness of her fingertips—just as he remembered.

Tom had met Bill when the family moved into his neighborhood. They'd hit it off immediately, so when the weekend came, Tom went to look for his new friend. To his surprise, the most beautiful girl he'd ever seen opened the door. Up until that moment, he hadn't known Bill even had a younger sister.

"Can I help you?" Jess asked with a smile he'd soon learn to appreciate.

"Uh... I was looking for Bill?"

Jess rolled her eyes and called toward the back of the house. "Mom! Where's your son? Someone's looking for him." She turned back to Tom. "My guess is he's anywhere but here. Bill isn't a fan of working."

Tom noticed she was wearing an old pair of pants splattered with paint, and when her mom, Amelia, appeared, she was dressed the same way, apron and all.

"Tom!" Amelia greeted with a warmth that matched her expression. "How are you this sunny early afternoon?"

Tom cleared his throat, but Amelia didn't let him answer.

"Bill had to leave early, but it would be wonderful if you could help us."

"Mom!" Jess crossed her arms, glaring at her. "You can't just assume people have time to—"

"I'm not assuming, I'm asking. Right, Tom?"

Tom nodded, intending to answer Amelia's question, but she took it as agreement and smiled even wider, ushering him inside.

"You're adorable, Tom! I'll make some food for you while you help Jess with these boxes."

Jess followed them into the large room, which was meant to be a family space but currently held at least fifty boxes and a pile of furniture. Unlike her mother, Jess's expression was cold, her arms still crossed as she stood by the door.

"I don't want to impose," Tom said, which made Amelia chuckle and Jess shake her head.

"Oh, sweetheart, you're so kind. It doesn't bother me to cook for you—it's the least I can do."

"Mom, you're abusing his kindness. I don't even know him, and you're already—"

"Of course!" Amelia interrupted cheerfully. "Tom, this is my daughter Jessica, and she'd really appreciate your help with all this heavy stuff."

Jess turned to her mother, and Tom was relieved that the angry look wasn't directed at him. But Amelia ignored her daughter and walked out. Jess sighed, her shoulders lifting as she let the frustration go. When she looked back at Tom, the anger was gone.

"I'm so sorry. My mother can be a handful. If you want to go, please do. This should be Bill's job."

Tom put his hands in his pockets and tried to sound serious. "Unless you want me to leave, I really can't. If my grandpa finds out I walked away without helping, he'll make me work extra hours in the shop."

Jess smiled. "A shop? What kind of shop?"

"It's a small workshop by the train station downtown," Tom said with a shrug, pretending it wasn't much—though he loved that place. "We fix mechanisms or build things from wood or metal—you name it."

"And you help your grandpa?" Jess asked, her tone filled with curiosity instead of the usual judgment he got when mentioning his family's trade.

"Yeah... he's been teaching me for a while now. It's not a big deal, really. We just figure out how to fix stuff."

She stepped further into the room, narrowing her eyes. "Just fix stuff? Do you know how many times Bill has fixed anything besides his hair? And my dad—Maker keep him at peace—wasn't a handyman either."

Tom laughed. She was right. Bill was a great guy, but not the kind who liked to get dirty. "So, where should I start?"

That was the first of many days they spent together, and over time, their friendship grew into something deeper—something amazing—that Tom eventually destroyed with his fear, doubts, and prejudice.

"I can't let you be blamed for this, Jess," Tom said, hoping, just like the day they met, she'd let him help her. It was his last chance to make things right.

"You've done nothing wrong. It was my decision."

"No." Tom ran a hand through his hair. "You know me, Jess." He pressed his lips together and took a deep breath. "I won't forgive myself if they... if you get in trouble."

Tears rolled down her cheeks, and he looked at the ground. For a moment, the only sound was the breeze brushing the tall grass around them.

He wished his argument was stronger—something that wouldn't hurt her—but in truth, he had no idea what else to say. He just knew he couldn't accept the alternative.

Jess moved closer. "You've never been to Chaos, right?"

"No! That's illegal! ...But I can if you— I will. I won't cause you more trouble. I promise."

"We'd better leave, then. We'll have to make an extra stop."

Tom couldn't contain his grin as he jumped to his feet. "Whatever you say."

She frowned, wiping her tears, and headed toward the parking lot.

"Aren't you going to talk to your mom first?" To Tom's disbelief, she rolled her eyes.

"You're joking, right? Don't you remember how much she loves my job? What will she say when I tell her: *'Mom, I'm glad Bill's better, but I have to cross into Chaos because I need to find a—'"*

"Got it." Tom raised his hands and nodded. "You're right. Let's just go."

<hr/>

Axiom

188A22 Year, Week 17

LATE NIGHT

Although years of scientific studies had advanced Axiom's medical knowledge, death remained part of existence. Most didn't think about it until their time came. The popular belief was that, after passing, everyone would move on to a greater level of life.

The nature of that level was up for debate. Some believed in the need to correct their failures before meeting the Maker, while others didn't. Most agreed that, no matter where or how this greater level was achieved, everyone would eventually meet again.

Marshall the Second had no questions about his future after death. He would not fail to reach his ideal status before his time came. However, the last few weeks had changed his current situation.

As the firstborn of Lezar Mos-Ium-115, the Corrupts' Chief, he had grown up with a clear understanding of how Chaos worked—who was in charge and what kind of business thrived in his realm. After he and his father secretly agreed to collaborate with the Agency, using Jess as his fake fiancée, his understanding of Axiom's legal and illegal systems had also become crystal clear.

Nevertheless, when Marshall's father went missing a little over two weeks ago, all the progress they'd made working with the Agency—as well as their own plans—was put on hold. The worst part was that the disappearance jeopardized the entire

Corrupts' structure. Marshall wanted to find his father, but he didn't have the luxury of losing control over Chaos. Bill had messed up his plan, and now he would have to pay for it.

That night, Marshall decided to pay a visit to the hospital.

Bill's family had taken their time leaving the viewing room, and the patient had remained unconscious for a while before being moved to a regular room. Neither Marshall nor Yttri were in any hurry. After all, there was no fun in simply adding a narcotic to the blood serum or subtly adjusting CLEO[1]—the trusted medical console—by recoding its mechanical bugs.

Once the rhythmic beeping in the room became steady, Marshall walked to the bed where Bill lay hooked up to tubes and machines.

As his shadow crossed the bed, Bill opened his eyes.

"What happened?" Bill muttered. "Arlett? Where is—"

"Hello, Bill. I'm glad you're awake."

As expected, his voice triggered CLEO's warning lights—an alert for increased heart rate. But to Marshall's surprise, Bill's eyes narrowed as he tried to sit up.

"You promised you'd leave her alone. You—" Bill's breathing hitched. "Where is she?"

"Well, that's interesting," Marshall said. "Are you hearing this, Yttri? We've got a runaway bride. I mean, who could blame her? You're not good-looking or strong or smart, or—"

"You kidnapped her!" Bill shouted. "We had a deal, and you broke it!"

Marshall grabbed Bill by the neck.

"I did what? *You* messed it all up! Let me explain this, little man—I've never broken a contract. It's what makes sense in my world. You changed the plan. My people told me your sister wasn't in the room where you said she'd be. In fact, there was an old alienist there, and we almost killed her! Why wasn't Jess where she was supposed to be?"

A light touch on Marshall's shoulder reminded him that Bill needed to breathe if he wanted answers.

"Thanks, Yttri." Marshall cleared his throat and released his grip. Bill's face had turned red, a fresh bruise forming around his neck.

"So you killed her?" Bill rasped. "You just—"

"Arlett? Why should I kill her? Are you blaming her? I mean, I'm not moral, but even for me, that'd be low. Yttri, do you believe this guy?"

"No!" Bill said quickly. "I would never! Arlett did nothing wrong."

Yttri didn't need instructions. He moved toward CLEO, opened the panel, and began recoding the system. With a few turns, Bill started coughing violently, his body convulsing until Marshall lifted a hand. Yttri adjusted the gears again, and the machine stabilized.

"I know it hurts, and it'll get worse. So just answer." Marshall smoothed his shirt. "What makes you think I killed Arlett? And what the photons happened?"

Bill coughed again, blood trickling from the corner of his mouth. His hand clutched his abdomen. CLEO flashed a warning—something that actually made Bill smile.

"I'll die soon," Bill whispered. "You can keep torturing me. I don't care."

"No, no, no. My sweet Bill, that's not how this works. Sure, you'll die, but *Arlett* will suffer more. When I find her, she'll know exactly who to blame for her torment."

Bill's eyes filled with tears, and he shook his head. "Please, don't. I'll do anything."

"No need for drama. Just answer my questions."

Bill rubbed his face, leaning back against the pillow. "Arlett heard my mom say Jess's flight was redirected. I told you that—remember? You said you weren't worried. Arlett was stressed about the wedding costs, so she canceled her room and someone else took it immediately. I didn't know until my sister showed up. It was Tom's idea to share his suite. But I called you! I left a thousand messages! You got them—you must have!"

"Oh, I got the messages," Marshall said coolly, "but it was too late. I like to plan things, Bill. It's very important they work *my* way."

"So... you don't have Arlett?"

Marshall clenched his fists, his jaw tight. The stupidity was painful.

"You're an idiot. Of course I don't have Arlett. I do business like my father—we don't appreciate complications."

"Who took her?"

"Think! Who *is* Arlett? I mean, who she really is." As Marshall spoke, Bill seemed to shrink into the bed. "Now you see. Your fiancée's daddy is a complication for me."

"Mr. Radnar won't—"

"Mr. Radium Radnar 88 must've been doing his job. Unlike you, he isn't an idiot. He'd never let his daughter marry a nobody from Axiom—not if he could help it. As you should know, he's a councilor of Chaos S-Group."[2]

"But he doesn't want her living there. She told me. He wants her here, in Axiom, with me."

"This dreamer!" Marshall laughed and clapped Yttri on the back. "Radnar wants *you* with his daughter? He wants your photonic last name, not you! Don't you get it? He knows who your sister is. He must have learned about the incident in Chaos a few days ago. That's why I needed to get Arlett as soon as she arrived. Your stupid messages were too late!"

Marshall walked to the head of the bed, grinning as his pulse quickened.

Bill's eyes widened. He tried to stand but fell out of bed. A loud crash echoed in the room, followed by a groan as Yttri silenced CLEO's alarms. The sudden quiet allowed voices from the hallway to carry in.

"Are you defending her?"

"Amelia, she's doing her job. Someone tried to kill Bill."

"Exactly, Dan! She *should* be here. And she shouldn't be fooling around with Tom. He doesn't even belong to our family status, for the Maker's sake."

"She's not fooling around. And our family status? Really, Amelia? The boy's just trying to help, and Jess is trying to find—"

"What? Did she tell you? No, she never does. Stupid Agency! I hate that she's there. I can't believe Tom's backing her up! He hates them as much as we do."

"That's my point! That's why he told me where they are. Did it occur to you she might be looking for Arlett?"

"In Chaos? Dear neutrons, Dan, Jess isn't looking for Arlett. Our security is. The Maker only knows what that poor girl is going through."

Marshall pointed at Yttri, who switched on the *No Visitors* sign outside the room. Moments later, CLEO's lights flickered back to life and the gears hummed as it resumed operation.

With no care or effort, Marshall tossed Bill back onto the bed just as Amelia began complaining about being kept out. He leaned close to Bill's ear.

"Say anything," he whispered, "and I kill them both."

Bill lay still. His knuckles whitened as tears rolled down his cheeks.

Marshall chuckled and shook his head as he stepped out of the room.

"Mrs. Hiem-Sagac?" he said smoothly. "I'm one of your son's doctors. Just wanted to let you know he's in excellent care. We had a brief glitch with the monitors. You can come in now."

Yttri lumbered past Bill's mother, earning a gasp from her. He was a sight—scarred, bald, and massive. But Marshall, all charm and poise, managed to draw a nervous smile from her.

Both men entered the elevator, waiting until the doors closed.

"Well, Yttri," Marshall said, grinning. "Looks like it's a good time to go home. Let's have a little chat with Randall."

1. CLEO, centralized panel utilized to guide the mechanical bugs in employing supplemental drugs, medications and electrical treatments to those in critical condition.

2. Chaos S-Group, one of the funder groups of Chaos. Descendants now possess the wealth and privilege that was promised to them in former treaties and agreements. Continue to have a considerable influence in the ruling of this realm.

10

Axiom Realm

188A22 Year Week 17,
Sixth day, Six hours before
sunrise

The Village was part of the outskirts of Main City, both praised sectors for their scenery and ambiance. The Center District was an exception, and most tried to avoid it. Its narrow streets and lack of landscaping showed the absence of care, and the particular neighborhood Jess wanted to visit was known for its questionable businesses and security.

"Explain again why we couldn't jump from the Village parking lot?" Tom walked to the other side of his vehicle.

"Are you worried about your truck?" She raised her eyebrows and tilted her head, but her door didn't make a sound when she closed it.

"Well, it's my baby!"

She rolled her eyes and kept walking down the darkest alley. Tom jogged to catch up, wondering how many times she had been in unsafe places like that one all by herself.

"No one would steal it," she said.

"And why is that?"

She turned to him, failing to conceal her smile. "It's so old. Only a miracle keeps it running."

"What? You can't be serious. It's vintage, Jess!"

"No, it's just an old piece of metal that happens to move."

He frowned and leaned down, staring straight into her eyes. "Do you know what happens to anyone who insults my baby?"

"I can imagine." She crossed her arms. "That doesn't mean it isn't true."

This time, Tom was the one rolling his eyes, moving away. "You just don't appreciate history as I do."

Behind him, he heard Jess laugh, and something warmed inside him. Years ago, it wouldn't have surprised him. They always had a good time together.

The alley went silent when she reached its end. Jess's features hardened as she examined the building from top to bottom.

"Are you sure you want to come?"

Tom's stomach felt uneasy, and he kept his hands in his pockets. His nerves had been up since they arrived, ready for someone to attack them—and they were still in Axiom. He could only imagine what to expect from a dark alley in Chaos. There was no way he would leave her alone.

"Absolutely. This is my fault."

"You did nothing wrong. You have to accept that."

Tom sighed. "Fine, I didn't. Still, I'll jump anywhere with you."

She stared at him long enough for him to recognize the same painful memories in his mind were filling her eyes.

"Jess, we need to talk about—"

"It's called crossing over." Jess cleared her throat. "Cross over. Not jumping."

He nodded. Talking to her would have to wait. A shiver ran down his spine as he wondered if they would make it back.

"Let's cross over, then." He clapped and stepped closer. "So, what do I do?"

She played with her fingers and bit her bottom lip—something she did when she was unsure or nervous. He started to wonder if she had changed her mind but didn't risk asking.

"All right," she said. "I have to use both hands, so you need to hold me close."

"Uh... say that again."

Jess exhaled, grabbed his hand, and pulled him to where she was standing. She turned him by his shoulders to face the building.

It was different when he was the one teasing her. Now that she had invaded his personal space, his senses sharpened, reminding him how much he enjoyed being with her. So when she placed his hands on her waist, Tom was certain she could feel his quick heartbeat.

"Don't let go, and as soon as you see the light, hold your breath. Got it?"

He nodded. "Yes. Got it."

She moved her hair to the side and pulled out a thin chain with a small charm hanging from it. He knew it very well.

Not long after he met the Hiem-Sagac family, Bill invited him for dinner. Tom didn't know it was Jess's birthday—the first one she celebrated in that house. Jess didn't mind him crashing her party and even spent some time talking to him.

Later that night, Tom climbed up to Jess's bedroom window for the first of many times and gave her a cuckoo clock charm with a rough handmade silver chain as a gift. He was surprised to see that she still had it.

A light shone in front of him as a heat wave pushed against his face. She didn't need to ask him to hold his breath, because he couldn't breathe. A gentle squeeze of his hand alerted him that Jess was moving forward.

He was sure the bright ray would kill him, and he only moved because he trusted her.

The light changed, turning to a soft orange with shades of red, very different from the one he saw when Arlett crossed over.

As his body moved through it, the heat became a freezing breeze, and the light shone so brightly he had to close his eyes. A buzzing filled his ears and echoed in his chest. He tightened his arms around Jess and moved closer, trying to protect her from it.

Seconds later, silence and darkness surrounded him. The breeze stopped, but the cold increased.

"Tom? Are you okay?"

He let go and stepped back. The ground seemed to move, and he stumbled, barely steadying himself.

"Take it easy. Things are different here."

Different was one way to describe it, and it was not at all what he had imagined.

In Chaos, hundreds of balconies stacked from bottom to top on each building in the alley. Everything was illuminated, and loud music and voices poured out of them. Between the structures, wires strung with colorful fabric and twinkling lights hung overhead.

There was a damp scent surrounding them, but above it he caught the smells of food, flowers, and things he couldn't identify. The smell of rain was the strongest. He walked backward, staring up, trying to figure out how those buildings could stand. Their asymmetric structures seemed to defy every law of physics.

The icy water wet his arms and face, making him smile. He had seen rain in the past, but it had been years.

"This is..."

"Weird? Bizarre and cold?" Jess said, and Tom noticed the colder, more serious tone in her voice. She was crouched by a black suitcase. Tom frowned at the sight of the Agency emblem: a golden circle formed by three embedded gears and an open book with a key in the center.

"Where did you get that?"

"You should get out of the rain." She pulled a jacket from the suitcase and offered it to him instead of answering. "It's hard to stay dry here."

Tom wondered about her experience in Chaos and her lack of enthusiasm for it. The thought sent another shiver through his body, and he shook it away.

He took the jacket from her and inspected it. It was black leather, with fur lining the inside—like a pilot's jacket, which he kind of liked. Right before he put it on, he noticed the Agency's logo on the arm, but it was the men's size that triggered his jealous side.

"Wait a second. Who owns this jacket?"

"It doesn't matter. You can't be picky here, and you don't want to freeze or get sick... especially not sick. Put it on!"

"Isn't it illegal to pose as an agent?"

"As of right now, you're an Agency's consultant."

"What? No, I would never—"

"Tom! It's for your safety."

Jess zipped up her own jacket and walked past him. He groaned and followed.

The rain continued to pour down, and at times he thought he saw snowflakes. His fingers were numb, and a pressure pushed on his head. He smiled at his boots—at least his feet were dry. Although he didn't say it out loud, after only a couple of blocks he was grateful for the stupid fur.

"Do you know where you're going? I remember you got lost often when we used to walk back from the train station to your house."

That was one of Tom's favorite memories. He'd been disappointed when he learned Jess wasn't going to enroll in his intermediate school and would stay at her boarding school. That left only two days a week to see her, and usually he spent weekends with Bill and their friends. Little did he know the Fifth days were going to become more special because of it.

His grandpa's shop was conveniently by the train station, and on a rare occasion when he was asked to work a half day on a Fifth, he spotted Jess arriving from Sector 4. Before he met her, he didn't work on those days and started his weekend early. After that afternoon, he rarely missed those half days.

Jess hadn't really been lost, but the street she took would add at least half an hour to her walk. Later, Tom learned she did it on purpose. She was never in a hurry to get home, and he couldn't blame her.

Tom rushed to close the shop and ran to find her. She looked so fragile, strolling with her suitcase down the cobblestone street and carrying a heavy backpack on her shoulder. She was still wearing the navy-blue skirt and white shirt of her school uniform.

"Are you trying to go home?" Tom said, making her jump a little. "Sorry, I didn't mean to scare you, but I'm sure that's not the best way to get there."

"Tom!" she said with a smile that made his heartbeat speed up. "What are you doing here?"

Tom rubbed the back of his head, surprised by his own reaction to her voice. "Well, my grandpa's shop is right around there."

He couldn't avoid a visit to the shop that afternoon, but he enjoyed the walk back with her. Tom always thought his old man liked that friendship more than Bill's.

Jess stopped and narrowed her eyes, bringing him back to the cold street in Chaos. "I know where we are and where we're going. I wasn't the lost one. That was your excuse to stay out playing."

"Funny. I could swear it was you."

She threw her arms up and walked ahead. Two steps later, Tom almost bumped into her when she spun around.

"I know how it looks, but it's dangerous here. Don't underestimate it. Just like a skilled predator, full of colors and attractive aromas, it'll kill you."

"So people in Axiom are right? This is hell. We're superior to—"

"Shh!" She covered Tom's mouth. "Don't joke about that."

Tom grabbed Jess's hand, and it took all his will not to kiss it. "I'm not joking, Jess. I'm asking. Is it true?"

She shook her head, and her shoulders dropped. "The people here have suffered a lot," she sighed. "I wish it were that easy. Just... please keep your guard up, would you?"

He passed his hand over his lips, pretending to seal them. "After you, Sunshine."

All around, laughter and voices followed them. The late hour or the freezing cold didn't matter. However, he soon realized everything came from the windows above. At street level, no one passed them, no vehicles drove by, and Jess's pace was far from a stroll.

They turned a corner and a plaza opened before them.

Thousands of tiny lights brightened the scraggy trees. The sound of running water from a cracked stone fountain echoed on the cobblestones. Around the square, metal curtains locked with thick chains served as doors. Tom knew they were stores thanks to the signs hanging above them.

He'd thought Jess was exaggerating, but there was something unsettling about seeing all the windows covered with wooden pallets and painted with threatening graffiti.

"Hold on, it's going to—" she said.

The ground under Tom's feet shifted, and he barely had time to grab Jess's hand to avoid falling.

As the buildings swayed, Tom noticed their different heights. The taller ones gained momentum, threatening to crush the shorter structures. Somehow, they avoided a collision, even though the movement lasted a while.

"What the photons! How didn't— Those buildings should have fallen."

"Oh, come on, Tom." Jess shook her hair, and white dust flew out of it. "I know they're ugly and old, but you shouldn't be so rude. Didn't you appreciate history?"

"Hilarious, Jessica. But I'm serious. How is it possible the buildings didn't collapse?"

"Well, I'm not an architect, but I believe it has something to do with the foundations or the structural flexibility—or both. And yes, before you ask, it gets pretty messy inside unless people nail their stuff to the walls and floors."

He looked up. Maybe the colors were related to different materials instead of just being funky?

"I'm not an architect either, but—"

"And why is that, Tom?"

His stomach hardened as he pointed at Jess with his index finger, but he didn't say a word and walked past her. Why couldn't she leave that alone? She never understood what it took to work around his problems with studying.

She was a brilliant student who could learn effortlessly. For him, it was a battle that started with the stupid letters bouncing around the page and ended with horrible headaches and failures. After his grandpa died, everything changed. He lost his main support and only family. What was the point of trying anymore?

For the next few blocks, the silence between them grew louder than the noise of Chaos. Sometimes he forgot their good moments were overshadowed by their struggles, and if it wasn't for the sharp pain that hit his stomach, he wouldn't have spoken so soon.

"Jess. Wait."

Tom kneeled, clutching his abdomen. Everything spun, forcing him to brace a hand on the ground, trying to make it stop. It didn't, so he closed his eyes to avoid throwing up.

He tried calling out again, but his throat filled with mucus, making him cough, and his breathing tightened. The jacket zipper gave him trouble when he tried to pull it down, and he was about to rip it when a soft breeze reached his nostrils. The sterilizing scent cleared his lungs but made him gag. His strength vanished, and he let himself fall. He expected to hit the ground face-first, but a pair of hands caught him.

"Tom..." He heard Jess's voice from far away. "Tom, don't take deep breaths."

He opened his eyes and was surprised to see Jess right in front of him.

"Jess—what is going..."

She helped him sit and rested his back against a wall. "I shouldn't have brought you here."

"Are... are you okay?"

She nodded as she touched his forehead. "You haven't spiked a fever yet. I thought we'd have more time. Photons! I'm so sorry, Tom. I'm not thinking straight, I'm..." She exhaled and sat on the ground beside him. "If something's true about Chaos, it's the level of poison. The atmosphere contains high levels of oxygen."

"Isn't that a good thing?"

"Well, no, not really. Think about your construction materials getting wet. The metal will rust, the wood will rot... you get the point."

"Isn't that because of the water?"

"Yes—which is partially oxygen, a highly reactive element. Here in Chaos, there's more of it, along with other reactors."

"And if it rains all the time..." Tom said.

He pressed his palms to his temples and rested his elbows on his knees. The pressure helped the throbbing in his skull, but his stomach was a mess.

"But why aren't you affected? I mean, it's a relief you're fine, but— Or are you feeling sick?"

Jess bit her lip and cleared her throat. "Well, I've been coming here for years, so my body's built-up defenses, and I have a ton of biochemicals in my system—along with a couple of bugs..." She looked down and pushed her hair behind her ears. "I'm so sorry, Tom. It's not safe for you here. It's a thousand times worse for you than for me."

"Hey, Sunshine, it was me who offered, and I'm not going back until we recover that thing." He smiled and leaned forward. "Plus, I remember you're an exceptional nurse."

Jess's cheeks turned red as she stood and looked away.

He shouldn't talk much about their past, but having her around made it impossible not to think about it. The last time she took care of him, they were still in intermediate school. He got sick and, according to his doctor, it was very contagious. That was Bill's reason for not visiting until they cleared him of the disease. Jess had seen him every day, though. She'd gotten the same virus years before and offered to help Tom's grandpa so they didn't need to close the shop. Those eight weeks with Jess were worth the dizziness, nausea, and fever.

"We aren't that far away." Jess's voice brought him back to the wet street. "Do you see that orange light in the high window over there?"

Tom stood and braced himself against the wall. The hardest part was not being able to inhale deeply to control his nausea.

"You think you can walk there?"

"Maybe." He nodded and leaned his head back. "I'm glad we didn't eat today."

She offered her hand, and he took it. "It's just a few more blocks, and we can go slower, but we need to hurry."

Suddenly, the street filled with a hissing sound, and Jess pushed him aside. The smell of damp and dirt filled the alley just as a hairy four-legged creature appeared only a few steps away.

"Stay in the light," Jess whispered.

He noticed they were both standing in a small but illuminated patch of pavement.

The creature crept closer until it reached the lit zone and looked up. Its teeth were sharp and cone-shaped. It was no bigger than a regular dog but had long, pointy claws, white pupils, and raised hair along its back. There was no denying it was dangerous—and still, the dim light on the ground stopped it.

Jess threw something away from them, and the creature sprinted after it with impressive speed.

"We'd better go. If it comes back, it won't be alone."

"What the photons was that? Was that a taxo— tadodum?"

"Takuosum. And no. That was hyaerodea[1]. Unlike the safety of Axiom, here in Chaos, besides poison, we have predators."

She pointed at the windows. "That's the reason for the noise and constant lighting."

Chaos

188Ch22 Year

Week 17, Sixth day, Four hours before sunrise

J ESS KNEW TOM'S CONDITION had worsened because his weight grew heavier as they approached the building. She only prayed he was strong enough to climb the ladder; otherwise, she had no idea how to get him up, and the last thing she wanted was to leave him alone on the street while she got help. Not for the first time, she hoped transmitters weren't monitored by the Corrupts in Chaos.

She understood Tom's awe of this place. She'd felt it the first time she stepped into Chaos. In that moment, Tom's presence only made the feeling of home that Chaos awakened in her stronger. It wasn't her born realm, but in Axiom—besides Tom's house when they were younger—she had never had the freedom to be herself.

"Jess?" Tom said, and when she looked at him, his smile only highlighted his pain, sweat beads traveling down his forehead.

She touched his face and her palm burned, so she helped him sit against a wall. Not for the first time, she questioned her decision to bring him here. She had a reason—someone had to return the relic to Axiom when she stayed in Chaos to find out who was behind the ambush and the robbery—but did her lack of trust in others justify Tom's pain and risk to his health?

"I thought you said we needed to get to the orange light."

"I did." She took the liberty of moving his hair away from his eyes.

"Isn't the door... behind, over there?" He pointed toward the way they'd come. She was shocked by how his hand trembled. It was a clear sign he was on the verge of collapsing.

Jess grabbed his hand and pushed it down but didn't let go. "You'll be fine," she said, swallowing a knot in her throat. "In Chaos, doors are almost prohibited. They're used by rebels, criminals, or crazy people. We have to use the outside ladder. We'll climb by the window. I'm sure you're used to that."

He rested his head on the wall and laughed. It was a weak sound, but it still woke the butterflies in Jess's stomach—something she didn't want or need.

She got up and stepped back. "It's right around this corner."

After a moment, Tom stood. He tried to walk without support, but when Jess moved closer to help him, he accepted without hesitation. Her worry about him only grew.

It didn't take long to reach the ladder, and Jess had no trouble setting the mechanical sequence that lowered the bottom section.

She looked around, trying to find some kind of step to make Tom's climb easier, but there was nothing aside from empty cardboard boxes and scattered garbage. The last thing people in Chaos wanted was to give predators an easy way into their homes.

"I can climb up there," he said. "I may need time to keep going after, though."

A peculiar scratching set Jess's nerves on edge. Only a few days ago, she had been surrounded by takuosums. She hadn't been their prey then, and there were more people around. Now, she and Tom were the dinner—and she wasn't looking to fight them, at least not without a gun.

"We have to hurry. I promise you can rest all you want once we get to the second window."

The high-pitched yelp of a takuosum got Tom's attention. "Please tell me that's normal here."

"It's normal... not good, though."

He exhaled and moved toward the ladder. It was a ninety-degree, half-rusted structure with a few missing steps. Tom looked down at her as he grabbed a higher rung. A low growl from the corner made them turn, and a pair of shiny eyes stared back.

"Climb slowly, and don't make too much noise."

He stepped back. "I won't go before you."

"Climb now, or we're dead." Jess didn't look at him; she kept her eyes on the creature.

"What in the Maker is—"

She didn't let him finish and jumped toward the opposite wall.

The furry creature hissed once and ran after her. As she expected, dozens of eyes from the pack glinted at the end of the alley and along the darker sections of the buildings.

"Photons Maker!" Tom yelled as the ladder cracked under his weight.

Jess grabbed a box from a garbage container and hurled it at the takuosum. It bought her a couple of seconds to find a glass bottle, which she held up so it gleamed in the alley's light.

"You need to get to the second level!" she yelled.

"I'll wait for you here."

One creature farther down the alley jumped and dug its paws into the brick wall.

Tom gasped. "Did you see that? Those things can climb walls?"

"Second floor, Tom!"

Jess didn't wait to see if he kept going. She threw the bottle and hit the second-floor window, splashing a few drops of orange liquid on it.

The creature in front of her ducked, expecting an attack, but when it found itself unharmed, it charged at Jess. The others followed.

Jess ran back to the ladder, and within seconds she was climbing the last steps to reach Tom. The window she'd marked with the bottle opened, and she barely had time to push Tom against the building and cover his head.

The creatures shrieked as gunshots filled the alley, then whined as they scrambled down the walls and fled along the street. As soon as the shooting stopped, Jess stepped back and found Tom staring at her.

"Do you know who the hell I am?" came a sweet voice from the second-level window above them, just before the woman racked her gun.

"Yes, Phoebe. I know who you are."

"Jess?" The woman's eyes widened. "Dear Maker! Jessica Hiem-Sagac—are you in trouble again?"

Jess waved and glanced back at Tom. "Ready to climb up her window?"

He didn't answer as he climbed the next flight of stairs ahead of her. His steps were clumsy, his trembling worse—but it was his cold expression that made her shiver. Bringing someone to Chaos who hated the Agency as much as Tom had been a horrible mistake.

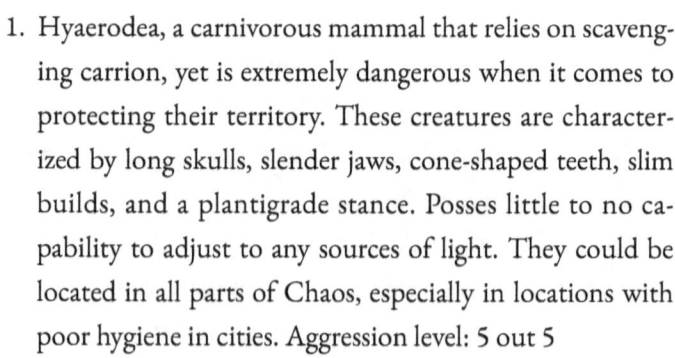

1. Hyaerodea, a carnivorous mammal that relies on scavenging carrion, yet is extremely dangerous when it comes to protecting their territory. These creatures are characterized by long skulls, slender jaws, cone-shaped teeth, slim builds, and a plantigrade stance. Posses little to no capability to adjust to any sources of light. They could be located in all parts of Chaos, especially in locations with poor hygiene in cities. Aggression level: 5 out 5

Chaos Realm

188Ch22 Year Week 17,
Sixth day, Three hours
before sunrise.

Tom didn't seem to have too much trouble getting into the apartment. He was tall enough to climb easily. However, once inside, he just sat on the floor, holding his head.

Jess wouldn't blame him if he threw up. Phoebe kept pacing around the room, making the light fabrics of her colorful dress swirl and releasing her perfume into the air. The flowery scent had already left a bitter taste in the back of Jess's throat. As if that weren't enough, Phoebe's long, almost white hair flew over her shoulders with every turn, and she brushed it back with exaggerated hand gestures that made her small frame seem larger in the tiny room. Sometimes Jess wondered how such an older woman could be so childish.

Jess kneeled in front of Tom and brushed the hair from his forehead. "Can you sit by the kitchen table? You'll feel better pretty soon."

"Of course, Jess. Forget all your manners here. This is just Chaos, anyway," Phoebe said, crossing her arms and shaking her head. "All of you have the same lack of manners."

"All of whom?" Tom asked as he stumbled toward the table.

Phoebe's features softened, as Jess had learned they always did when she spoke to a man. "The agents, of course," she said—and her tone shifted to one of genuine concern. "Jess, how are you holding up?"

"I'm fine, Phoebe." The last thing she needed was to talk about her failed extraction or Karen's death. "Where's Holm?"

"He's out." Phoebe sat at the table, brushing a hand over the colorful tablecloth that was barely visible under the piles of vases, papers, and plates. "He'll be back soon. He's still trying to figure out what happened this Second." Her tone dropped lower. "I don't know how things went so wrong. I'm sure it'll get worse if we don't discover the... umm... traitor?"

Jess's hands froze by the open pantry full of containers, cups, and bottles. She had to inhale several times before picking out the herbs for the remedy[1]. It was an old recipe that would help Tom build resistance to the environmental toxins. It wasn't permanent, but it would protect him for a while.

"So, who are you?" Phoebe asked, turning to Tom—and Jess was grateful for the distraction. Phoebe could be irritating, but she never forced a conversation on anyone who didn't want one.

"This is Tom Umbrar-Ment, an Agency consultant."

Phoebe covered her mouth but failed to muffle her laugh. Before Jess could intervene, the apartment door opened.

Phoebe was instantly on her feet, shotgun aimed at the entrance. At the same time, Jess reached to her side and swore under her breath when she remembered her gun was locked in a safe somewhere in a hotel in Axiom.

"It's good to know you're ready for intruders, honey," a man said as he stepped into the room.

"Holm," Phoebe said, lowering the weapon and stepping forward to hug him. "The door again? I'll accidentally kill you one of these days."

Jess exhaled and glanced toward the window.

There was something odd about watching those two embrace. Phoebe looked years younger than her husband—whose white hair and hunched posture revealed their advanced age—but it was more than that. The way Tom sat silently at the nearby table only heightened the strange atmosphere.

After a moment, Holm set an umbrella by the door and looked at Tom and Jess.

"Jess, I'm glad you're back. We need to talk." His hard expression, along with his tone, put her on edge again. "I'll be in the office when you're done with your... visitor."

Jess exhaled and turned back to the kitchen to finish the remedy.

———◆◇◆———

"Y OU WANT ME TO eat that?" Tom said, ready to stand up.

Jess rolled her eyes and set the bowl on the table in front of him. "Yes." She pushed it closer. "If you want to move around without getting sick or dying, you have to eat it."

He stared at the bowl and groaned. "I saw what you put in it." He pointed at the jar full of green water resting on the window ledge. "You see that mold? I'm not eating it."

"It's not the kind of fungus you think it is," she said.

"So, I can drink from a puddle here?"

"No! That would definitely kill you." Jess placed a spoon in Tom's left hand. "The atmosphere here causes the rain to become acidic—not to mention the millions of germs and poisonous bacteria. This is a special mildew to help your system adjust to Chaos."

Tom frowned but let the steam reach his nostrils. He wasn't wrong—the bitter, rotting vapor coated the back of his throat, forcing him to lean away from the bowl.

"The aroma is worse than the flavor," Jess said. Phoebe laughed. "Come on, Tom. Just eat it, please."

He grabbed the bowl, ignoring the spoon, and forced himself to gulp the thick, gooey stew. The rotten flavor burned his taste buds, and its bitterness glued itself to his insides, bringing tears to his eyes. Between gagging and coughing, he finished it all.

He rested his forehead on the table. The cold surface, along with the warmth from Jess's hand on his back, helped his stomach settle.

"Quantum Photons, Jess. I'm even sweating." He rubbed his face and stood up. "I'm sure you just killed my palate!"

"It'll get better after you have more—"

"Have more? Now you've lost it! There's no way I'll eat that mold ever again. No way!"

Jess bit her lip, her eyes shining under the dim light, pinching Tom's heart. He was about to tell her he'd drink that slop for the rest of his life if she asked him to—but then the old man appeared in the doorway.

"Jess?" Holm's deep voice was all it took for her soft expression to vanish, replaced by tension and worry.

Without a word, she walked toward the other room and closed the door behind her. It surprised Tom how such a small apartment could be so soundproof.

"Sit down, handsome. You need to rest. The remedy won't do all the work," Phoebe said.

He didn't argue. His legs were weak and sore, as if he'd been laying floors for a month, and his stomach was a knot of nausea and bile. The constant spinning sensation didn't help.

As he sat back down, he rested his head in his hands.

"So, who are you?" Phoebe asked.

Tom looked up and found the strange woman sitting across from him. Her palms rested on the table, and her smile was the kind he'd learned to fear—too confident, too knowing, as if she already had the answers and was just testing him.

"I'm Tom."

"Ha!" She leaned back, resting an elbow on the top of her chair. "That's a tiny name. Only Axiom people use such weak names."

He cleared his throat and straightened up. "But Phoebe is way longer?"

For a fleeting moment, she frowned, the wrinkles on her face revealing her true age—a couple of decades older than Tom had guessed. Probably more dangerous, too.

"It's Phoebe-82, handsome." She spelled it out for him. "Axiom people are ignorant about naming. In Chaos, everything has meaning and lineage. My number tells you who my family is and why I may—or may not—be important. The name Tom says nothing."

"Interesting." He grabbed the spoon from the table and spun it in circles. "So, are you important?"

Phoebe laughed, shaking her head with an almost angelic sound, then stood and moved to the kitchen. She served a plate of steaming vegetables and meat that made Tom's stomach growl, reminding him how long it had been since he'd eaten.

"This," she said, placing the plate in front of him, "is a piece of heaven... well, I guess you don't know what that is." She giggled. "Heaven is the best food in Chaos. Only the Corrupts and diplomatic officials can afford it. I can't tell if anything in Axiom tastes this good, but compared to what you just ate, this *is* heaven."

He chuckled and inhaled the salty, earthy aroma that reminded him of a stew his grandfather used to make. It had never been his favorite, but now he savored the rich flavor and the crisp bite of the meat. The meal was indeed delicious.

"I told you," she said, leaning forward. "Isn't it better than the food in Axiom?"

He'd eaten plenty of meals as good as this—some even better—but he was smart enough not to offend her.

"Nothing like this, Phoebe-82."

She smiled. "You aren't that bad, Tom."

"That's what I tell myself every morning in front of the mirror."

Her laughter was contagious, and it felt good to laugh again.

"Peter wasn't this nice. He always complained about Chaos—the people, the food, everything."

"Who's Peter?"

"The owner of that jacket."

Tom's smile faded as he looked down at the dark fur-lined coat he was wearing.

"Oh..." Phoebe said. "Well, I guess Jess will have to answer more questions. I can't go breaking Agency secrets again." Her tone turned teasing when she mentioned the Agency.

"That's impossible!" Jess's voice cut through the room as the door slammed open, hitting the wall. "You know her as well as I do, and—"

"Believe me, Jess, I know. But there's something to be said about evidence. You can't deny that," Holm replied.

Jess closed her eyes, exhaled sharply, then walked over to Tom, shaking her head. "How are you feeling?"

It took him a second to realize she was speaking to him. "I'm better. You?"

Holm sat down on a ripped couch. "Let's close all the gaps, Jess. Find our deserter and ask him what happened."

"That's the plan," Jess said, crossing her arms. "I'm sure he's involved in this—in *everything*."

"Do you think he betrayed the Agency?" Holm asked. "Was it his intention all along?"

Jess rubbed her eyes with her palms.

"Jess's fiancé has never been trustworthy," Phoebe said. "I'll say it was his plan from the start—and his father's too."

Tom set the spoon down slowly. The room felt suddenly colder. "What? Fiancé? Who are you talking about? This Peter?"

"Oh, poor thing," Phoebe said, patting his hand. "Jess's fiancé is not a good man. Well, not that Peter was any better—but no, not him."

Jess growled and walked to the window. "Marshall must be involved in part of it, but I don't think he planned it all. I truly believe his father's disappearance scared him away."

Tom's nerves came alive—not just from this new revelation about Jess.

"Which is justified," Holm said. "And my point to mention that—"

"No, Holm." Jess glared at him, anger flashing in her eyes. "She didn't betray the Agency. There has to be another explanation. I'll figure it out, but I need to recover the relic first."

"You lost the relic?" Phoebe shot up so fast her chair crashed to the floor, startling something outside the window into a shriek. "For the Maker's love, close that window, Jessica!"

Tom wanted to defend Jess and admit it had been his idea to hide the relic, but Jess's hand on his shoulder silenced him.

"That's why Tom is here," she said firmly. "He'll help me find it and return it where it belongs."

Phoebe shook her head, but Holm spoke instead. "Be careful, Jess. Not everyone deserves to be trustworthy—and even fewer should be given the chance to take advantage of it."

Jess pressed her hand down on Tom's shoulder, keeping him quiet—though he would have gladly yelled at the old man.

When Phoebe and Holm finally left the room, Jess walked into the kitchen. She took her time serving herself a bowl of stew, then sat across from Tom.

"There's nothing we can do this late," she said, staring at the food but not eating. "You must be exhausted. Resting will help you adjust. Tomorrow morning, we'll keep looking."

He reached out and touched her hand, but she pulled away and met his eyes. "You can trust me," he said softly. "I'd do anything to—" He stopped. Their past hung between them, heavy and unresolved. He should've apologized years ago—for his silence, his mistakes, and for letting Charlotte come between them. That weekend he'd shared with Jess should have meant more. It *had* meant more.

"Tom," she whispered, her eyes brimming with tears. "Holm was talking about me, not you. It's me you shouldn't trust."

"Why would he say that?" Tom straightened, arms crossing as despair crept into his chest.

Jess bit her lip. "The reason I accepted your help... something happened here, and I have to figure out who did it—in this realm. The Agency will want me to stay in Main City," she sighed. "I can't be in two places at once. And I don't trust many people anymore. But I trust you, Tom. I can count on you to bring the relic to the right person."

"You're not coming back to Axiom?"

As he said it, all his hopes of mending things—or even restoring their friendship—faded. Self-loathing filled him for not finding a way to keep her close.

"I'm sorry. I didn't mean to lie. Well, technically, I didn't. I wanted to say more outside the hospital, or in the truck, but... I'm still figuring it out."

"Jess." He grabbed her hand and didn't let go this time. "I'll do anything for you. Just tell me what I need to do." He tilted his head, fighting back tears. "I'm going to miss you, Sunshine."

Tears rolled down her cheeks, but a smile broke through them. "I wouldn't stay if I had another choice."

"Like I said, I'm happy to help you, Jess. Not the Agency. Not these people. You." He hesitated, then added, "I do have one question, though."

She nodded.

"Your fiancé?"

A soft chuckle escaped her. "Marshall the Second. It was part of my undercover job. I was supposed to pose as the fiancée of the Chief of the Corrupts' son."

"Not sure how I feel about that." A memory surfaced. "I met a Marshall a few months ago."

Jess frowned. "That's not a common name. Where?"

"He's our new client—our biggest contract. Bill said he'd take our company to another level."

"Wait. Bill introduced you?"

Tom nodded. "Not long after he got engaged to Arlett."

Jess's expression hardened. "Describe him."

"About your brother's height. Dresses like him too—way too formal, thinks he's God's gift to humanity. Self-centered, smug. And he had a huge bodyguard with him."

"Many scars on his skull?"

He nodded again.

"Yttri." Jess rubbed her eyes and pushed her hair back. "That's bad. Marshall is dangerous. Whatever Bill was involved in, it can't be good."

"I figured that much when I met him. I tried to warn Bill, but you know your brother." Tom's eyelids grew heavy, his thoughts slowing. "The only thing I could do was to fulfill the contract by building that huge house and get us out of it. But then the wedding happened and..."

"You need to sleep," Jess said. "I can't believe it took so long for the potion to work. I'm glad it's working now."

He got to his feet and stumbled but managed to make it to the couch, where he flopped down. Before sleep overtook him, he looked at her and murmured, "You won't leave without me, will you?"

Jess shook her head and laid a blanket over him, just like she used to—bringing back memories of a simpler, happier time.

1. Remedy, an archaic phrase used in Chaos to describe a concoction of antibiotics, probiotics, and antidotes to increase the tolerance to the high levels of oxygen and other toxins within the domain.

12

Axiom Realm

188A22 Year Week 17, Seventh day, Sunrise

BILL STOPPED AT THE edge of the bed to catch his breath. A gnawing pain stabbed at his side, and his heart raced as if he'd run a marathon. His mother's constant reprimands only increased his desire to leave.

"I told you, Mom, if nobody's looking for Arlett, I will."

"Bill," Dan said in his usual condescending tone, "I'm sure the Agency is trying to—"

"The Agency?" Bill raised his voice, and a wave of dizziness forced him to grab his head and hold his breath for a second. "You mean the stupid place where my sister works? By the way, where is she again?"

When neither of them answered, he stood up. Though he had to use the mattress for balance, he was grateful his legs were holding up. He had no time to waste—too many hours had already passed. If Marshall didn't have Arlett, her life could be in even greater danger. A shiver ran down his spine.

His mother placed a hand on his shoulder. "Jess isn't the only agent. They came earlier and asked questions. I'm sure they're looking—"

"My sister couldn't care less about my wife—about Arlett!"

A soft knock on the door cut through the tension, followed by a woman stepping into the room. Her posture, her calm confidence, and the faint air of superiority instantly marked her as an agent.

"Bill Hiem-Sagac?" Her voice was flat, emotionless, and her sharp eyes locked onto him. For a moment, he thought they'd found out—that somehow the Agency had learned about his and Arlett's plan. His hands began to tremble. "I need to ask a few difficult questions. Are you going somewhere?"

Bill crossed his arms and glared at her. "And you are?"

"Of course." She smiled, nodding politely to his mother and Dan. "I'm Agent Millie Gaia-Ico."

"Go figure! Another agent."

"Bill!" his mother scolded, shaking her head before turning to the visitor. "Please excuse him. He's under a lot of stress and has forgotten his manners."

The agent nodded but fixed her gaze on Bill again—this time harder. "You said another agent visited before?"

"Visited?" He let out a bitter laugh. "That's a funny way to put it. Do you people ever just *visit* anyone?"

"Bill!" his mother snapped, moving toward him.

"Whatever," he muttered, scanning the room for his clothes. "My sister's one of your kind, and no, she isn't even here. Apparently, more important things than my fiancée went missing this morning."

"What things?" Dan asked.

"Where is Jess?" Agent Gaia-Ico interrupted.

Her posture stiffened, and her voice sharpened. Bill instantly knew he'd said too much. He kept his eyes down and let his mother speak.

"We believe she went to... she crossed over to that other... place."

"She's in Chaos?"

Dan placed a hand on his mother's shoulder, and bile rose in Bill's throat. He'd always hated how Dan pretended to play the role of father.

"A friend called a few hours ago and said she was going there," Dan said. "He didn't explain much, but we're hoping he'll talk her into changing her mind and coming back to support her family."

"Her family?" the agent repeated, frowning. After a pause, she nodded. "You said some things were lost, Mr. Hiem-Sagac?"

Bill's muscles tensed. "Obviously." He forced a smirk, trying to look both arrogant and clueless. "Only an idiot wouldn't notice. This was supposed to be the Wedding of Main City. We had priceless items in every room. Criminals walked into the Village because of the Agency's lousy security."

The agent's half-smile unsettled him. "Of course. You poor citizens always suffer from our lack of work. Yet, neither the hotel nor your guests reported anything missing. You're the only one who mentioned a robbery. Perhaps—"

"What are you getting at, Agent?" Bill snapped, crossing his arms. "Do you have a real question for me, or are you here to waste my time while my fiancée's out there in danger?"

"We're doing everything we can," she said evenly.

"All you can do to *find her*?" Bill's voice cracked, his anger giving way to desperation. "My best friend's grandfather was murdered, and you people did nothing. A stupid report—that's what you called justice! I don't need your excuses. I need my fiancée back!"

His mother caught his arm, rubbing his hand to calm him. "Agent, perhaps you should come back later. My son isn't well, and your questions are upsetting him."

Agent Gaia-Ico smiled at her, but there was no warmth in her eyes when she turned back to Bill.

"I'll come back later, Mr. Hiem-Sagac." She paused in the doorway, her voice soft but sharp as glass. "You'd better be here when I do."

CHAOS

188Ch22 Year

WEEK 17, SEVENTH DAY, SUNRISE

HOLM-67 SET HIS CUP down and studied the new arrival again. He didn't like meeting strangers—especially those from the other realm. As a man of Chaos, he had good reason to judge them harshly. Visitors from Axiom were never tourists. They were agents or government workers who came to *fix* Chaos, and, in the best scenarios, they left confused and disappointed when reality hit them.

But there was something different about Tom.

Considering it was his first time in Chaos, the man looked more alert than sick. The shifting ground and tilted gravity should have made adjustment difficult, yet aside from a minor fever from the night's poison, Tom seemed remarkably steady. His amiable smile, his humility in admitting his ignorance, and his ability to laugh at himself—traits that should have marked him as prey in Chaos—instead gave him an odd edge of danger.

His name, however, told Holm nothing. No ascendency, no inherency, no trace of family improvement over generations—just *Tom.* A meaningless, one-syllable name, and a last name, *Umbrar-Ment,* that said even less.

Holm would never understand it. Chaos shaped its inhabitants, starting with their names. To him, names carried weight, legacy, and worth—especially as a descendant of the Ium's family[1], one of the oldest in Chaos. Shouldn't Tom's name carry something stronger? Or did its simplicity perfectly match the stupidly curious way he stared at everything?

Jess grabbed a pistol from the table and held it out to Tom.

"Jess, I'm telling you, I won't be carrying that thing." Tom took two steps back. "I'd be more danger *with* it than without."

"You need to protect yourself here," Jess said firmly.

"What if I shoot *you* by mistake?"

Phoebe's giggles only deepened Jess's frustration. Maybe Holm's mixed feelings about this newcomer had less to do with Tom himself and more with how he *interacted* with Jess. Watching them was like seeing a reflection of his own life—Jess in his place, and his beloved Phoebe in Tom's.

"I've never shot anything in my life, and I'm not starting now," Tom said. People in Axiom didn't need to be armed.

"What if you have to protect Jess?" Holm asked.

Tom's features hardened as he stared at him. It was unsettling to feel a flash of fear toward someone from the so-called *weaker realm,* but Holm was old enough to acknowledge his limits—and Tom's sudden, dreadful intensity sent a chill down his spine.

Tom took the pistol from Jess's hand. "All right. What are the instructions for using this thing?"

Jess's expression softened. With more kindness than patience, she explained how to release the safety and pull the trigger, then gave an extremely basic overview of aiming and firing with the backlight.

"You're so cute," Phoebe whispered in Holm's ear.

He groaned, which only made her giggle harder.

"Isn't your problem with this fellow because of how much you care about that girl?" she teased.

Holm turned toward her, narrowing his eyes and pressing his lips together—but he didn't argue. His wife was far too observant, and she was right more often than he liked to admit.

"It's irresponsible for Jess to bring him here," he murmured.

"Is it?" Phoebe countered softly. "Or is it just that you don't want to see her get hurt again?"

Holm shook his head, unable to refute her. Just the night before, he'd had to deliver unpleasant news about the ambush during Jess's extraction. He only hoped things would turn for the better—soon.

1. Ium's family, the original rulers from Chaos, separated their legacy into 15 different groups and became lost during the early 120A era. As dictated by their earlier statutes, each group within this family was expected to specialize in a fundamental service for their people, for instance, housing, exploration, heritage, resources, nourishment, transportation, etc.

13

AXIOM SEA PERIPHERY

188A23 YEAR WEEK 24, THIRD DAY, AFTERNOON

I T HAD BEEN TWO days since Jess started her job at the Square, and it already felt like a lifetime.

The prison had only one entrance—a narrow, half-mile bridge stretching over the ocean. Her stomach had twisted with nausea the first time she crossed it, just as it did every time she had to climb somewhere high. Maybe it was the dizzying view of the terraces surrounding the prison—or the sight of the dark, endless water below.

All four walls of the Square had outer decks along its seven levels. Electrified nets wrapped the structure, sending a shiver down Jess's spine. She doubted they were meant to prevent intruders. More likely, they existed to stop anyone from jumping out.

The massive, double-height doors framing the entrance were legendary within the Agency. During training—and later, during her years of service—Jess had seen countless photographs of the train station and the distant view of those iron gates, symbols of justice and order. The Square had represented everything the Agency stood for: success, control, victory.

Now, as she walked from the pitiful excuse for a station toward those doors with the other guards, the weight of the metal seemed to press against her shoulders and bow her head. For the first time, an undercover mission was taking a toll on her soul.

The interior was worse. A dark, electrified dome sealed off any trace of sunlight. The official reasoning was to control airflow through small vents, trapping the stench within so it didn't escape. The result was a suffocating nightmare—a toxic stew of sweat, rust, and despair.

Jess's heart sank the first time she saw it.

Tom loved the sun. Now, he had none. The prisoners of the Square lived in darkness, cut off from every hint of the outside world.

Her duties were simple: as a new guard, she was to patrol a single sector on the third level, then log her reports into the archaic system. If she could just stop seeing the prisoners as people, maybe she could stomach the work.

As an agent, she had sent dozens of criminals here—but she'd never seen their destination herself. She had never questioned what happened to them once they were gone. Now, she wasn't sure any of it had been fair.

The seven-level facility stood on Axiom's southern islet, at the far edge of the sea line. It was hard to believe this prison belonged to a realm that prided itself on higher learning, justice, and civility. There was nothing humane about the Square.

Jess preferred walking close to the outer railings where she could hear the waves below. The sound reminded her that life still existed somewhere beyond the concrete. The walls themselves unsettled her more than the void beneath.

Unlike the first time she entered—when she'd nearly thrown up—she now took a deep breath, filling her lungs with what little fresh air she could before pushing open the heavy metal door.

A deep clang echoed, vibrating through the walls, and the atmosphere shifted instantly.

Salt from the sea had crusted over the concrete, the thick acrylic windows, and the metal bars of the cells. The prisoners barely glanced at her as she passed, but she couldn't help noticing their cracked lips, their hair and skin damaged by the acid air, and the raw flesh on their bare feet. The sight turned her stomach and weighed down her heart.

Jess used her keys to unlock a second door—a seven-inch slab of solid steel. It took all her strength to pull it open.

The central core of the Square was an open corridor running around the inner perimeter. Unlike the outer terraces, this one had an open view on three sides, giving her a grim sense of how vast the place really was. The deeper she went, the thicker the humidity became. Sweat dripped down her forehead, and the stench clung to her clothes.

Other guards had warned her: stay near the railings, or the prisoners might reach through the bars and grab you. She didn't need to test that to believe it.

Unlike the earlier section, where no one paid her much attention, the middle levels erupted the moment she stepped in. Prisoners shouted, cursed, and hurled every vile insult she'd ever heard—and some she hadn't. Jess kept her gaze forward, focusing on the flickering bulbs that lined the narrow corridor.

When she reached the third flickering light, her hand slipped into her pocket. She touched the small black mechanism Holm had given her—a fragile piece of a much larger system. Once all the components were in place on each level, the device would generate enough energy to attract the wave deep beneath the ocean and open a rift between realms.

As she removed the old bulb, her mind lingered on the consequences. The opening would collapse a section between the worlds. Months of calculations had gone into ensuring minimal damage. An air bubble would shield the Square—technology Holm had developed after the Disruption, thanks to Tom's accident.

Suddenly, someone yanked her backward by the shirt. Jess slammed into the metal bars of a cell. The impact rattled her teeth. An arm snaked around her waist and tightened, but she somehow kept the small sphere secure in her pocket.

"You're new here," a man hissed in her ear, his breath hot and foul.

In any other situation, Jess would've broken free instantly. But as part of her cover, a new and clumsy guard couldn't fight back too easily. Too many watching eyes could spread word fast.

"I think your fellow guards will be disappointed when I steal your keys," the man growled.

Jess struggled just enough to make it look real—then used his grip as leverage to push herself up. She kicked the lightbulb she'd been working on, shattering it.

The old electrical circuit plunged the corridor into sudden darkness.

"What the photons!" the prisoner shouted.

Jess seized the moment. She grabbed his arm, twisted, and slammed his head into the bars. He screamed, but the noise was lost under the uproar of the other inmates, who were shouting and pounding on their cells.

She yanked his arm through the bars and drove his head hard against the metal once more. The emergency lights flared to life, bathing everything in a dull red glow. The hatred in his eyes burned for an instant before she knocked him out cold.

Jess took the mechanism from her pocket, her jaw tight. To work, the device needed a conductor—something attuned to the wave's frequency, like an agent's key. The thought of leaving behind part of the silver chain Tom had made her for her birthday broke her heart. But saving him mattered more.

A heavy clang echoed from the far end of the corridor—the sound of the main door opening.

Jess hid the mechanism behind the lamp's casing and resumed her cover. She took a fresh bulb from her work satchel and screwed it into the socket just as the flickering lights came back to life.

"What's going on?" a guard called, striding toward her.

"Ah—no, nothing!" she stammered, forcing herself to sound panicked. "Sorry, my hands aren't as steady as they used to be!"

She stepped aside, careful to block the unconscious prisoner from view, and prayed the guard couldn't make out the shouted accusations echoing from the cells.

14

Chaos Realm

Tom followed Jess down the ladder and onto the street. Funny how something that had seemed nearly impossible the night before now felt simple. Whatever awful concoction she'd forced him to drink had worked wonders.

Though he still lost his balance now and then, he didn't mind—it gave him an excuse to hold on to Jess, more for enjoyment than necessity.

A sudden, loud buzzing made him glance up. Instinctively, he pulled Jess close and covered her with his arms. To his surprise, the "predator" was a modest-sized hot-air balloon gliding along a zipline strung between two buildings. Jess's laughter caught him off guard.

"I don't think those will attack us," she said, chuckling.

"What in the realms *is* that?"

"That," she replied with a smile, "is part of Chaos's transportation system—which you're about to test." She looked back at him with one eyebrow raised and a teasing grin. "I'm curious to hear the vintage expert's opinion once we're done."

Tom tilted his head, studying the balloon as it drifted away. Platforms dangled from the rooftops, suspended by steel cables.

A few looked stable enough. Most did not. His mind immediately filled with ways to improve them—better counterweights, reinforced joints, maybe even a braking system.

As they walked, a quiet nostalgia crept into his chest. Strange, but Chaos made him feel at ease. Jess was part of that, of course—but not the only reason he knew he'd miss this place.

"Vintage is the way to go," he said with a grin. "Wait. Isn't this exactly the kind of thing you'd hate?"

Jess pressed her lips together, keeping her gaze on the ground. "Didn't you once tell me fear of heights is just the void calling you?" she said. "I hope you weren't lying, Tom. That's how I've managed to survive this realm."

He laughed, raising his hands in surrender. "I might've read that somewhere." He had—at the library, of all places. He'd gone on his own just to find that book about phobias. It seemed only fair after she'd spent hours researching dyslexia and alternative learning methods for him.

"So," he said, gesturing around, "you can't use doors in Chaos, you have to climb everywhere, and now you travel *by air*? How big is this place?"

"Big?" Jess asked. "The hot-air balloon?"

"Chaos," he clarified. "How big is *Chaos*?"

Jess shrugged. "Hard to say. There are sections no one's explored yet, and parts that overlap with Axiom. My guess? At least as big as Axiom—probably bigger."

Tom's eyes widened. "As big as the *entire* realm?"

"Of course. And this isn't even one of the major cities. The ones here are smaller but denser. Lots of people—but they live upward."

The buildings around them loomed high, nearly as tall as those in Main City.

Then the ground trembled. Tom stumbled as loose stones and shattered glass crashed around him. How anything taller could stay standing was beyond him.

Jess grabbed his hand to steady him. "I don't like Elemental-1," she said. "Too many people, too many bureaucrats, and traffic jams that make you question reality."

"In the *sky*?"

She laughed. "There's also the water system and a top rail."

"A what?"

"Picture a sidewalk a few stories high—two lanes, crammed with motorcycles."

Tom frowned, and her laughter doubled.

"Tell me about it," Jess said. "No vintage cars here."

He grinned. "Then I'm done. Where's the exit to this madness? Or better yet—where's the food? I'm starving."

Jess looped her arm through his and guided him toward the next building. She turned the gears beside a wall panel, and the ladder descended with a hiss. Tom caught it before it hit the ground. It was the least he could do—and maybe it would earn him lunch.

"We can grab something at our next stop," she said, climbing up. "But I wouldn't recommend eating before your first ride."

F ROM THE ROOFTOP, CHAOS looked different—more dreadful. Tom didn't fear heights, but he understood construction. Most of the surrounding buildings were ancient, fractured skeletons threatening to collapse. The cracks running along their sides were bad enough, but seeing the exposed steel supports beneath the crumbling concrete set his nerves on edge.

"The balcony's near the end of the line," Jess said, pointing to a group of people waiting to board the hot-air balloon. Some wore smiles; most didn't. "We get to skip the line."

Jess strode ahead toward the rooftop platform, erasing what little joy remained in the passengers' expressions. Tom avoided their eyes. It was moments like this that made him resent the Agency. Who were they to decide whose time or business mattered more?

As if she'd heard his thoughts, Jess glanced over her shoulder. "They're a lot like you," she said. When he raised an eyebrow, she added, "They hate agents."

Tom stopped in front of her. "First of all, I don't *hate* agents. I hate the *Agency*. Big difference. And second, maybe they have a right to be mad. How long have they been waiting to board?"

She brushed past him and pushed open the door, shaking her head. "They don't want to ride with us. They'd rather we leave. Agents bring bad luck."

Tom sighed and followed her out.

The wind hit him hard. It wasn't a pleasant breeze—it shoved him. The high-altitude air buzzed in his ears, but what truly made his stomach twist wasn't the height. It was the sign posted ahead: a cluster of identical letters listing rules and safety guidelines. The sight dragged him back to school days filled with frustration and failure.

They approached the roof's edge, and Jess grabbed his arm. "No one reads that. Honestly, I don't think it matters."

Tom was about to ask why when he felt the building shudder. Jess clung to his arm with both hands and buried her face against his chest. He looked up just in time to see the neighboring tower tilt and collide with theirs. The roof trembled violently. Screams rose around them as chunks of concrete sheared away and crashed to the streets below. Somehow, the structure stayed upright.

"Boy, sweet Barrier!" the balloon operator shouted, wiping sweat from his forehead. "That was a big one! Let me run a few empties first before you board. Don't wanna send you up on a weak line, right?"

Tom didn't argue. The hot-air balloons were tethered to steel cables that spanned the rooftops. If the quake had loosened one, the whole system could fail.

Jess exhaled shakily. "None of those rules mentioned what to do in case of an earthquake."

"Are you all right?" Tom asked, noticing her grip still firm on his arm. He knew what it felt like to face something that exposed your weakness. Every time he struggled to read, his old failures came rushing back. She must've felt that same helplessness every time she faced her fear of heights.

"I'll be better once we reach the market," she said, inhaling deeply before stepping toward the ramp.

She climbed first, moving with practiced precision. If he hadn't known her phobia, he'd never have guessed. Hiding it was probably a necessity for an agent in this city. The thought of anyone exploiting that fear sent a chill down Tom's spine.

He followed her onto the platform. He wasn't fond of fairs back in Axiom, but he'd been on a few carnival rides—none as high as this. The same hollow drop opened in his stomach as he prepared to step into the basket, suspended hundreds of feet above the ground.

"Watch out!" Jess shouted, yanking him down.

The heat from the balloon's burner singed the side of his face. He collapsed onto the bench inside the basket.

"I believe that was in the instructions," he said, rubbing his temple. "Why do I keep hitting everything that hangs?"

"Your fault for being tall."

He chuckled and leaned back, taking in the view. From up here, Chaos spread below them in winding, irregular lines. The cobblestones glistened green with moisture. Keeping anything dry—or warm—in this humidity must've been a daily battle. No wonder Jess's skin was so pale.

"The rain really never stops?" he asked.

"Sometimes it snows, but not often." She stuffed her hands into her jacket pockets. "You'd miss Axiom's sunny days if you lived here."

"Maybe I don't like the sun."

Jess laughed, shaking her head. "You? Not like the sun? Impossible. Look at you—you probably work outside all day."

Tom glanced at his hands, noticing the difference in their skin tones. "I have to build a roof before I can get inside most days."

The basket tilted sharply as the balloon changed direction, sending his heart into his throat. They drifted along the edge of the city, where thick foliage bordered the urban sprawl. A translucent barrier shimmered from the basket's side, shielding them from overhanging branches. Jess didn't seem to notice, her eyes fixed on something distant.

"What's the plan?" Tom asked. "Besides breakfast, obviously."

She shifted in her seat and cleared her throat.

"Because you're thinking about food too, right?" he added.

Jess smiled faintly—too faintly. A polite, weary smile he despised.

"You're not keeping secrets from me again, are you? I mean, I followed you through a collapsing building and flying baskets. I think I've earned a few answers—nothing top secret, just... something."

"I wasn't thinking about breakfast," she said softly.

Tom crossed his arms, narrowing his eyes. "So that's still the game? I thought you trusted me."

Jess rubbed her face and rested her hands on her knees. "Do you know why your mom's so hard on you?" she asked, meeting his gaze.

"It's exhausting trying to talk to you without asking questions," he replied.

"I doubt that's her problem with me," Jess said. "She never had trouble being nice to *you*."

"Are you saying I'm difficult to talk to?" Tom leaned closer, lowering his voice. "Coming from the girl I used to talk to for hours every day? That sounds made up."

Jess met his gaze, unflinching. "You're not that person anymore. That guy stopped talking to me the day I joined the

Agency." She turned away, staring into the clouds. "Why did you leave engineering school?"

Tom looked down. It wasn't a time he liked to revisit. Once, he'd dared to dream—then everything had fallen apart.

"See?" she said quietly. "Easy to ask. Hard to answer."

She wasn't wrong. He had changed. And, in many ways, it had started because of her.

He remembered that day as vividly as if it had happened yesterday—the end of their last year in intermediate school. The sun had been warm but not oppressive, the kind of perfect day that made the world feel possible. Then Jess came running toward him, waving a paper in her hand.

"Tom!" She threw her arms around him, nearly bouncing with excitement. "I did it! They accepted my registration!"

"Who accepted what?"

She tucked a strand of hair behind her ear, grinning. "The research program! Remember? I applied weeks ago. They'll train me to help protect resources and species in *both* realms. Isn't that amazing? I'll get to—"

As she spoke, his smile faded. He snatched the paper gently but urgently from her hand and scanned it. The words blurred and jumped. *Resources. Program.* He recognized a few, but not enough. The paragraphs bounced on the page, unreadable chaos.

He shook the sheet, furious at himself for not understanding, furious at the document for taking her away. He forced his eyes to the bottom line, just enough to recognize the Agency's signature.

When he looked up, she was watching him, her excitement faltering. "Are you mad?" she asked, her voice trembling.

"Mad? No," he said, handing the paper back. "Why would I be mad? I only told you a thousand times *not* to join the Agency."

"Why are you yelling?"

"Right." He lowered his voice, folding his arms. "You just ignored my opinion—and my grandpa's. But sure, why would I be mad?"

Jess clutched the paper to her chest. "It's not about the Agency. It's about protecting our world. This program works across realms. It's meant to bring balance, to—"

"*Save* the realms? That's exactly what I was trying to do—save you from joining that cult." He stepped back, his voice shaking. "Did you tell my grandpa? I'm sure he'll be thrilled."

She wiped at her tears. "I thought you'd understand."

"I could say the same to you, Jessica."

The tears streaming down her cheeks stopped him from shouting, but not from hurting. She wasn't just ignoring his warning—she was leaving him behind. Deep down, he knew her new role would elevate her, while he remained... ordinary.

"There you are!" Bill shouted from the gate. "Come on! We're starting the fire!"

Tom nodded and stepped away from her. It was easier to walk off than admit his heart was breaking.

After that, he stopped calling her *Sunshine.* At first, he thought she deserved it. Later, he realized his silence had pushed her even deeper into the Agency's arms.

It had all gone wrong. And even now, years later, his anger wasn't about her decision—it was about the danger she lived with, and how powerless he felt to protect her.

Because the truth was simple. He didn't hate the Agency. He hated what it had taken from both of them.

15

CHAOS REALM

188Ch22 Year Week 17, Seventh day, Morning

T HE HOT-AIR BALLOON SLOWED as it approached a lower platform, just a few inches above the ground. Jess stood and walked toward the gate.

"Watch your head," she said, and once she stepped out of the basket, she looked back at him.

Tom's legs felt strange for a second, as if the ground were about to move, but when nobody seemed concerned, he kept going. It took him a few quick steps to catch up with Jess, and he was relieved when he did. He'd been right—dark alleys in Chaos were way worse than the ones in Axiom.

The streets narrowed, and without cobblestones, the ground was a mess of mud and things Tom would've preferred not to smell. The buildings were shorter, but in this part of town the windows were blocked with lumber and chains. The walls were covered with obscene, cruel graffiti. For once, he was glad it wasn't easy for him to read them. A chill crawled down his spine when he noticed the scratches along the wooden and concrete walls. Those marks weren't made by humans and were probably too big for the two kinds of creatures he'd already seen.

"The windows here are just illegal?" Tom asked.

"Not illegal, just unsafe. Most of Chaos isn't friendly. From the windows, you have a better view for stopping any attack. The doors behind you are a vulnerable point of entry. Business-es use appointments. Even knocking is extremely dangerous."

"So you'd better avoid all social interaction?" Tom said, try-ing to steal a smile from Jess, but he failed this time.

"That's one way to put it. This is Elemental-6," she said, as if that were enough explanation. "We're here to meet the Tracker. He isn't a nice man, and he's not fond of agents. But like most around here, he owes his life to some of us."

Smoke and dust covered the door where Jess stopped.

"You mean the Agency?" Tom asked.

She grabbed the handle and stared at him. Her eyes were cold and her voice severe, like the agent he'd never met before. "No, Tom, I meant agents. We. A few of us saved his life." She knocked twice, hard and clear, before opening the door. "Just don't talk about your preferences here, please. This guy—these people—aren't the kind you make friends with."

He wanted to defend himself. He wasn't stupid. Obviously, he wasn't going to say anything, especially if he was posing as an agent, but he lost the opportunity.

At the end of a chamber, a scraggly guy with long, dull hair and a dumb smile that showed the gap between his teeth stood with a knife in one hand and a whetstone in the other.

"Look who's here this morning, Silvie." He passed the knife along the stone, sending yellow sparks across the otherwise dark room. "It's one of our favorite agents. And why is she here? Because the day wasn't gloomy enough! We needed the extra cold around our pit."

"I need to locate something," Jess said.

The guy shook his head and made a hushing noise, swiping his finger across his mouth. "Silvie isn't feeling good, Agent. We can't help you today. Come back—"

"I find it irritating having to talk to you. I don't have to listen to you talk to your disgusting knife."

"How dare you?" He nearly bumped the whetstone into his face as he put a hand over his heart. "This knife is my life and history!" He looked down at the blade and ran a finger along it. "Of course you won't get it. Nothing is sacred to you."

"I saved your life a few weeks ago—and other times before that. What was it, two months ago, when I had to drag you out before Marshall—"

He slammed the whetstone onto the table, then cradled the knife as if it were a baby. Tom knew he loved his truck, but he wasn't that crazy. Was he?

"Fine! Allow me to guess. You're looking for a metal from Axiom, correct?"

"Not exactly." She placed her hands on the table. "I need to find a black epoxy case."

The man burst into laughter, flashing his crooked teeth. In one swift movement, Jess yanked him down by his hair and smashed his face on the table, then held him there, making sure the blade of his beloved knife was almost touching the tip of his nose.

"Agent." His voice sounded muffled and full of fear. "Silvie—my knife—it's poisoned."

"Good. I won't have to drag you down to Marshall's home then." She pushed him down but kept the knife away from him.

"Are you going to help me, He-li-3, or should I use Silvie to slice open your face?"

"No! I can do it," He-li-3 said, struggling to hold the table's edge as his feet slid in the mud. "I'll do it. Black epoxy. Got it."

Jess let him go, and he scuttled to the other end of the room. He was shaking as he rubbed his face, as if trying to clean something off it.

"I'll look, but... Agent, you must know: one of the few things we can sell to Axiom is our resins—the epoxies. It'll be impossible to identify—"

"I don't need an economics lesson on how our realms' commerce works. I know when this specific epoxy case crossed to Axiom and then back to Chaos. That will narrow our search."

"But—"

Tom stepped forward and crossed his arms. He only wanted a closer look at the knife, but the movement made the guy shiver. Making someone so afraid was a strange feeling, but he wasn't going to waste it. He'd watched enough entertainment to know how to be intimidating.

"I'm starving," Tom said in a low tone. "Better hurry."

A small cry escaped He-li-3, and he jumped to the table, tapping a few gadgets that turned its surface into a small screen. Jess kept an eye on him—and on the door behind them.

He remembered the sweet girl who used to help him with assignments and even read him the classics. The strong woman in front of him hardly resembled that delicate memory. Was it the same for her? Had he changed that much, too?

The table lit up with thousands of points of light, forming a map of what Tom guessed was Chaos. Unlike Axiom's maps, this one displayed an area on the right side of the Barrier, with a gray zone on the left for Axiom. Tom shook his head. It was an illusion to believe the realms really worked that way.

He leaned in, studying the details. The strange traces of the streets made no sense—they formed half-circles or polygons that led to dead ends. Like Jess had told him, the inhabited area sprawled larger than the clustered cities that concentrated everything together.

"All those are black epoxies, Agent," He-li-3 said, lowering his voice. "I'm not sure how—"

"Which of those crossed to Axiom on the Second night?" Jess asked.

He-li-3 exhaled.

"Don't test me," she said. With quick hands, he worked the controls again. Over three-quarters of the lights vanished.

"Hey, I recognize many of those may not be legal, but—"

"Now, from those, which came back on the Fourth? And you'd better not lie. My partner here"—Jess pointed at Tom without taking her eyes off He-li-3—"has many skills. He'll know if you miss one or try to play games. And let's just say Yttri will seem like a loving mother compared to what my partner will do."

"No, no!" He-li-3 rushed the gears. Sweat beaded on his forehead. "I'll give it straight, Agent."

It took longer, but eventually the table darkened, leaving only three lit dots.

Jess turned to Tom. He could've been wrong, but he thought she nodded. His bloodstream pounded in his skull as he spoke.

"Looks good," Tom said, and only when Jess turned back to He-li-3 did his heartbeat ease.

"Let's see," she said, leaning in to study the map—putting Tom's nerves back on alert. The guy behind her might look weak, but he was a borderline lunatic.

"Could I offer you something to eat?" He-li-3 asked.

Tom's stomach rumbled, but there was no way he'd eat anything in here. Now that he was closer, he understood the guy's role better. Animal carcasses hung upside down from hooks on the wall—good reason to become a vegetarian.

"That won't be necessary," Jess said, turning to Tom. "Let's go."

"Is that all, Agent?"

It wasn't the stupid smile on He-li-3's face as he picked up his knife, but the sudden joy in his tone, that made Tom aware of the coming danger.

Beside him, Jess must've sensed it too, because instead of opening the door to leave, she shut it and slid the wooden bar across to lock it from the inside.

"What's wrong, Agent? Need something else?"

Jess looked around, stirring the hay and mud on the floor.

"I told you, Silvie, it was a good day." His tone turned mocking as he began sharpening the blade again. "Not every day we see stupid agents get killed."

That was enough for Tom. In two strides, he reached the table and knocked the knife from He-li-3's hand. He bent the man's arm backward until the whetstone clattered away and a scream tore out of him.

Tom grabbed the whetstone and smashed the knife, shattering the blade into hundreds of pieces.

"No! You bastard! My... Silvie!"

He-li-3 lunged for the broken blade, but Tom punched him in the nose, sending him flying backward into the hanging carcasses.

"I'm sure Silvie will enjoy the show," Tom said, hauling him up again. "What if we hang *you* with your food and see if your friends eat you?"

He-li-3 clawed at Tom's arms, trying to free himself, mumbling through blood and panic. Tom knew the cruelty behind the threat—but at that point, he didn't care. He was ready to teach the photonic bastard a lesson about messing with him—or Jess. A loud knock at the door, followed by a heavier crash, cut him off.

"Let's go," Jess said, showing him a gate in the floor.

Tom hurled He-li-3 against the wall and sprinted to Jess. As soon as he reached the gate, the door burst open and someone—or something—fired at them.

Jess yanked him down. Ungracefully, he dropped through the opening and landed in a slimy puddle he wanted nothing to do with.

"Come on!" Jess said, helping him up.

The moment he stood, she grabbed his hand and they ran into a very dark tunnel.

Tom had no idea how Jess didn't stumble at every step, because even when his eyes adjusted to the dim light, it felt like an obstacle course. Shots cracked behind them, but no one seemed to be following. It should've been good news, but the screams of the creatures he'd met in the alley the night before echoed around them.

Jess pulled harder, forcing him to speed up. She kept turning through the tunnels, which didn't help. He only hoped his head wouldn't slam into some low-hanging thing down there.

His feet began splashing through larger puddles, and soon he was fighting a strong current. When Jess stopped, the water was up to his thighs.

"This is our exit." Jess moved his hand to a cold steel pipe. "Climb the ladder behind me as quietly as possible."

She didn't need to say it twice. He could hear splashes approaching. The last thing he wanted was to find out what was following them.

The ladder rose at least three stories. He couldn't see much; the tunnel wall scraped his back as he climbed. He wasn't claustrophobic, exactly, but he didn't enjoy tight spaces—especially in the dark, expecting something to grab his ankles at any second.

A latch clanged above, echoing down the shaft, and a moment later a weak light spilled in as rain fell on his face.

He kept climbing until Jess crawled out. The yellow gleam of too many pairs of eyes below made him move even faster.

Once he emerged from the tunnel, he looked around. The line of hot-air balloons was gone. In their place, large trees with strange, curving branches and roots crowded the horizon.

"Are you all right?" Jess asked, scanning him head to toe. "Did you get shot?"

"I'm fine," he said, taking in the bright green landscape. "What is this place?"

Jess looked skyward. "It's the back of Elemental-6. We aren't that far from—"

"Someone was shooting at you—at *us*!" He shook his head as understanding dawned on him. "Jess, are you hurt? Did we get ambushed?"

"I don't know. Back there I... What were you thinking, Tom?" Jess cleared her throat. "I've never seen you fight before. I never thought you would get— Were you really going to hang him? That would've killed him..."

"No! Of course not." Tom forced a chuckle. He'd never considered himself violent, but he couldn't deny how good it felt to shut that bastard up—to make sure he stopped laughing at Jess. And if something had happened to her, his answer might be different.

"I don't know, Jess. I wasn't thinking. Who was shooting at us? And what were those screams following us?"

Jess rubbed her face and sighed, but instead of her usual avoidance, this time Tom got answers.

"The screams were the takuosums. They live in this region. We're closer to the Barrier, and it's a smaller city." She started down a dirt path. "The shots... I don't know. They could be from anyone."

"Anyone?"

She smiled, nodding. "You're hardly the only one who hates agents." She shrugged. "Or it could be personal, although I doubt it. I don't think anyone has figured out the truth about Marshall and me... yet."

Tom pressed his mouth shut and followed in silence for a while.

The trees were majestic—huge, vibrant—and just like Jess said, perfect for hiding predators. Before long, the rain washed the mud from his clothes and boots, and the puddles became a small stream. If it weren't for the freezing cold, his numb fingers, and the hunger sliding into outright starvation, he might've enjoyed the quiet walk.

"I don't hate agents, Jess." He didn't dare meet her eyes. "I'm sorry I haven't supported your choices, but I've been shot at twice in two days. I've never been shot before. Those weird creatures are trying to hunt us so they can eat us. You know how crazy that sounds? And I can't—"

"I'm sorry, Tom. You shouldn't be here. Chaos isn't a nice place. I didn't use my best judgment bringing you." She sighed. "I promise I'll protect you while I—"

"No, Jess." He stepped in front of her. "It isn't me I'm worried about. It's you. Don't you see? My problem with the Agency isn't the theories and made-up conspiracies we've heard about. It's the danger it puts your life in. It's always been that."

For a second, the way her eyes held his made him step closer and reach for her hand. "I should've explained it like this before. And for all the time we—"

"There you are!" a woman shouted, hurrying toward them. "Holm sent a message hours ago! What the photons happened?"

When she reached Jess, she hugged her tight. "I'm so sorry. Oh, Jess, I can't believe it."

The woman broke into tears, and Tom thought Jess might cry too, but she pulled back and, with a nod, brushed the topic aside.

"We had some issues with the Tracker, but I think he found the right epoxy."

"We? Right. Holm mentioned you were with someone." The woman finally looked at Tom. Without warning, her gaze sharpened, and she pointed at him. "How dare you wear his jacket? You can't just take it. Did you kill him? Where is Peter?"

"I didn't kill anyone!" Tom said, stepping back with his hands up. "I don't even know who the photons Peter is!"

"He's my brother!" she yelled. "Son of the void, what did you do to him?"

Jess blocked the woman before she could smash a branch over Tom's head. "Gall-I, Peter isn't here. He's in Axiom. Tom did nothing to him. He's just borrowing his jacket."

Gall-I backed away, wiping her tears, but still narrowing her eyes at him. "I don't trust this Tom, Jess. He has the look."

"What look?" Tom asked, but she ignored him.

"Let's get out of here," Gall-I said, clutching the branch and frowning at Tom. "The takuosums have been crazy since... you know. Better stay out of the forest for now."

Jess turned to Tom with a shy smile and whispered, "This is Gall-I 31. She's a good friend, but life here toughens you up."

16

Axiom Realm

MILLIE GAIA-ICO STOPPED HER car, hoping her instinct was wrong. After meeting Bill, she knew the guy was hiding something. Considering the events of the week and what had happened before the wedding, she was certain it had to be important.

Millie's job within the Agency was to keep track of Lezar Mos-Ium-115, the Chief of the Corrupts, and his moves in Axiom. Her team had tracked some of the illegal exchanges, and on some lucky days, they stopped them. Naturally, when they received news of the man's disappearance, things got complicated. He wasn't a good person, but at least they knew him and most of his intentions: to move potable water into Chaos and illegal items into Axiom.

With the head of the Corrupts missing for a couple of weeks already, things could get dangerous.

The obvious suspect should have been his older son, Marshall. He would've taken control of the Corrupts in his father's absence. Strangely, he'd vanished a few days after his father, and his younger brother, Randall, was not reliable. No one in Chaos respected Randall, and his lunatic ways didn't help him reinforce his domain.

Just a week ago, she had no idea where or what Jess had been working on. She was following a lead to find the Chief when Peter, her captain, called for an emergency extraction from Chaos. It wasn't until she got to the plaza that she realized they were extracting Jess from an undercover job—and worse yet, they had killed Karen.

Karen was Millie's coach during her years in the Agency's training program. After Millie graduated, she applied to become an active agent but was rejected twice. Not everyone was as lucky as Jess, who'd been recruited as an agent from the ridiculous research program.

Karen developed a special bond with Jess—more like she adopted her as a daughter than as an apprentice. It was clear that Karen had broken many rules to get Jess out of Chaos. Usually, to extract an agent, the Agency worked for days, if not weeks, to make sure all the agent's contacts and assets were protected before the undercover agent could leave their position. This hadn't been the case. In the end, they saved Jess, but Karen didn't make it.

On the day of the extraction, it only took one look at Jess to know she had ignored her partner's plan. Obviously, Jess knew how the Agency worked, and even when Marshall had vanished a few days back, she should have stayed in Chaos, closing all loose ends.

Getting ambushed the way they did was the most questionable move Millie had witnessed from Karen during her years of service. Her former coach wasn't an amateur. The missing Welder just added more questions to the already hazy situation.

The tall, impenetrable building where the Welder worked stood in front of her. A few decades ago, it had served as an old clock tower for Main City, but the Agency decided to move the Welder's location after they purchased the place. A small door to the side worked as the entrance. The appearance didn't match its status as one of the most dangerous places in Axiom, but it helped with security.

Inside, the energy from the Barrier made Millie's nerves stand up and kept her on edge. She hated being so close to the powerful wave, and if it weren't for the emergency at hand, she would never have set foot in here.

Peter had been very clear with his instructions: after she finished her verbal statement at the Agency, she would meet him at the Village to support Jess until the First, when Jess would return Karen's relic to the Welder.

Millie didn't argue, but she disagreed with the instructions. After all, Karen's death needed to be investigated. Jess shouldn't need help. She was being rewarded with a luxurious weekend and the opportunity to be at her brother's wedding. Millie had missed so many family events that now they just sent her pictures of smiling faces instead of invitations.

However, by the time Millie arrived, someone had shot the groom and kidnapped the bride. There was no sign of Peter or Jess, and now she understood many other things.

Jess's brother was a jerk, and Millie couldn't understand why Jess's mom didn't even ask about her daughter's whereabouts and seemed more upset at Jess than worried for her. A weekend with those two looked like a punishment. More importantly, in the end Jess had needed their help, and neither Peter nor any other agent had been around.

The Welder's tower was nothing like what Millie had imagined. Sure, from the outside it was a block of bricks, but she'd pictured the inside more glamorous—sophisticated, expensive rooms. The truth was that the front was more interesting than the interior. The building was empty inside but for a spiral staircase.

As she approached it, she drew her gun. She tried the light switch, but nothing happened, so she turned on her flashlight and crossed the room. The concrete floor was bare. Above her, she could only see the brass railing of a balcony halfway to the ceiling. A weak light shone from the top of the Barrier, probably from the heat wave behind it.

Millie took a deep breath and headed for the stairs.

The metal steps were loud and cracked under her weight, which didn't help hide her presence, but aside from the broken door, it seemed like the place had been abandoned for a while.

After a couple of minutes that felt like an eternity, she reached the top step and lunged onto the balcony. A large, tinted glass wall faced her. If it weren't for the glass, the light from the energy wave probably would have blinded her.

She frowned and noticed a table with two chairs. One chair lay upside down on the floor. A plate and a candle rested on the table.

As she walked farther in, she kept the glass wall at a distance. Previous generations had built a container to protect their cities from the energy wave—the Barrier. Now that she was looking at it, everything made sense, and she wondered if she should be wearing a special protective suit for her body and eyes.

"Just don't stare at it," a raspy voice said, making her jump back and lower her gun. "Don't! No, Millie! It's me... Peter."

Millie didn't holster her weapon and stared at the weak man cornered against the wall.

He looked nothing like her captain. He couldn't sit up straight. His skin, even under the strange light, looked gray. Deep bruises covered his face and arms, but the most shocking part was his eyes—bloodshot and sunken.

"Peter!" She kneeled beside him and tried to help, but he pushed her away.

"No. They did it." His voice cracked, and his lack of breath made it hard to understand him. "It wasn't me... Millie, don't look at me. I'm done."

"Stop," she said, grabbing his arms and looking straight at him.

Long ago there were rumors about Peter—rumors she didn't want to believe. Now, seeing him like this, it was clear the rumors were real. Peter was an addict, and he had been using something. Part of her wanted to punch him, but mostly she just wanted to help.

"What happened?" She sighed and helped him rest against the wall. "You told me to meet you at the Village."

Peter leaned his head back and closed his eyes. "I'll answer everything, but... Millie, please... can you get rid of those?" He pointed with a shaky hand.

She followed his gesture and saw a bent spoon, a syringe, and a few packets, most of them filled with something she wished weren't there at all.

"Where—why did you—"

"Marshall." Peter shivered, and to Millie's surprise, tears leaked from his closed eyelids as he clenched his fist until his knuckles turned white.

He didn't need to explain further. She'd been following Marshall's father and knew their techniques of persuasion. She gathered everything and moved toward the opening in the Barrier, where she guessed agents returned the relics. The heat from the energy felt like fire, but her fingers went numb, as if it were freezing in there.

Peter's warning came to mind, so she looked down quickly. The energy waves bounced with colors that reminded her of portals when they crossed realms. It made sense. The keys pushed the energy from one realm into the other, like pouring oil into water, creating a bubble of a portal. For a second, she hesitated, but the syringe leaked a few disgusting drops onto her hand.

She tossed the stuff into the energy waves, and for a heartbeat, nothing happened. It looked as if the syringe had just melted, but then a blob formed among the waves. It seemed to vibrate, building momentum, and turned bright red. Millie turned and covered her head just in time.

The explosion echoed around the tower. Its heat burned and froze Millie's back at the same time. A strong smell of sulfur made her gag, and she tumbled to the floor.

"Millie!" Peter crawled toward her and, with a trembling hand, brushed the hair from her face. "What were you thinking? That thing is pure energy. Anything hitting it will accelerate its particles until they explode."

Millie coughed, scooting farther from the pit. "You told me to get rid of them."

"Sure, but I was thinking more of a garbage can."

"Peter, what the hell is going on?"

Peter sighed and lowered his head. Millie had never seen him like this. He wasn't only her superior; he'd been with her ever since she joined the training program. They were friends. She was one of the few who didn't believe the rumors. It would be a lie to deny how mad, confused, and worried she felt. But she needed to focus on why she was here.

"I went to the Village," Millie said. "Someone kidnapped the bride, the groom is a piece of neutrons and is hiding something, and there were no signs of Jess... or you."

"Jess isn't there?" At the mention of her name, as usual, Peter's expression changed—something that made Millie's blood boil. Jess and Peter had been romantically involved until she broke his heart so badly he left for a couple of months. Millie never liked Jess, but now she wondered if Jess had known about Peter's addiction and preferred to let the story grow rather than destroy Peter's career by telling the truth.

"Jess wasn't there and, according to her family, she crossed to Chaos with a friend." She shook her head. "I thought she betrayed us. It would explain everything."

Peter's eyes darted to her, but he let her continue.

"But if Marshall isn't with her, and he attacked you, do you think they took Jess against her will, too? Her family was there... all of them. It would've been easy for the Corrupts to threaten her."

"I know." Peter used the chair to pull himself up. "Any idea who the friend is?" Millie shook her head, and he nodded. "Who told you Jess crossed to Chaos with a friend?"

"Her dad—I mean, her mom's boyfriend. Her mom was more concerned about Bill and how he was talking to me."

Peter snorted. "I'm sure he was a delight."

Millie glanced at the waves again, recalling another issue—probably a bigger one. "Where is the Welder?"

"I don't know." Peter shuffled toward the stairs, then stared down the steps. "When the High Office ordered me to have Jess wait until the First to bring the relic, I knew something was wrong. It had happened before, but never with such a powerful relic. They must have known the danger of having it in the city."

"Marshall attacked you in here?" Millie asked.

Peter nodded and stepped onto the first stair with a grunt.

"What did Marshall do to you?"

"You really want to know, Millie?" he said as he kept descending.

"What did he want it?"

Peter sighed and stopped descending for a second. "The relic... and I—" his voice cracked before he continued. "I told him what he needed to know about it."

Millie swallowed a nod and thanked the Maker for the darkness. It was too painful to see him like this.

"Who knows what Marshall did to our Welder!" Peter said, stopping again to catch his breath. "It must all be connected—but how? The door was broken, yet there was no sign of a confrontation."

"It looks abandoned," Millie said, walking close behind him. "I doubt the Welder has been here—who knows how long ago."

Peter turned to her. "This isn't good. We need to find out who's with Jess, and why she's in Chaos."

She nodded and walked in silence toward the last turn of the spiral stairs. Once they both reached the bottom and stepped onto the floor, she forced Peter to let her help him walk.

"Good thing you need a hospital," she said, and at his skeptical look, added, "You've been beaten up, and who knows what that bastard put in you."

"Millie," his tone lowered, "I know exactly what Marshall did."

She stopped in front of him. "We have no idea what that bastard put in you. Understood?" When he nodded, she moved back to help him again. "After we solve all of this, we'll deal with it."

"We'll deal with it?"

"Yes," she said. "We, Peter. That's what friends are for."

Her heart ached as she wondered if she should've known about Peter's addiction—or if they were true friends, because he should've trusted her. However, there was no point in worrying about hypotheticals.

Axiom

188A22 Year

Week 17, Seventh day, Morning

"Y ou don't have to go home, Marshall." Randall's voice sounded slightly higher than usual, which meant he was losing his patience.

"Randall," Marshall said in the controlling tone he always used with his younger brother. "You know better than anyone how important it is to find Jess. Especially now."

"I get it." Randall paced across the pristinely clean carpet of their house in Axiom. "She's in Chaos, snooping around, and you want her... um... safe?"

The smile on his brother's face affirmed how little he knew Marshall. It also confirmed how long and hard Marshall would have to work before allowing Randall to collaborate with him once he took over the leadership of the Corrupts. Worse, it reminded him how much he needed his father's guidance.

"I'll find her and keep her in Chaos," Randall said. "You need to find our father, dead or alive—which is our priority."

It was difficult to tell if Randall was smiling while he put food in his mouth.

Marshall's jaw tightened. The idea of his father being dead was unacceptable. The night seventeen days ago, when he arrived at his father's airship, was still fresh in his mind. His father wasn't the kind to leave doors open, and the second Marshall saw his office ajar, he knew something bad had happened. He thought about his health, though the old man had seemed fine. He even thought about depression—that the years of hiding his past had finally caught up to him. It had never crossed his mind to find signs of a struggle, splashes of blood, and his father missing. Whoever had dared to take him had better kept him alive, or Marshall's revenge would be legendary across both realms.

"Marshall," his brother said, stepping closer, "we need to consider both possibilities."

Marshall was about to stand, but Yttri's hand on his shoulder stopped him, giving Randall a chance to keep talking.

"I'm not you, and I won't pretend to be, but you can't be in two places at the same time. Let me help. You can find Father, and then you can settle down all the agitators once and for all."

Marshall sat back on the couch and rubbed his temples. His brother was right. Finding their father was their number one priority.

"All right, Randall. I'll stay here, but you—"

"Yes! I'll handle things in Chaos while you manage Axiom... like the brothers we are, correct? Divide and conquer?"

Although Randall's excitement was concerning, Marshall didn't have a strong reason to second-guess his decision.

Over the years, Marshall had learned that his little brother had some questionable ideas and impulsive tendencies, but he always followed their father's instructions. It was his immaturity that excluded him from some business decisions—like working with the Agency and knowing Jess was a fake fiancée.

Randall wouldn't understand that passing some controlled information from Chaos could give them great intel from Axiom—weaknesses, corruption, potential blackmail material. Personally, Marshall would have protection from an agent, something valuable in both realms.

But for his brother, Jess really was Marshall's true love—and it should remain that way for a while.

"Do not harm Jess, Randall. She is my problem."

"What about the other dude? She left you for—"

Marshall stood and crossed his arms. "No one left me for anyone. And I'll learn more about the other guy when I talk to him. Do not hurt them."

Randall rolled his eyes.

"I'm serious, Randall. That's an order."

"I would never betray you, Marshall," Randall said with a smirk. Yttri stepped closer to him, and Randall raised his hands before leaving the room.

Marshall watched his brother's back as he closed the door, but the seed of doubt had already settled in his mind. "He wouldn't betray me, would he, Yttri?"

17

CHAOS REALM

188Ch22 Year Week 17,
Seventh day, Midmorning

Gall-I 31 only stopped staring at Tom when it was absolutely necessary, and her expression never softened. Despite being a small person, she knew how to put anyone on edge.

"How bad have the attacks been?" Jess said, while handing him a brown bomber jacket and a pair of pants. It was an older, warmer fashion than what they wore in Axiom, but similar to the outfits he'd seen in that realm. "You can change in that room." She pointed to a door—and only because it was Jess who said it, he walked toward it. In this house, and with this host, he could easily expect a murderer on the other side.

The room wasn't bigger than the last one, and the thousands of newspaper clippings nailed to the walls made it feel smaller. He stepped closer. The small fonts of the articles and the sheer amount of information made him groan. The photos, though, caught his attention. The people's features and the angry expressions told him they were Gall-I's relatives.

As he walked around the room, the scent of ink and old paper reminded him of his grandfather's shop—and to avoid the immense pain and regret that usually followed those memories, he quickly got dressed.

When he finished, the photos near him drew his attention again. All of them had been taken at a construction site. Everyone in the pictures held either a hammer or a shovel and stood by dirt piles or compacted ground, waiting for a foundation.

He tried to read the headlines, but his eyes refused to focus. With a groan, he let it go and focused on the details instead. The photos had been taken in different places—he guessed they were in Chaos because of the surrounding vegetation. However, the lining of the foundations and the materials used seemed odd to him.

As far as he'd seen, the buildings in Chaos were bizarre. This design, though, was similar to an Axiom complex. That was when he noticed the last picture. It was the only one where the people were smiling, with no tools in hand, standing before a completed construction.

The Barrier. In *his* realm—Axiom.

The Barrier was a massive concrete wall that ran along the energy wave crossing both realms. Most people mistakenly believed the Barrier worked as a border between them. He finally confirmed his lifelong suspicion: Axiom and Chaos overlapped in different sectors.

The concrete wall in Axiom formed a straight line that contained the world's energy wave, keeping it from bouncing into the sectors. The best developments to live in Axiom were closest to the Barrier, because of the stable weather and cooler temperatures. He had worked on several of those constructions, and the permit requirements were notoriously difficult to meet.

So far, he hadn't seen a Barrier in Chaos. Jess mentioned they were closer in the city, but now he wondered if there even *was* a barrier—or how deep into the jungle it might be. Maybe the wave just ran free in Chaos instead of being contained like in Axiom.

He thought about asking Jess, but discarded the idea. What was the point? She had probably sworn never to disclose it.

When he stepped back into the main room, Gall-I stomped toward him.

"If you touched anything, you will pay for—"

"Gall-I!" Jess yelled as she came down from the narrow stairs.

Like him, she was now dressed in the older style of Chaos. Though the clothing made her look beautiful, it was the way she moved—at ease, as if she belonged in this realm—that made his heart ache. If she was serious about staying in Chaos, there was nothing he could do to stop her. Worse, she might never go back to Axiom.

"Jess, I'm sure he messed up all my stuff."

"I didn't touch anything," Tom said, crossing his arms. "But I can't imagine how you'd know if anything's missing in that—"

"Shut up!" Gall-I snapped, rushing to grab the wet jacket he'd left hanging on the back of a chair. "You sons of Axiom's particles are all the same—so fast to show your cleverness and superiority. But listen to me: Chaos is, and always will be, better. Way better."

"Gall-I, please." Jess touched her shoulder. "Do you think I would bring those people into your home?"

"But he *looks* like them."

"He's new to all of this. You gave me a chance before. Just give him a pass this time—for me?"

Gall-I narrowed her eyes at Tom but finally nodded. "It's better now that he isn't insulting Peter, anyway."

For some strange reason, Tom became convinced that he hated Peter—and he had no intention of ever meeting him.

Jess walked toward the wooden table in the middle of the room and unrolled a map on top of it. "Let's find the relic, shall we?"

18

Axiom Realm

D AN HAD NO OPTION but to drive Bill to Arlett's father's home—a man who, until that morning, Bill had believed was dead, or so Arlett had told them. If Dan had known who the man really was, he probably would have sedated his future stepson and kept him in the hospital. Not for the first time in his life, he wished Amelia were his wife. Years ago, he would have set some rules and boundaries in that family.

Radium Radnar 88 was a diplomat from Chaos with a position in Axiom's parliament and had direct contact as an advisor to Axiom's leader, the Prime Commissioner. He was one of those people you would never meet unless you belonged to their social circle—and neither Dan nor Amelia belonged there.

He had no idea how Arlett could be related to that man. He hoped Bill was wrong—or that she had lied to impress her future family—because if Radium Radnar 88 didn't want his daughter marrying Bill, there was no way they would end up together.

"Did you ring the bell?" Bill asked from the passenger seat without taking his eyes off the large, decorated metal gate.

"Yes. We need to wait."

"Ring it again."

Dan sighed, and when he didn't move, Bill pushed himself between Dan and the steering wheel and pressed the speaker button.

"Bill! You need to be careful with your wound!" Dan shouted.

Even though Bill pretended to be strong, Dan could hear him gasping for breath and straining with every word.

"I need to save Arlett, Dan. These people kidnapped her. I will not be polite with them."

Dan wondered when the last time Bill had been polite to anyone was. He adored Amelia, but she always let Bill get away with his bad behavior and mood swings. They were always arguing about it, and it had really taken a toll on him—but nothing ever changed.

"Bill, you've been shot. None of the doctors agreed with you leaving the hospital. I won't have your mother worrying sick over you again. Kidnapped or not, you need to—"

A knock on his window made Dan jump in his seat, and the sight of an arm by his door didn't make him feel any better.

"This is private property," the guard said, inspecting the back of the car. "You can't see the Commissioner without an appointment."

"I couldn't care less about your photonic policies," Bill said, more from Dan's seat than from the passenger's. "I came to get Arlett back."

"Sir, I'll call the police if you don't—"

"Great!" Bill said. "Call them so they can help me save my fiancée."

The guard shook his head and stepped back from the car. He said something into a transmitter, but Dan couldn't hear over Bill honking at the gate.

"Bill! Stop!"

From inside the fence, three more guards approached. All of them were armed and as serious and annoyed as the first, who kept talking over his radio.

"What are you gonna do?" Bill yelled over the honking. "Shoot us?"

"For the Maker's sake!" Dan pushed Bill back, making him groan and press his side. "Sorry, I didn't mean to hurt you, but you can't—"

The metal gate opened just as the first guard approached Dan's window.

"The Commissioner will see you now." He gestured to the other guards, who stood behind the car. "Follow the path and park at the first roundabout. Someone will meet you there."

Bill hit the car's dashboard. "Well, what are you waiting for?"

Dan swallowed down bile and drove along the perfect gardens that blocked the view from the street. As the path curved, the mansion came into sight. A shiver ran down his spine, and he tightened his grip on the steering wheel. The estate was as big as a hospital but far more luxurious, surrounded by immaculate landscaping.

The first roundabout led them to a staircase at least twenty steps high and a door nearly two stories tall.

A guard in a high-rank uniform decorated with dozens of medals descended the stairs.

Dan pulled up to the entrance and turned off the car. The guard opened Bill's door. For a moment, Dan was thankful his stubborn passenger was still recovering from surgery; otherwise, Bill might have slammed the door into the man's face—and they already had enough problems.

Without a word, the guard walked up the steps while the others stood near Dan's car, weapons slung over their shoulders.

Dan hid his shaking hands and cursed himself for not telling Amelia where he was taking Bill. He hadn't wanted her following them, but now he feared the Commissioner might make them disappear.

"They want to intimidate you," Bill said, failing to hide the pain each step caused him.

Dan expected to see a massive vestibule outshining the grand exterior, but instead, a tall, overdressed, gray-haired man stood in the doorway, blocking their entrance.

"Look at you!" The Commissioner shook his head, curling his lip as he pointed at Bill. "I suppose Arlett was trying to humiliate me when she befriended you."

"Where is she?" Bill tried to take another step forward, but a guard pushed him back, and Dan rushed to catch him before he fell.

"There's no need for that," the Commissioner said, though a wide smile spread across his face. "This fool is so weak he can't hurt me."

Bill pulled his arm free from Dan's hold. "You son of the photons! Where is your daughter? I won't let you hurt her!"

The Commissioner laughed—clutching his abdomen and shaking his head as he tried to catch his breath.

"You can't do a thing! If I wanted it to be so, my daughter would never have met you." Once he regained composure, his tone hardened. "Lucky for you, I don't care a photon about her. She's a disgrace, and I'd rather see her buried underground than—"

"You killed her?" Bill took two steps forward. This time, the guard had to use full strength to restrain him. Dan felt a flicker of pride seeing the Commissioner take a step back. Bill's behavior was reckless—but the man deserved it.

"Are you mad? I would never get my hands dirty for such scum. Never," the Commissioner sneered.

"So where is she? I know you kidnapped her."

"You should know I had nothing to do with this." Hatred burned in the Commissioner's eyes. "My daughter died to me the moment she partnered with her mother. Everything Ar-Earth Radium 18—or Arlett, as you know her—told you is a lie."

"You're the liar! I know you have her, and I will—"

Behind them, the sirens of police cars filled the air, and soon flashing lights surrounded Dan's vehicle. At least twenty officers got out, but only one approached the stairs.

"Captain, I'm glad you're here," the Commissioner said.

"Yes, we are," Bill snapped. "This man kidnapped my fiancée!"

The captain looked at Bill, then removed his hat and turned to the Commissioner. "We received a call that someone was trespassing on your property, sir."

"Oh yes." The Commissioner smiled, his tone suddenly polished.

Dan recognized the shift immediately—the diplomat's mask sliding into place.

"I'm sorry to trouble you with such a minor issue," the Commissioner said, "but I'm glad you're here so we can put this gentleman to rest." He pointed at Bill, voice calm but cold. "Apparently, my daughter has gone missing, and her fiancé believes that I took her."

"What?" The captain scoffed, rubbing his neck. "That's ridiculous! You're one of the most decent men in Axiom."

Dan hadn't believed Arlett's father was involved until that moment—but now he was convinced. The Commissioner may very well have kidnapped her. Some of Tom's absurd theories about the realm's leaders conspiring to maintain control and hide corruption crept into Dan's thoughts. He only hoped Jess really was looking for Arlett—and that's why she hadn't spoken to the police.

Bill shouted, "This man has threatened Arlett before! She was hiding from him. You must look inside—"

"My daughter doesn't fear me."

"Of course, Commissioner!" the captain said. "Maybe she came to her senses and left this poor man. Who would blame her?"

The guards laughed, joined by a few officers, but not all—giving Dan a flicker of hope. "Bill," he said quietly, "we should go."

"No!" Bill and the Commissioner said at once, making Dan's heart pound.

"Captain, I don't like misunderstandings or vain accusations. Since your officers are here, I want you to search my house so this sad young man can see that my daughter isn't here."

The captain shook his head. "Commissioner, please. I would never dare invade your privacy. You have rights! This guy is just a loser."

"Captain, you're not questioning my decision, are you?"

"No! I'm sorry, Commissioner, that's not what I meant."

"This is stupid!" Bill said. "Obviously, she isn't in the house then. But you own more places!"

The Commissioner stepped so close to Bill that he had to move down a step and grab Dan for balance.

"Listen to me, Billy. You can search all my properties—here and in Chaos—and you won't find her. Like I told you, she's dead to me, and she knows it. If she tricked you into marrying her to live in Axiom, that's between you two. I didn't kidnap her, and I don't ever want to see her again." The Commissioner stepped back and smoothed Bill's shirt. "If you were smart, you'd leave her to her luck."

Bill shook his head, and as the truth settled over him, his weight collapsed into Dan's arms.

"You... no. It can't be. If you didn't take her, then who did?"

The Commissioner straightened, his polite tone returning. "Poor guy," he said to the captain. "Love is a problem for many." Then he turned to Bill. "If you want to find her, look for her mother. That bitch has a heavy agenda, and I'd bet my life she's behind this."

Bill's body shook in Dan's arms until Dan couldn't hold him anymore—they both fell. Dan caught himself before rolling down the stairs, but Bill tumbled over the stone steps, unconscious.

Alarmed, some officers rushed to help. It was the Commissioner who ordered them to call an ambulance and offered Dan his hand to stand.

"I have nothing against Bill. I feel sorry for him," the Commissioner said, helping Dan down the steps. Then he lowered his voice so only Dan could hear. "I don't know what Arlett's mother is playing at, but she's dangerous. I'm afraid my daughter tried to outsmart her and now..." He shook his head. "Well, she may be dead." He opened Dan's car door. "Good luck to you—and never come back."

Chaos

188Ch22 Year

Week 17, Seventh day, late morning

R ANDALL SLAMMED THE TRANSMITTER on the table and groaned. What was it about that stupid brat Jessica that no one wanted to hurt her? Before this year, he had never even heard her name. Marshall swore he had met her, but Randall was certain she would have been hard to forget. Not only because of her peculiar hair color but also because, to his great annoyance, he found her very attractive.

Marshall was stupidly in love and blind—but Randall's new ally too? What was the reason to spare Jess's life? She only meant trouble for their business and nothing else.

"Sir," his administrator said from the door, "something happened down in Elemental-6. An agent visited the Tracker this morning."

Randall raised an eyebrow and rubbed his chin, half his attention appreciating the smooth growth of his beard, the other half analyzing the situation. "I'm guessing we lost them?" he said.

"Yes, boss—sir."

"Watch out, Ta-llum, we have another boss, remember?"

"Sure, but come on. We all know where our loyalty lies. Sir."

Randall couldn't help a wide smile and sat up taller. Chaos was a tough place to grow up, and being part of his family wasn't easy. People expected things from them. Soon, when he finally took control of the realm, even Marshall would understand.

A pinch in his stomach made him shake his head. He loved his brother, but he needed to save Chaos—and Marshall had become weak, just like their father. At least the old man was out of the picture. He could only hope Marshall would forgive him for keeping his alliance and movements a secret. It would all be worth it in the end, when both ruled Chaos.

"Did we find what the agent wanted?"

"No, sir." Ta-llum closed the door behind him and approached. "Some of the witnesses—their description of the agent is... very suspicious."

"What do you mean?"

"There were two of them. The guy sounds like a regular Axiom resident, but the girl had the same strange hair color as Marshall's—"

"Photons!" Randall slammed his hands on the desk. "That daughter of the void is an agent! I knew something was off. What else do we have on them? What does she want in Elemental-6?"

Ta-llum stayed where he was, arms crossed and jaw tight. "Nothing yet. We're still talking to witnesses. I'm sure they'll have to use the boats to leave."

"Wait, no one has seen them leave?"

"Correct. We think they may be in hiding."

Randall chuckled, shaking his head. "That bitch."

He had known Jess was a problem. Now that he knew she was an agent, there was no doubt she had gotten involved with Marshall to snoop around. It explained why his new boss didn't want to touch her either. She was a loose end for the new people—but not for him.

In fact, he would redeem himself by saving his brother.

"You're certain our people know who the real boss is?"

"Absolutely, sir." Ta-llum stepped closer. "We know who the person in charge is."

Randall clapped his hands and moved toward the window. Below, the streets of Chaos were packed with people moving about, busy with their daily lives—lives he owned, and would soon change.

"Ta-llum," he said, his tone calm but sharp, "I think our boss may not have the same level of loyalty required here. It's time we spread our wings."

19

Chaos Realm

188Ch22 Year Week 17,
Seventh day, Late morning

As they walked down a hill into the abandoned side of Elemental-6, Tom followed Jess mostly in silence. He noticed how her steps grew slower, heavier, and how the dark circles under her eyes deepened. He doubted she'd slept much at Holm's house, and although he didn't know what had happened, it was obvious it affected her. The only thing he knew about the lost relic was that, according to Jess, in the wrong hands it could become a deadly weapon. He didn't care much about that, but he agreed with her—they needed to find that stupid relic soon, for Jess's sake.

"What is it, Tom?"

Tom shook his head, surprised she'd noticed his concern. "Nothing. I didn't say anything. Why do you ask?"

She frowned at him. "You have that look."

"You too? What look?"

Jess glanced at him while crossing the street. For a moment, Tom's mind traveled back to the days he used to wait for her on the Fifth day to walk her home from school. Who knew how many times they'd crossed streets together—but back then, they were having fun.

"You want to ask something?" she said, bringing him back to the present.

Tom pressed his lips together, remembering when talking to her hadn't been so hard. Now he second-guessed everything he wanted to say.

"Just ask," Jess sighed. "Or not."

"All right, I'll ask—but you can't get mad at me."

"Mad?"

"Is it comfortable?" he blurted out quickly, barely containing a smirk.

Jess's eyebrow rose as her eyes narrowed slightly.

"That." Tom pointed at her clothes, careful not to let his eyes follow her silhouette. "The thing you're wearing. Is it comfortable?"

"The corset?" She looked down at her outfit. "I guess so. I have to get used to it. But wait—why do you ask?"

Tom's smile widened. He leaned closer to her ear. "You always look good. And those few times you dressed up for formal dinners and things..." He straightened up, deliberately making sure she noticed his gaze on her. "Well, I like how much more of you I can see now."

She crossed her arms and stepped back.

"I told you." He took a small step back too. He'd experienced how strong her arm was, even when she wasn't trying. "You can't get mad."

Jess threw her hands in the air and walked past him. "Believe me, that was not what I thought you were going to ask."

Tom followed her, feeling slightly at ease. It was nice to know he could still take her mind off her worries, even for a moment.

"Do you get seasick?"

This time, it was Tom's turn to look confused. "No, I don't think so. Why, do you?"

As they turned the corner, a river replaced the street in front of them. Small canoes floated up and down the channel in a complex traffic system. Some boats stayed still, filled with products, while others carried far too many passengers. Like the hot-air balloons, wires hung above the boats—he guessed they worked like power lines on a rail system. A massive steam wheel churned on the riverbank, providing the city's energy.

A loud whistle from the wheel made Tom cover his ears. The ground shook moments later, and waves rocked the boats, sending a few crashing into each other. Some people fell into the water. Instinctively, he took a step forward to help them, but Jess grabbed his arm.

"No, Tom. They'll be fine. The water isn't a problem for them, but it could be lethal for you."

The trembling stopped, and as the noise faded, a foul odor from the river hit him. He turned away, afraid he might vomit on Jess.

"I still hate this part," Jess said. "The smell is too much, no matter how long I've lived here."

"They probably don't have a sense of smell anymore."

She chuckled. "Are you ready?"

As she stepped toward the river, Tom caught her arm. "I thought you said the water could kill me."

"Ah..." Jess bit her bottom lip before smiling. "Well, just don't fall in."

"Jessica!" He groaned as she guided him toward a line of people. Once again, they made their way to the front.

"What about the hot-air balloons?"

"Wrong direction," she said. "We need to go south."

This time, she showed the boat attendant her official insignia—one Tom had never seen before. The man looked down at her. He was at least a head taller and twice her size, but Jess didn't care, nor did she act intimidated.

"Do you have a problem with this?" she asked as the man studied Tom.

To Tom's surprise, the attendant unfolded his arms, cleared his throat, and stepped aside to let them pass. As Tom walked by, the man kept his eyes on the ground and touched his hat, almost like a salute.

"Just like with the hot-air balloons, the boat won't come to a complete stop," Jess said lightly. "So you'll have to jump on. Do not fall, Tom."

He smiled, though his attention was on the people nearby. Most didn't seem to care about Jess, but when he met their eyes, they reacted the same way as the attendant—either hiding or offering a strange, shy gesture of greeting.

"Are you ready?" she said.

An empty little canoe floated toward them. He followed Jess and jumped onto the platform, gripping the railing. This was easier than their last mode of transport. As soon as they were both aboard, Jess closed the gate. In one swift motion, the boat sped up, and fresh air cleared the stench from Tom's nose.

"We won't be disembarking at a port," Jess said, pulling a rope from under a seat and nodding at its edge. "The station hasn't worked for years. We'll have to cross part of the jungle. Make sure your sleeves are down and most of your neck is covered." She paused. "Are you all right?"

Tom rubbed the back of his neck. He wanted to ask why everyone saluted him instead of her, but he focused on not falling into the river. "Cover arms and neck. Got it."

Jess sat across from him. "You've been out in the sun."

"Excuse me?"

She stared at the channel, then back at him. "I'm sure you've noticed Chaos isn't exactly sunny. The people here don't get bright days—unless you're part of a select group." She glanced at him again, her eyes softening. "The diplomats from here live mainly in Axiom. If they come to Chaos, it's only to adjust... deals, contracts. The Corrupts—at least the higher-ranking ones—move between realms too. When you had Peter's jacket, everyone assumed you were an agent. But now they don't know what to make of you."

"And you are—"

"Pale?" She pushed her hair behind her ears and looked at the water. "The Maker knows how many times my mother pointed that out. I've been here long enough to pass as one of them."

Tom exhaled, resting his arms on his knees. "And how long has that been?"

Jess stood and grabbed the rope again. "Do you see that peninsula?"

He nodded, hiding his frustration.

"I'll hook the rope to the pier. It'll stop the boat for a few seconds."

"Let me guess—I need to jump and not fall into the water?"

"You got it."

Tom eyed the peninsula. The old pier looked half-destroyed and barely wide enough for one person. Tree branches and thick bushes grew around it, making the jungle beyond impossible to see.

He thought about the creatures in the alley, and a shiver crawled down his spine. He really didn't want to meet any more of them—or whatever had growled at them in the tunnels that morning.

"Do you remember the dinner when Bill told us about his engagement?"

Tom stared at her, his chest tightening. That night was one he'd rather forget. Bill had made reservations at a fancy restaurant in Main City and, of course, invited Arlett and Charlotte. At that point, Tom had been trying to figure out what kind of relationship he had with Charlotte, and the last person he'd expected to see was Jess.

She'd walked into the room, and all their past had come crashing down on him. In a way, Charlotte's rude, possessive behavior that night made up his mind to leave her for good. Still, it hadn't given him the chance to talk to Jess—and somehow, he'd managed to hurt her, to the point where she'd walked away from the table, and from him.

"Well," Jess sighed, "I arrived in Chaos the day after. I've been here since then—until the day before you picked me up at the airport."

Although the peninsula was closer now, and the pier's landing was clearly narrower and full of rotted boards, the reason Tom's stomach twisted was the math in his head. He didn't have time to ask, though—Jess tossed the rope, hooking it around a broken pole.

The boat stopped abruptly, throwing him forward, but he managed to keep his balance.

Jess pulled closer to the pier while the river's current pushed the boat sideways. Tom stood behind her and grabbed the rope, helping her angle it. Together, they pulled again, shifting the boat back toward the dock. Once it aligned, Tom wrapped the rope twice around his wrist and braced against the pull of the current.

"Tom, you should go first. We have to move before the next boat catches up with us."

Tom glanced back and saw the outline of another vessel in the distance. "Jump. I'll follow you."

He liked Jess's common sense. Once they were both safe, she'd yell at him—but for now, she didn't argue, something Charlotte had never learned to do.

Jess landed on the pier with ease, but as soon as her feet hit, the boat tilted and water splashed over the sides. Tom climbed up using the rope, but the unstable boards made him crash against the pier, pain shooting through his chest. He grabbed the edge as best he could, feet dangling above the water.

The boards cracked beneath him. A loud snap warned he had little time before he plunged into the river.

Each board split, the steel poles bending outward. He looked down at the dark, churning water striking the rocks—it didn't look safe or appealing. Maybe the poison wouldn't kill him, but the fall definitely would.

His wrists were suddenly seized in two strong grips. He looked up—Jess was lying flat on the boards, holding him.

"I can't pull you up," she said, tightening her hold.

He adjusted his position, and for a moment, Jess's hand slipped.

"No, Tom, you need—"

Tom's plan wasn't to let her go. He quickly tightened his grip, clasping her hands again. By his feet, he spotted a small hook once used for tying ropes or fishing poles. He used it for leverage, pushing himself up while Jess pulled with surprising strength.

Once half his body was on the pier, he crawled to where the boards looked sturdier and had fewer gaps. As he moved forward, something tore his side, leaving a burning pain the cold quickly numbed. He rolled onto his back, catching his breath—until Jess leaned over him.

She brushed his sweaty hair from his face, inspecting him. Then she opened his jacket and patted his sides. He groaned when she pressed near his ribs.

"Oh no," she said, pushing his jacket aside. "You're bleeding. Can you breathe?"

If Jess hadn't turned him on his side, he might not have noticed more pain. He was so cold he could barely feel anything—but yes, he could breathe.

"I'm fine. I'm sure it's just a scratch."

"I have to check this." She moved to the side, glancing around frantically. "We can't let it get infected."

As far as Tom could see, there was nothing but trees, bushes, and rotting wood.

"Maybe there's a patrol house nearby." As she stood, her head brushed a branch—and a low hissing sound followed.

"Jess, wait!" he said, trying to get up, but she pushed him back down.

"Don't move! You'll open the wound."

Suddenly, a dark, sinuous body shot from the trees and lunged toward Jess's head. Tom grabbed her, yanking her aside. The ophident's jaws caught his arm instead, its teeth sinking deep into his muscle.

"What are you—" Jess started.

Tom groaned as the poison burned through his veins like a thousand needles.

"For the Maker's void!" he yelled.

Though the glossy, sticky creature made him want to shake it off, he forced himself to grab it by the neck and squeeze until it released him. Then he flung it into the river.

"Tom, no!" Jess dropped beside him and grabbed his arm, making him wince. "You need the antidote!" She ripped the bandanna from her hair and wrapped it tightly around his arm. "This is bad... I can't believe... I'm so sorry." Tears filled her eyes.

"Stop. Jess, stop." Tom gently pushed her hands down and held her face between his. "What's the matter?"

"The poison! It'll kill you."

"You remember where I work, right?" He smiled faintly. "These things love the Barrier—but you know that. It won't hurt me." He lifted a shoulder. "I'm a contractor, Jess. I pretty much live outdoors, and there are ophidents in Axiom too. I get shots every year to keep my permit."

For a second, she just stared at him. Then she dropped to her knees, covering her mouth to stifle her sobs.

That was it. Tom needed to know what had happened to her. He moved closer and, barely touching her arm, whispered, "Please, Sunshine. Tell me what's going on. You're falling apart in front of me, and it's more than I can handle."

Jess closed her eyes and bit her bottom lip. For a moment, she said nothing. Then she sat back, tears spilling down her cheeks. "Karen is dead..." Her voice broke. "And it's my fault."

Tom had no idea who Karen was, but in that moment, he didn't care. He wrapped Jess in his arms and let her cry against his shoulder.

Around them, clouds thickened, darkening the sky. Wind picked up, stinging Tom's face. He didn't need to live in this realm to know the storm rolling in wasn't good. They needed to get off the half-destroyed pier and find shelter soon—but he didn't want to let Jess go.

Gently, he brushed her hair back and tightened his hold. "I'm on your side, no matter what."

She nodded but kept her face buried in his shoulder until thunder rumbled in the distance.

Jess pulled back and wiped her eyes. She pointed toward the foliage where the pier disappeared into the branches. "The station should be close. We'd better get there."

Tom wanted to scream or swear but did neither. He wanted to ask about Karen, to know what had really happened—but for now, he followed, the questions burning in his chest.

J ESS PUSHED ANOTHER BRANCH out of their way as she guided Tom into the jungle. A long time ago, this path would have been a wonderful walk to one of the most important stations in Chaos. Now, everything had been abandoned for decades.

She wasn't only concerned about falling and injuring herself, or Tom getting hurt, touching a poisonous plant, or crossing paths with a predator. She also needed to control herself. Her hands trembled, and her eyes kept blurring. She hated it. Being broken and vulnerable had always bothered her, and this wasn't the time to fall apart.

Tom was right. She felt her judgment slowing, her thinking getting harder. Her common sense was running away. It wasn't until she said it out loud that she understood the pressing weight in her chest. She wasn't just grieving Karen's loss. Guilt was eating her up. No matter how much she needed to figure out what went wrong that night, Karen would be alive if Jess hadn't been extracted from her undercover job.

"Is that the place?" Tom called over the loud rain, trying to shield his head with his jacket.

The broken entrance of the old station gaped a few feet ahead. She swore at herself for being so distracted.

The steel-and-brass gates were ornate, now rusted. One door hung crooked; the other was missing its bottom panel. Beyond the gate, a massive stone building smothered in plants barely resembled the magnificent place it had been. Windows were shattered, and branches invaded the openings.

Inside, the only relief was the roof. Broken as it was, it kept most of the rain off. The entrance was in better condition than the rest. A vast chandelier—one Chaos had once used as an example of greatness in their paintings—lay in pieces on the floor.

Tom stood beside her, hands on his hips, staring at the ruined foyer. "It'll take a while to find anything here," he said, turning to her. "Do you have a trick for that?"

Jess pressed her lips. "Kind of. The Tracker—He-li-3—found the epoxy case in a tunnel. According to Gall-I's maps, it should be about a mile from the platform."

Tom sighed. "Jess, you're talking to the guy who can't find his wallet on his desk."

She smiled, pulling a compass from her pocket and a flashlight from her belt. Thunder boomed, and dust and bits of debris sifted down.

"Let's find the tunnels."

"Wait. What?" He raised his voice. "You mean the train goes underground? This place is full of earthquakes! Who thought burying the trains was a good idea?"

Jess's heart lightened and she let herself laugh. "Well, this is Chaos. Almost nothing makes sense here. But to ease your mind, the trains don't run anymore. Now we use the hot-air balloons and the boat line."

He rolled his eyes and followed. "Right—safety first around here."

"For someone who drives like you, that sounds a little hypocritical."

Tom waved a hand, pride edging his smile. "If I remember correctly, I used to stay late at the shop so you didn't have to wander home alone. Talking about safety!"

Jess's throat tightened and butterflies filled her stomach. Those days were her favorites, and she hardly ever let herself think about them. She tried to speak, but the knot in her throat stopped her. So she started walking.

Tom trailed her down the dark tunnel in silence, even after she'd told him about Karen. He didn't press for an explanation. He just kept pace beside her, trying to help—because of her job. It had been her decision to join the Agency, and it had destroyed their friendship. Again, her fault.

"Tom?"

"What is it? Don't tell me. This dirt wall could also kill me?" he asked, and when she didn't answer, he turned around.

She had forgotten how well he knew her. The second he saw her face; he walked back and rubbed her arms.

"It's all right, Sunshine." No doubt in his voice. "We'll find it. You'll see." He smirked. "It takes a while, but in the end, I always find my wallet."

Jess pushed her hair back, nodding. "You deserve an explanation."

Tom kept his eyes on hers.

"Karen was my partner. My mentor. I met her when I enrolled in the Agency's research department. Her late husband was one of my professors. She always thought I was wasting my time there, but she supported my decision—our 'delusional ideas,' as she called them. I really believed we could help fix both realms. I was so wrong."

Jess looked around and sat on the tunnel's narrow ledge, resting against the concrete wall. Tom stood in front of her.

"When your grandpa died, I asked Karen to investigate it. I needed to make sure it wasn't what you thought. You had to be wrong." Jess sighed, staring at the ground. "Karen agreed, but in exchange, she ordered me to join her on a mission."

Tom's jaw tightened; he crossed his arms, shifting his weight.

"I agreed. It seemed fair. She had to lose an agent to look into your grandpa's death; I felt I should fill the slot. That's when I changed departments. She took me under her tutelage and eventually I became her partner. You met her once when you visited the Agency?"

Tom's eyes widened. "Was she the one who asked for my name? Or the old lady who came and interrupted our conversation?"

Jess chuckled. "She wouldn't like being called an 'old lady.'"

Tom shrugged. "I didn't like that she didn't let me talk to you."

Jess didn't let her mind wander down that road. It was pointless to think how things might be different if they'd talked that day—if she hadn't been so hurt and mad.

"Hey," Tom said, moving closer to take her hand. "I didn't mean—"

"I know." She covered her face for a moment, steadying herself. Tom needed to know, but continuing was hard. Years of keeping everything to herself set off all her internal alarms.

He had changed, though. The anger in him was gone. Otherwise, he would have interrogated her already.

"The deal with Marshall involved his father, too," she said, fully aware how many rules she was breaking. "We—the Agency—protect them so they can establish clean commerce between realms in exchange for intel from the Corrupts. It was the Chief who came to the Agency with the offer." Jess fidgeted with her fingers. "I know what you're thinking. Too good to be true, too easy. I had doubts. But you don't get deals like that often. After Marshall's father disappeared a few days ago, Marshall vanished too. I knew he was leaving, but I couldn't talk him into staying."

She bit her bottom lip, unsure he'd understand what came next. "My job was to protect Marshall's life, not his father's. After the Chief was kidnapped, Marshall was in danger, and the Agency needed to know who did it. We had a fake relationship, but my mission was real—protect his life."

She rested her head against the wall and closed her eyes. "My job wasn't done. I had to figure things out. The Agency counted on me. I shouldn't have left. Holm told me they'd expected me to stay a few more weeks. All those months working connections, finding clues, gaining trust... It was bigger than me. Others were involved. Their lives are in danger, and Karen had to have known."

Her voice broke. Tom stepped closer; confusion shadowed his face.

"Karen showed up at my apartment in Chaos. She was in a panic," Jess said. "Less than an hour later I was following her through the streets of the city, but we got ambushed by the Corrupts—or so I thought. Karen called for backup, but we were outnumbered, and she was shot. She died there in the street." Her voice cracked as she covered her mouth. "We couldn't even bring her body back..."

Tom wrapped his arms around her again, his warmth and strength making her want to stop time—to stop running, to stop fighting a losing battle.

"When did this happen?" he asked, not letting go.

"Ah…" She cleared her throat. "The Second day. I reached the coast the Third morning and flew to Main City. Then you picked me up."

"Jess," he eased her back to meet his eyes. "This week? Like four days ago?"

She nodded. "I didn't even know I was missing Bill's wedding. Peter ordered me to wait until the First to return the relic."

"But Bill and your mom knew you weren't coming. You responded."

"Yeah, that was Karen." She sighed, lowering her voice. "She managed my life here. Part of the job. It's better not to know unless it's a life-or-death emergency."

Tom hugged her again, which helped; she didn't want to see accusation in his eyes.

"I know nothing about undercover stuff, but I know lost, Jess," he murmured in her ear, voice warm. "You shouldn't be here. You need time to rest… to think. All those questions deserve answers, but you have to take your time or you'll land on the wrong conclusions—like I did."

A sudden rumble cut him off. Before Jess could process it, Tom shoved her against the tunnel wall just as a fast wagon screamed past.

"I thought you said the tunnels are no longer in use," he said, scanning both ways down the track.

"They're closed…" Jess kept her eyes on the retreating wagon. "This isn't good."

20

Axiom Sea Periphery

188A23 Year Week 24, Fourth day, Morning

Unlike the middle section of the Square, setting the dark, small mechanisms on the rest of the levels and around the perimeter was relatively easy. Jess didn't have to encounter any of the prisoners there, and the guards tried to do as little walking as possible during their shifts. Her only real obstacle was her fear of heights—but since her motivation was critical, she forced herself to work fast and ignore her shaky, sweaty hands.

She couldn't blame the guards for their lack of commitment. They all had keys and a time to leave, but the feeling of being trapped was overwhelming at times. Even she felt anxiety in the mornings when she faced the prison entrance.

Because of that, it surprised her to find most of the guards leaning against the railing when she came back from the outside deck.

"Showtime!" a guard yelled, smiling at her for a second before turning his attention to the opening below.

Jess took a deep breath, acutely aware of how high up she was. Ignoring her wobbly legs, she walked toward the deck.

"You think HC-3 will scream today?" one of the guards asked no one in particular.

"That'd be great!" another replied. "He deserves that and more."

One of the hardest parts of this mission for Jess was the loss of proper names. Part of the prisoners' punishment was to lose their identity, starting with their name. Inside the Square, even the guards used nicknames based on rank or position to keep anything personal outside those walls.

"Way more!" said the guard who had smiled at her. "I mean, we keep the worst crap here, but come on. The bastard who crashed the Barrier? He should be thrown into the wave! He killed so many innocent people."

Jess's heart sped up, her throat tightening. She looked toward the hanging cages in the center of the Square.

A massive gear dangling from the dome engaged, and a metallic grinding filled the air. The chains holding the cages began to move upward in unison, like a slow park ride, swinging loosely hundreds of feet above the ocean below.

When the gear stopped, an open elevator rose to the seventh level on the far side of the chamber. A narrow bridge extended toward the first cage—no handrail, barely wide enough to stand on.

Jess had seen the cages before. Holm and Phoebe had warned her about them. Still, watching them move—watching the guards and prisoners eagerly await the spectacle—made the cruelty of it all painfully real. A small bunk fit tightly inside each cage, and she doubted anyone of average height could stand upright.

"Are we half full?" someone asked.

"No, just three," another guard said, shaking his head. "Two losers died last week, remember?"

"Right! One jumped off, and the other got sick."

"I told the boss to leave them there, but he insisted they needed to stretch. In my opinion, it makes things worse. They dwell on what they can't have and... well, they give up."

"Who's in the cages?" Jess dared to ask.

"Who knows," said the guard beside her, lifting his shoulders. "The only one for sure is the Disrupter. Maybe the Corrupts' leader too. But who cares?"

A loud crash made Jess jump. Another mechanical arm extended toward the cages. At its end was a hook and two dangling cables. Seconds later, a man appeared on the narrow edge between the cage and the bridge.

He wore the same dirty white uniform as the others—short-sleeved shirt, pants—but his hair was long, and a beard covered most of his face. A guard on the far side of the Square attached the hook to a chain on the man's belt and the cables to his handcuffs.

The prisoner walked hunched over, eyes on the floor. Without the hook supporting him, he would've fallen from the bridge several times. Once he reached the deck, the hook mechanism turned him, forcing him to face the massive opening at the center.

The guards shouted and cursed at him, and soon the other prisoners followed their lead from within their cages.

Jess swallowed bile and forced herself to stay in control. The mechanical arm locked two more chains onto the prisoner's ankles. There was no doubt—it was Randall. Her false statement to the Agency, claiming he had been the driver who caused the Disruption, was the reason he now stood here, punished in this horrifying cell.

The uproar grew. Prisoners slammed the bars of their cages. Some threw things Jess didn't want to identify; others spat at him. The commotion spread to the lower levels, where convicts crowded their openings or gripped the railings to catch a glimpse. They couldn't see Randall, but that didn't stop them from joining in.

"How long before he cries?" the guard beside her said.

She couldn't take her eyes off Randall.

"That guy?" someone answered. "Five minutes. Tops."

For the next hour, she watched the second son of the Corrupts' Chief—Marshall's brother—stumble through the seven corridors of the Square. Behind him, three more prisoners from the hanging cages joined the walk, though she didn't recognize them. The mechanical arm pulled them forward, guiding them along the bridges down the levels. They only paraded them along the far side of the building—giving the guards a perfect view of the show.

"Do the other prisoners know what he did?" Jess asked.

"Photons, no!" a guard said. "If they knew that bastard was the one who destroyed Axiom, no one here could stop the massacre."

Jess turned to him. "Then why do they seem to hate him?"

The guard chuckled. "It's their entertainment. This is their break time."

21

AXIOM REALM

188A22 YEAR WEEK 17, SEVENTH DAY, AFTERNOON

PETER HELD HIS STOMACH and bent down. For the last hour, the cramps and nausea had stopped him in his tracks, and only shame had kept him from screaming. Millie stared at him. She hadn't said a word, but he had a good idea what she was thinking—and he hated it.

"Are you sure this is the address?" Millie asked as she pulled up to a small cottage on the outskirts of Main City.

The house had no lights and looked abandoned, yet the garden in front was in pristine condition.

"If you got the coordinates right, yes. The order to wait until the First to see the Welder came from this location."

She turned off the engine. "Let's check it out, then."

She jumped out of the car and slammed the door shut, startling Peter. He swore under his breath. Millie was great with directions—it was stupid to doubt her—but the constant nausea and pain kept him on edge and irritable.

He held out his hands, hoping they would stop shaking, but it only made it worse. What he needed was a hospital—and probably to be locked down—but first he had to figure out what had happened. That was why he'd persuaded Millie to change her plan. It was his job as captain, and he owed it to Jess. After all, Marshall had gotten the answers he wanted from him.

He sighed deeply, opened the car door, and half slid, half crawled out.

"It looks empty," Millie said, walking back from the other side of the house. "Still, I don't like this."

Peter stepped onto the porch and knocked on the front door. A second later, he tried the handle. "Can you—"

She pushed him aside. The easiest way in would have been shooting the lock, but Millie disliked violence—probably the reason the Agency had kept her in the lower ranks and rejected her first two applications to become an agent.

With a small gadget and two thin steel picks, she had the door open in under a minute.

"I should call you the next time I lose my keys." He wiped the sweat from his forehead, trying to smile.

"You lose them often?" she said, stepping inside without waiting for an answer.

Peter sighed and grabbed the flashlight from his belt but left his gun holstered. In his state, he was more of a danger with it. Millie could easily protect herself—and him—if it came to that, something he wasn't sure he could do anymore.

Inside, the place looked surprisingly ordinary: a few chairs, a table, a couch by the fireplace, and a desk. But the next room reminded him of the Agency's archive.

Large drawer cabinets lined the back wall, all sealed with high-security locks. Pictures of train wagons and an old station covered the other three walls. He moved to the desk, where several folders lay open, each filled with photos of the same place, marked with numbers along the bottom.

He picked one up, and a paper slipped out. It showed an underground tunnel with something scrawled across it in terrible handwriting—something that looked like "parcel eleven." He guessed the images were from Chaos, judging by the sky, though he wasn't familiar enough with that realm to be certain.

"Peter?" Millie called, and the concern in her voice made him drop the paper and follow her. "You have to see this."

He expected a dead body—but instead found another room like the first, this one filled with photos of people.

He recognized the quiet neighborhood in Axiom, and a knot twisted in his stomach when he realized it was Jess's childhood home. His only consolation was that the pictures were old—too old to be from her lifetime.

As he moved along the wall, the photos changed. Newer ones were taped over the old, and the neighborhood shifted to one of the most privileged areas in Axiom. The photos centered on a young woman who, if she lived in the mansion behind her, had to belong to a powerful government family.

"We need to figure out who this is," Peter said.

"My guess?" Millie replied, leaning in to study the pictures. "That's Arlett—the fiancée of Jess's brother."

"How do you know?"

"Because in this last one"—she pointed with a disgusted look—"she's getting very cozy with that guy, Bill. And yes, I know it's him. I just talked to the jerk."

Peter stared at the photo. Millie was right; that was Bill. But what caught his eye was the name written underneath, circled several times in bright red ink: *Thomas.*

Axiom

188A22 Year

Week 17, Seventh day, Afternoon

B ILL DIDN'T REMEMBER THE ride back to the hospital or the new surgery in the emergency room. His proof of the visit was the pain in his chest where wraps now covered a large scar. The worst, though, was the desperation filling him. He was now certain that Arlett's father had nothing to do with the kidnapping. It was hard for him to accept that Arlett had lied to him. He had understood that her mother had died when she was only a child, or so she'd told him.

He closed his eyes, resting on the pillows while his mind replayed the conversation from when he decided to ask Arlett to marry him.

Tom had been right; Bill wasn't a fan of attachments, and he didn't care about exclusivity while dating. But all that changed when Arlett, with a broken voice and tears streaming down her face, described her future.

He learned that her father, the Commissioner, had questionable business between realms. Arlett explained that her father was forcing her to move to Chaos and marry a powerful man from that realm. She asked for nothing from Bill; she was just saying goodbye.

Until that day, he hadn't cared about their relationship. They had a good time together, and she always showed up. But in that moment, he realized he loved her, and he didn't want to go through life without her.

So he came up with the idea for them to get married, but it didn't convince Arlett it would be enough. She feared her father. As a solution, she suggested talking to Marshall. Bill wasn't stupid and had plenty of questions, starting with how she had met that criminal, but in the end it all made sense. Arlett's father had all these trafficking business deals, and she met Marshall at one of her father's business parties. She knew Marshall was one of his father's unhappy customers. A powerful man as an ally seemed like a good idea—at least that was what she told him.

"You should be careful. Those medicines can really put you down."

Bill opened his eyes, and between the light from the window, the pain all over his body, and the dizziness, he could have sworn it was Tom sitting in the chair for visitors.

"I thought you were in Chaos."

"Well, I was there, but meeting you became my priority in the last few hours. After all, your sister is a...umm...how to say it? A hazy variable in my plan."

Bill half pushed himself up, and the shape of Tom that had been as clear as water a moment before transformed into a stranger—someone Bill knew he should fear. Another man stood at the door, arms crossed, and two others guarded the sides of his bed and the window.

"Who—" Bill cleared his throat and tried, but failed, to sit up. "What are you?"

"Of course, how rude of me." The man in the chair leaned forward, and his eyes looked exactly like Marshall's. "I'm Randall-O 86. You have business with my brother, Marshall? I can't believe we haven't met before, Bill."

Randall stood and walked closer to Bill, which caused Bill's heartbeat to rise. At his side, the CLEO device beeped faster, and an alarm went off as his breathing constricted and his throat closed.

"I'm not sure how you do business, but I want you to understand how we do ours." Randall smiled and patted Bill's hand. "What do you know about your fiancée?"

Bill gasped, trying to rip his throat open with his hands and nails to get air.

"That's not good enough," the man said, signaling a guard who moved closer and forced Bill to sit up. Suddenly, his lungs were hit by a cold mist that burned his throat but cleared his mind and vision.

He leaned over in pain; his voice was barely a whisper. "Her father—he didn't kidnap—he told me her mother—"

Randall nodded, looking at the group around Bill. "Ah, so Mr. Radnar is not an idiot, after all."

"Ar—she—upset her mother—" Bill made another attempt, but the metallic taste of blood in his throat choked him.

"Right," Randall said, unsurprised. "She—your fiancée—chose the wrong man to marry, and her mommy wasn't a fan of the idea." Randall shook his head. "The woman didn't approve of you."

"You know"—Bill's blood dripped from the side of his mouth—"her mother?"

Randall shook his head from side to side. "That's a complicated question, Bill. If you want to know where Arlett is, that'll be an easier question."

Bill's throat opened at the same time CLEO stopped beeping. He inhaled even though the cold made him dizzy. He feared having that conversation without a clear head, but his priority was to save Arlett.

"I need to find her. I have to—who—"

"Who took her?" Randall said. "It was me!"

Bill stared at the men and then at Randall. His nails cut into his palms when he closed his fist. "Why?" His voice was low, carrying the frustration and anger burning inside him.

"Aww! I like that question more. Still, I have a better one." Randall sat back in the chair without taking his eyes off Bill. "Do you know who your sister is?"

"My sister?" Bill's blood rushed. "Of course, she had something to do with this. That stupid bitch."

The man by his bed moved an inch closer while Randall leaned forward. "Perfect! We agree so far. Your sister should pay the ultimate debt."

Bill fought to stop shaking. Marshall's last call a few days ago and his involvement in their plan came to mind. He was going to ambush Jess because he believed she had something he needed in Chaos. Randall wasn't speaking hypothetically. He really wanted to kill his sister.

"Oh Bill, yes, I met Jess. In fact, she is my brother's fiancée. Imagine this: we are supposed to become a happy family...or not."

The words felt like a punch in Bill's stomach and confirmed how stupid his sister had been. One thing was doing business with Marshall, but marrying him? And now he learned that Marshall's brother had kidnapped Arlett and was probably working with her evil mother. He would not let Jess bring scum into his family.

"I think not," Bill said, his voice regaining strength. "Last I heard, she was fooling around in—"

Randall giggled, shaking his head. "How little you understand things, Bill. I envy your ignorance—so innocent, so uninformed."

Bill narrowed his eyes. "I don't care about Jess. I want Arlett back. Where is she? Did you hurt her?"

"No, I didn't even touch her. I simply delivered her into her mother's loving arms. Now, I'm feeling betrayed by your sister, but I have a plan."

Bill swallowed bile, looking down at the sheets over his legs.

"Interesting," Randall said, standing. "You didn't hesitate to ask my brother for help, right? We are the same family and want the same thing. Well, you and I crave the same thing: our lives back in our control."

The man by the bed grabbed Bill's hand and placed a small black box in it, folding Bill's fingers around it until his palm stung against the edges. The others moved to the door and pulled out their shotguns.

"We don't—I can't—" Bill began.

"You'll love the plan, Billy," Randall said. "Arlett's mom is a bitch and is torturing her for the disappointment she's caused their family."

The air around them thickened, and it had nothing to do with CLEO or the drugs in his system.

Randall sighed. "Not every mother is as sweet as yours. In any case, things are happening in Chaos—things that will affect your realm—but don't despair. If everything works out for me, I'll make sure your little fiancée comes back into your arms."

Bill looked at the box in his hand, then at Randall. "What do I have to do?"

"Not much, Billy. I have to tie up some loose ends. If it isn't me bringing Arlett back, I'll need to have a conversation with whoever delivers your fiancée. So, the next time you see Arlett, you open that box. That's all."

Hate and anger froze through Bill's veins.

"As soon as Arlett walks into this hospital room, you open that box. You got it?" Randall took a step toward the door.

"Whoever brings Arlett?"

"Yes, Bill. Whoever: Marshall, me, your sister, your stupid friend, your mother... whoever is with her."

"But what if no one—"

"Do not question me, Bill." Randall tilted his head and smiled. "If it isn't me, most likely it will be your sister, who will become my problem, and you'll get your fiancée back. Is that clear?"

Bill's mouth went dry. Although he wanted to deny it, he had feared for Jess's life when he made a deal with Marshall. He had convinced himself it was just a robbery and that she would be fine. Now he was certain his sister could be killed, and he would be the one handing her over. But what choice did he have?

He nodded.

"Excellent!" Randall said, not looking back. "If you betray me, I will tell Arlett about our conversation, and you will witness firsthand the extent of my proficiency with the Corrupts' practices."

All the guards left, closing the door behind them.

Bill covered his face, trying to block his thoughts. This time, they involved not only Arlett but Jess—and even Tom, who had nothing to do with this...

22

CHAOS REALM

188CH22 YEAR WEEK 17, SEVENTH DAY, AFTERNOON

TOM FOLLOWED JESS THROUGH the train tunnels. After the first wagon passed them, nothing else had moved around them, not even rodents. What bothered him more was the change in Jess. Once again, his friend had vanished, and a cold-hearted agent was walking at his side.

Her attention was on the road, her expression hard. She hadn't said more than necessary, and all the tiredness seemed to have disappeared. He was almost certain she would slap him if he made a joke.

After a mile and a half, she slowed their pace and pulled out the note Gall-I had given her before they left her house. From time to time, she would take a few steps back to check, then shake her head and continue.

"What the void!" she said. "It crossed over here! At least there should be a sign that something happened, not just...dirty."

Tom frowned. Aside from the vague description of a box, he had no idea what they were looking for. Nevertheless, he knew better than to ask.

Jess's story kept his mind busy, and every time he went over it, the pressure in his heart grew—not just for what she had lived through in the last week, but for the silent months she'd omitted to mention.

A strange shadow caught his attention, and when he looked up, he saw a half-fallen sign hanging from the top of the tunnel's arch. The letters were blurred beneath dust, burn marks, and grease, but even he could make out the word "Parcel" and two bars.

"Jess," he said, walking toward it. "Did you see this?"

He stared down at a chamber too small for a train station. It had no platforms or stairs, as far as he could see. A smell of dirt and steel reached him along with something familiar he couldn't identify.

As he moved farther in, he noticed the tracks multiplied and crossed over each other, sketching a spiderweb on the ground.

Hundreds of wagons were parked on the tracks, blocking most of them. He doubted the wagon that had passed them was able to leave the chamber.

"A depot?" Jess said, without taking her eyes off the space below.

"Probably," Tom said.

He knew little about trains, and less about how they stored anything. Still, he had a feeling that what they were witnessing wasn't normal, not even for Chaos.

"I suppose they needed a place to put the equipment after the station closed," Jess said, walking down the tunnel.

Tom stared at the view a little longer. The tracks in the middle looked like a stabling area. There were also high tracks along the walls that would work as inspection lines. He couldn't think of a reason they'd need that section so deep inside the tunnels.

Adding the random arrangement of wagons and the thousands of crates all over the ground, he had a bad feeling.

"The problem is what's missing," he said, jogging to catch up. If this was the central train station, he would expect to find the workshop and the wash plant, but those were missing.

"What do you mean?"

"I can't be certain, but do you see any coal bunkers or steaming tanks?"

Jess looked around, crossing her arms. "I'm not sure. Do you need any of those?"

"You're the agent here, but if I were going to smuggle anything without being noticed, I wouldn't have the luxury of much fuel or motors. You keep those safe and moving," he said.

Jess narrowed her eyes and stepped so close to him her sweet aroma reached his nostrils. "And you don't know this because of experience, right?" she said.

"What? No! You know I wouldn't—"

Her laugh echoed in the chamber, and Tom loved the sound of it.

"You're not funny, Jess," he teased. "Now, you owe me an—"

A shot echoed around them. They barely had time to drop. A second later, pieces of rock fell from the chamber wall—too close for Tom's comfort.

Jess dragged him behind a wagon to hide, just in time to avoid another shot.

"Are you all right?" she said, taking out her gun and flicking off the safety.

"I'm fine," Tom said, trying to see where the shooting was coming from.

Jess yanked him down as another shot exploded.

"Are you out of your mind?" she said, doing exactly what he was doing and getting the same answer.

She peeked out again and fired six times. In reply, a loud scream echoed in the chamber. Then a rumble of bullets bounced around them.

"Did you just kill—" He didn't finish. He shouldn't point out the obvious, and the hail of bullets that followed blocked his thinking.

Jess leaned against the wagon, checking her gun. From the look on her face, Tom understood they were in trouble. He remembered that Holm had given him a gun and reached back to take it, but Jess's hand on his arm stopped him.

"No. If you aren't sure how to use it, don't—" More shots surrounded them. "We need to get out of here."

Tom knew they were in deep trouble. They'd come from a tunnel with no side exits. The rock and dirt wall set in front of them and behind them was just a dead-end trap. Hundreds of wagons surrounded them; they couldn't tell if someone was behind them. And judging from the number of shots whizzing by his head, they were outnumbered.

Jess turned and opened fire again. Tom tried to pretend he hadn't heard the loud cry that followed. Any doubts as to why Karen had taken Jess as her partner were utterly silenced.

Another shot struck near them; this time rocks tumbled from the ceiling. He threw himself over Jess, and although she protested, he didn't move, making sure nothing hit her.

A larger chunk smacked his ear and his vision blurred.

"Tom! You're bleeding."

The next thing he knew, a hard pressure clamped his skull as Jess pressed a piece of cloth against it. For a moment, he thought he'd spotted a faint light emanating from a tiny ledge on the wall behind them.

"Tom!" She helped him rest against the wagon. "Please, answer. Tom—"

"I'm fine. Just a scratch," he said, though he wasn't so sure. Tears filled his eyes; he rubbed them and tried to move, but had to stop to regain his balance. Again he saw the light—and this time, trees and a lake on the other side.

"Jess, what is—"

More shots reached them, and now there were voices shouting orders—moving closer, faster.

"We need to go back to the tunnel," she said. "Can you walk?"

Tom nodded and followed her, crouching as she moved slowly among the wagons. He kept a hand on the side of his head and tried not to tumble, while a desire to run crept up his spine and only intensified when he figured out what one of the men was shouting.

"Photons! It must be Marshall's girl. Few have that aim."

A discussion followed, but as much as Tom tried to listen, he caught only random words: little brother. Too bad. The boss is happy. The last phrase was crystal clear, though: "Let's kill them."

Just after that, a growing buzz filled the chamber. Tom tried to turn back, but Jess grabbed his arm and pulled him against a wagon.

A loud explosion shook everything, more powerful than the earthquakes. Rocks, sand, and pieces of metal rained around them, but Tom couldn't hear them hitting the ground, which confused him. His vision worsened as a cloud of dust covered him, making him cough. At his side, he felt Jess grab his hand and try to haul him up. The second he stood, she pulled him and ran.

They couldn't have run for long—Tom's balance wasn't good and he stumbled at every step. When they stopped, she dropped to a knee.

He realized part of the chamber ceiling had fallen, and now they were hiding inside the tunnel. They had little time. Footsteps and shots moved closer, and he was certain another explosion would demolish the underpass over their heads.

"Jess, we need—"

A strange, wavy light up a sand slope by the tunnel caught his attention.

"I know," she said, and fired back toward their pursuers.

Tom stepped closer. It looked like an opening—and the lake and trees on the other side were painfully familiar and real.

He remembered reading the Agency's report about his grandfather's attack, and suddenly everything made sense.

"Jess," he said, crouching beside her. "Are there takuosums around here?"

"What?" She glanced at him, and both covered their heads as bullets whizzed past.

"The animals, takuto—"

"Takuosums? Yes... probably. Why?"

"Follow me," he said.

"What?"

"Do you trust me?"

Her expression was hard to read, but he hoped it meant he was an idiot for asking—not that she doubted him.

He crawled as close to the ground as possible toward the light.

As they moved up the slope, the rocks and dirt were looser, making the climb harder. Tom lost sight of the opening until more shots hit around them and part of the dirt wall collapsed beside them. Up close, it seemed smaller than he'd imagined, and he wondered if they would fit through it.

But there was no time. He recognized the buzz filling the place. Without a second thought, he turned and grabbed Jess by the waist. The tunnel rumbled as the missile approached; Tom rolled, holding Jess between his arms, toward the opening.

The force of the explosion felt like sudden heat burning his back, but it propelled him forward. He wrapped his arms tight around Jess and closed his eyes, waiting for the weight of the rocks to crush him. Instead, the air went cold, making it hard to take the next few breaths. After a few painful coughs, a warm breeze—clean with the scent of fresh air and water—filled his lungs.

Axiom

188Ch22 Year

Week 17, Seventh day, Late Afternoon

T OM OPENED HIS EYES, and the light—bright and warm—shone on Jess's hair the way it had over the years, making him believe, for a second, that he had to be dead. He rolled to the side and sat up when he realized he was still on top of her, but there were no bullets shooting at them.

"How in the..." Jess stayed on the ground.

A throbbing pain pulsed at the side of his head as a horrible fear crawled up Tom's spine. He turned around, ready to grab her and run away from their pursuers. To his surprise, there was no opening—just a bizarre rock formation growing among the brush.

"Tom?"

He looked at Jess, who was still lying on the ground. He crouched beside her, dreading the thought that she might be injured.

"How are we—Is this Axiom?" She got up on her elbows, frowning, either from the light or at him. "Am I dead? That has to be it."

He chuckled. "I had the same idea, but..." He sat back, resting his arms on his knees. "I doubt I'd be this lucky."

"What do you mean?"

"My head's still bleeding," Tom replied, ignoring the question.

She moved closer and pushed his hair out of the way. This time she was gentle, her hands warm and careful. "You're right—it's just a scratch. A deep one." She sighed and sat back. "How did you—how did we get here?"

Tom nodded as the memory came to him.

"What is it?" Jess said in an alarmed tone.

"Nothing. This is where my grandpa got killed."

Jess's eyes widened as she stared at the lake behind her.

"It's kind of hard to forget," he said.

She didn't ask questions, which he appreciated. Most of the time, he was the happy guy who made people laugh, whose work kept his hands and clothes dirty. Few had met his other side. Jess was one of them.

"Can you see that?" He pointed at the distance, where a pile of broken wooden boards with peeling paint lay half-buried under weeds and tall grass.

"Is it a tree house?" she asked.

Tom stood up and helped Jess to her feet. He felt slightly bad about moving her—she was tired and needed the sun—but he didn't want to be here.

"That was my mom's playhouse. Decades ago."

She looked around again. "Wait... Is this the lake behind...?"

"Yeah, these are the woods behind Grandpa's house." He shoved his hands into his pockets, walking with sure steps. "Your old house isn't far from here either."

Jess walked toward him, matching his pace without complaint. She probably had plenty of memories from that neighborhood—hopefully not as painful as his, but he wouldn't count on it.

After she got accepted at the Agency, things got rough at home, and Tom hadn't made things easier. Not long after, she started avoiding him, giving him no chance to apologize. She changed—spending most of her time at her school in Sector 4, coming home only for extended breaks and weekends. Then she moved to the Agency. He could count on one hand how many times she'd visited after that.

"I'm sorry about the tree house. It must have been a pretty one."

Tom smiled. "It was—before I demolished it."

He didn't dare look at her.

"Grandpa got killed here. At least that's what the police report said and what the doctors told me, but... well, you know, I didn't believe it."

He pushed his hair back and cleared his throat. "I didn't accuse the Agency for nothing, Jess. It's all blurry, but a few days before Grandpa was killed, I came home all excited because I got accepted into the engineering program. I found him all worked up, shouting that a woman had been interrogating him. I don't know—he made it sound as if she wanted to know too much about our family or his shop. I told him to file a report with the police, but he was certain she was an agent. The police wouldn't be able to do anything. He pretty much ordered me never to talk to an agent in my life."

Tom slowed down but kept his eyes on the distance. "I got so upset and yelled at him, and once we both calmed down, Grandpa, of course, dismissed you from his hated list." Tom lowered his voice. "He said you weren't a real agent—that research wasn't part of that deal."

Jess was looking at the ground. He wanted to find her eyes and ask what she was thinking or feeling, but he wasn't that brave—or that stupid.

"When I read the report," he snorted, shaking his head, "boy, that was hard to read. It took me hours of struggling, gathering pieces, and re-reading them. I guess I should've asked for help, but I feared what I'd find out." He sighed. "Anyway, things made more sense when I saw those disturbing creatures last night."

"Tom," Jess said, touching his arm.

He patted her hand and took a deep breath. "So back there—" he pointed toward where he guessed the portal should be "—the report finally made sense. Also, my grandpa's wounds..."

A heavy silence fell between them. The worst part of his old man's death were the hours in the hospital, watching doctors and nurses try to close the wounds. Part of him was glad to learn they weren't human-made. Now he knew the truth—that his grandfather had been killed by those disgusting creatures. And even though it was terrifying, it brought a certain peace. No one had hated his grandpa that much to kill him in such a horrific way.

After a while, when he felt confident his voice wouldn't betray him, he continued.

"There was this light in the tunnel, and when I saw the lake and the tree house... well, I got it. Those creatures don't have a key to cross over between the realms, so I figured if they could do it, then we could too. And, well, we did, right?"

Jess pushed her hair behind her ears and nodded without looking at him.

In the distance, he could distinguish the lights of houses, windows, and streetlamps. If he'd wanted, he could've found his house and Jess's without trouble—but he didn't. Too many memories weighed on that place.

"Do you still want to come?" she finally said.

"I'm here to help you recover that stupid thing. Sorry we ended up in the wrong realm, but we didn't—"

Jess blocked him and looked at him for the first time in a while. "You saved our lives. Never apologize for it." Then she bit her bottom lip, and a shy smile illuminated her face. "If you're this crazy to come... I know how to get back from here, and I think I know where the relic is—and who took it."

Tom clapped his hands. "Let's go back, then."

23

Axiom Realm

188A22 Year Week
17, Seventh day, Late
Afternoon

MARSHALL KNEW IT WASN'T good to find an Agency car parked in front of his father's gateway. But the most concerning part was the agent who had come out of the house.

He'd confronted the captain the day before. As he suspected, the man cracked under his own faults. His father had been right: knowing people's weaknesses was powerful, especially when those flaws made temptation easy.

He waited a few minutes before walking into the old cabin with Yttri. The house was a box of memories. It was where his father hid from everyone except his children, and, when she was alive, Marshall's mother.

It was here he'd learned most of the important lessons his father taught, and where he'd met the man who hid behind the powerful figure he showed to others. Marshall owned many houses in Axiom, and even more mansions, zeppelins, and airships in Chaos. Still, this modest wooden cabin was his only home.

He ran his fingers along the main door lock; the small indentations from forcing it open made his heart pound. The next time he met those two agents, he'd remember their intrusion—and they would pay for it.

"Yttri, why were they here?"

The boards creaked beneath his footsteps as he moved from the family lodge to the studio. He took a breath before opening the door. His father wasn't there, but the scent of old leather and linseed oil hit him like always. He needed a moment to compose himself.

Familiar photos of the Chaos train-tunnel system lined the walls. He found one photo out of place—its folder left in the middle of the table. Again, he took a deep breath to contain his mounting anger. Parcel 11 had been an extensive project. For years his father had tried to shut down the train system; a few years back he finally succeeded. The old man was wise—such an expansive network would erode his control over Chaos. It was virtually impossible to protect and contain the perimeter of those lines, so he closed them for the wellbeing of the Corrupts' business.

Marshall suspected it was also tied to his father's past. His father had lived between realms and had split his soul in two. Marshall hated the other room in the cabin but understood how important it had been to his father.

Yttri stood at the doorway, so Marshall followed him into his least favorite place in both realms. Not two steps in and a weight settled on his chest; his breathing grew difficult.

Newer pictures—mostly of Arlett and her family—covered the walls. All the old man's work, all his research, had been obscured by colorful, glossy photos of smiling people who seemed blissfully unaware they were being watched.

He took a step forward, but Yttri crossed his arms and blocked him.

"You're right." Marshall opened and closed his hands, trying to quell the heat rising inside him. "Of course. It's evidence, but..." He paced, his voice rising. "There are too many questions, Yttri. Who contaminated this place, and how did they know about it? Why were those two morons here, and—" He shook his head and stepped out of the room. "Where is Father, and why was the door forced open just now?"

Marshall crouched to inspect the lock more closely. That was when he noticed the shattered glass in the family room.

At first glance, he'd missed it—a small shard on the dusty wooden floor. As he moved closer, a sickening fear washed over him. He wished he could be a child again and close his eyes to the evidence, but he wasn't. He needed to see.

On the mantel shelf his father kept only two framed photos: one of their family and the other from the old man's past. His mother had hated that second picture—had fought with his father over it—but in the end she'd accepted it. It was from before her time. Now Marshall understood why the younger members of his family had problems with it as well.

He passed his fingers over the clean spot where the frame had rested for years. The memory of that other woman holding a child that looked too much like his father sharpened everything into terrible clarity.

The door puzzled him. Previous vandalism had involved keys. As with all their properties, his father had designed special locks for the family: some sent notifications when opened by a non-member; others wouldn't open without a drop of family DNA.

Yttri's hand rested on Marshall's shoulder as his world collapsed around him. His knees failed and he sank to the floor. He screamed and struck the wooden boards so hard one cracked. His fist bled; an electric pain ran up his arm, but he didn't care.

His father was dead. He would never find the body—the killer knew his family very well.

Randall—his brother—had killed him. He'd gotten rid of the "weak old man," as he called him, and Marshall had been foolish enough to ignore it. Love for his family had blinded him—and it had cost him everything.

Marshall wiped his eyes and rested on his heels. The smiling family photo made bile rise in his throat.

"He'll pay, Yttri." He grabbed the frame and, perhaps mimicking his brother, smashed the glass and tore the photo from its backing. "Randall is an idiot—and he'll learn why Father made those plans. He'll learn what real power feels like."

24

CHAOS REALM

188Ch22 Year Week 17,
Seventh day, Early evening

J ESS WAS GLAD TO be back in Chaos.

That section of Axiom was full of memories she disliked thinking about, especially with Tom at her side. She understood he wanted to talk about their past, but even if she opened herself to being hurt that way, she needed to have the conversation with a rational mind. Having him here was proof she wasn't thinking clearly.

"Tell me again why we're going to meet Ronald?"

"Randall," she corrected. "The people shooting at us kept talking about the baby brother and the boss."

Tom stuffed his hands in his pockets. "How do you know they were talking about Marshall's brother and not somebody else?"

For a moment, Jess considered the question, making Tom sigh and shake his head.

"Never mind. You've got this," he said.

She couldn't blame him for getting frustrated. For years, she'd answered no questions about her job. In fact, she shouldn't even consider talking about it now. But she'd broken so many rules already—and Tom had been shot at and nearly died from poisoning. He deserved an answer.

"When I met Marshall, he explained a lot about his business. We had to share—"

"Jess, no. No, no, no. I don't need all the details."

"Yes, you do." She cleared her throat and slowed her pace. Tom's expression was unreadable, so she focused on the road ahead. "Marshall explained how the train system in Chaos was a hazard to his family's business. In short, it ran around the perispherical line of all the cities and even into parts of the jungle, making it hard to protect and control."

"Protect and control?" Tom said. "Sounds delightful."

Jess pushed her hair back. Marshall had never hurt her or been outwardly cruel, but he had a way of making her fear everything around her just by talking. He'd forced her to witness the despicable things he did to others. Still, some of his father's ideas about safety and order made a twisted kind of sense. Chaos would've been pure anarchy without their control. She hated the Corrupts, but if people stayed out of their way, they could live as peacefully as possible in that realm.

She wasn't a naïve girl dreaming of fixing the world anymore. Long ago, she'd learned how ridiculous that was. Sometimes she wondered whether living in Chaos had forced her to give up those ideals—or if her life in Axiom had made her dream of a better reality.

"Jess?"

"Sorry. Where was I?"

"The trains? Protect and control?"

"Right." She nodded a few times, hoping this information wouldn't put Tom in greater danger. "Marshall's father closed the tracks a few years ago. The boats and hot-air balloons were part of his replacement plan. If you want to travel to another city, you need a permit and a good reason."

"All but agents?"

"Kind of." Jess glanced at him. "There's supposed to be diplomacy between the realms. It doesn't work, of course, but they have a deal with Axiom. We protect resource trade, and they give us a free pass into their realm—as long as the Corrupts aren't in charge where you're headed or you don't get in their way."

"Then what do you do?"

She lifted one corner of her mouth. "You've already experienced what happens."

Tom nodded, crossing his arms before letting them fall. "All right. What do the trains have to do with Marshall's brother?"

"Randall isn't a big fan of his father. He has his own theories, and though I don't know the details, his main goal is to oppose him. So when I heard people talking about the 'little brother' and the 'boss,' I figured it had to be him. Marshall never doubted his brother's loyalty. Ironically, he has a better family relationship than I do."

"Does he have that much power? Would people really betray his father and the brother in charge?"

Jess shrugged. "I'm sure Randall isn't working alone, but I have no idea who's helping him. Holm will probably figure that one out."

"Holm?"

She nodded. "He's our informant—one of them. I trust him."

After a few steps and a long silence, Tom said, "It's worth checking out. Sounds like a solid lead."

"You're not convinced?"

"It doesn't matter, Jess." He chuckled. "I don't understand this place or its people. But I don't doubt your conclusion."

It should have comforted her, but it didn't. Did she want to know who else was involved? Of course. But there was no time. The relic had to be recovered before anyone opened that box. It was a massive source of power that should be in no one's hands.

J ESS STOPPED AT THE bottom of the building and forced her breathing to slow. Her hands were sweaty and her knees shook—just like every time she climbed those big zeppelins. The hot-air balloons were bad enough, but the airships always tested her will. So far, she'd hidden her fear from most people in Chaos. Only Holm knew, and by default Phoebe. Of course Tom knew too.

"I'll be with you," Tom said, placing his hands on her shoulders. "I won't let you look down."

Jess bit her lip and exhaled. "We're taking the wire ride to the other level."

"What other—" His eyes widened as a large airship rounded the corner, casting a greater shadow over them. Jess shivered.

"There?" he asked. "Why?"

"Did you think the influential people of Chaos live in the shaky buildings?" she shot back.

The peculiar hour had gathered many travelers. Randall was famous for parties and large dinners, so even when staff balloons arrived, they were full of workers and delivery people.

The wire ride was as awful as Jess remembered. High-speed winds slammed the small basket, which bounced wildly at a steep angle. Every part of her screamed to close her eyes, but her time in the Agency taught her that fears were her enemy's strength. If she hadn't learned to resist them in Chaos, she wouldn't stand a chance now.

Tom didn't look happy either, but she suspected his discomfort wasn't about height. His hand gripped the basket railing; Jess's heart skipped imagining how close he was, and how much she wanted to reach for him.

"That balloon looks bigger and more stable," Tom said, pointing to a larger hot-air balloon approaching the airship's landing deck.

"Yes, but that one's knocking at the front door. We can't do that."

"Are you sure?" His eyes met hers and a smile brightened his expression. "All the shooting could be a misunderstanding."

Jess wanted to be angry at the joke, but a larger, sillier part of her wished they could be laughing somewhere far away—even if that meant attending her brother's wedding.

She looked away. It was already the seventh day. If things had gone according to plan, Bill would be on his honeymoon with Arlett—and she doubted Tom would still be around.

A horn honked, announcing the landing. The basket tilted even more to force a jump onto the higher pier. The crate barely stopped before everyone gathered their things to disembark.

She pulled up her hood and signaled Tom to follow. If she'd had time, she would've done something with her hair—easy to recognize—but she didn't. She only hoped Randall wasn't expecting her.

It was different walking in Elemental-1 or 6. In that airship she moved among people she'd probably met with Marshall—except Marshall wasn't with her.

"We need to get to the kitchen's entrance," she said, moving quickly down the bottom-level corridors.

Unlike the spotless, impressive hallways of the upper decks, the workers' levels smelled of things that should've been discarded long ago and were packed with people hustling about. The better halls stayed empty; guests spent their time in the dining room, ballroom, or on deck.

"How can you be sure this contact will help you?" Tom asked.

She took a breath as she gripped the metal door knob. "I'm counting on Yttri's family."

"Who's family?"

"Um... it's complicated. He's Marshall's common sense—yes, that's a good way to put it."

"Marshall's what? Jess, that doesn't make sense!"

She ignored him and opened the door. Maybe Tom was right and they needed a better plan. But she was close to solving the case, and her body and mind were fraying. Her shoulders ached, her head had been pounding for days, and the constant need to stop was growing. She couldn't pretend for much longer.

The kitchen was as full and chaotic as she'd hoped. People had precise tasks on tight schedules. Patience wasn't a virtue in the Chief's house; Randall was notorious for rage when dinners went wrong.

Jess walked to the small office. The aroma of grilled meats and fresh bread made her smile at the thought of Tom yelling at her for skipping a meal.

She didn't knock.

The woman inside jumped and clutched her chest. "For the Maker's life, would it kill you to knock?"

"Sorry, Hafni, but I need your help," Jess said as Tom stepped in behind her.

Hafni-Um 72 crossed her arms and narrowed her eyes at them. "Listen, I'm not one to judge, but I don't help traitors."

Jess glanced at Tom. "No! He isn't—I haven't—" She shut her eyes. Unlike Gall-I, Hafni wasn't a friend; she knew nothing about Jess's arrangement with Marshall.

"I don't care, Jessica. I won't betray my boss."

"Yttri is in trouble."

Hafni stared and spun toward the wall behind her. "No. It can't be. Yttri knows how to protect—"

"If you want to help your brother, I need you to—" Jess began.

"Liar. That's it. Just like Randall's people were whispering. You're cheating on Marshall and now—"

"And now what?" Jess crossed her arms. "I walked into Randall's kitchen with my lover to ask for your assistance? How ridiculous does that sound, Hafni?"

A sob escaped; she muffled it with her palm. "You probably work for the Agency, and they're going to kill my brother."

Jess stepped closer. "I work for the Agency, yes. But my job is to protect Marshall."

Hafni shook her head.

"Listen, Randall is behind the Chief's disappearance, and I'm afraid he'll hurt his brother too."

"No," she whispered, backing away. "Not possible."

"Hafni, I didn't believe it either, but Randall tried to kill me."

"Because he caught you with your lover!" Hafni blurted.

Jess heard Tom move behind her but didn't look. If she had, Tom would have seen exactly how she still felt about him—feelings she was certain she needed to bury.

"Yes. He found us in the working train tracks of Parcel 11."

A gasp escaped her lips and she sank into the chair. "It can't be. Marshall will kill Randall—"

"Only if Marshall learns about this, and I'm not sure he knows." Jess exhaled. "Marshall only trusts Yttri, and he'll send him after Randall. My brother hates me—he always thought our father preferred me. He blamed me for refusing to join our dad on the trip where he died. We haven't been civil in years. Still, I'll do anything to save him. No hesitation. Yttri knows you've got his back, and I have a plan, but it requires your help."

When Hafni didn't answer, Jess pressed on. "I must get into the vault. I need to get inside Randall's suite."

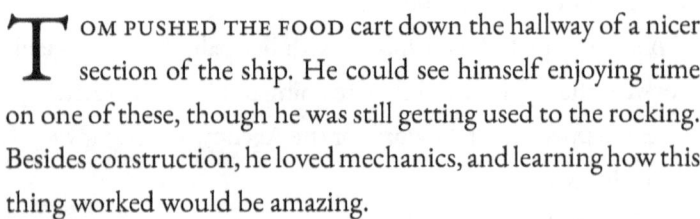

TOM PUSHED THE FOOD cart down the hallway of a nicer section of the ship. He could see himself enjoying time on one of these, though he was still getting used to the rocking. Besides construction, he loved mechanics, and learning how this thing worked would be amazing.

A couple came out of a room laughing and clinging to each other. The guy glanced at Tom for half a second, then jabbed a thumb toward the closed door behind him.

"The place is disgusting. It better be clean by the time we're back."

Tom didn't bother to answer. He'd dealt with people like that plenty of times. The guy pretended Tom didn't exist as he passed, but the girl hanging from his neck turned and winked at Tom.

He chuckled and kept walking, counting the doors before his turn. It wasn't the moment for distractions, but it was easier to focus on numbers than on what he was doing here.

He'd asked little about Jess's plan because he preferred not to know. The sweet girl he used to visit at her bedroom window was very different from the woman who now shot—and killed—people. He was prouder and more impressed by her than ever, but he was also afraid of who she'd become.

Jess had said the corner where he needed to turn would be easy to spot, and she wasn't wrong. An enormous chandelier hung from a three-story ceiling, and tall mirrored columns lined the corridor—exactly the arrogant aesthetic he imagined the Corrupts liked to flaunt. It reminded him of plans for the house he and Frank had been building for Marshall. Now he understood the over-the-top design choices.

He opened the small compartment in the cart and took out the master key Hafni had given him. Before he could use it, one of the double doors flew open, slamming the cart and nearly making him drop the key.

"What the photons?" said a forgettable man in a pristine dark-blue suit. "Trying to knock me down?"

Tom pulled the cart back and lowered his head. The man swept past, adjusting his jacket, followed by two large, ugly bodyguards.

"Don't ever cross my path again or I'll have you killed," the blue suit said.

Tom waited for the other two to go. One kicked the cart so the plates and glasses rattled; the other laughed and muttered what sounded like another threat.

He took a breath, slipped into the room—grateful he hadn't needed the key—and eased the door closed. The last thing he wanted was those idiots returning.

Jess emerged from her hiding place in the bottom of the cart.

"Delightful friends around here," Tom said. She didn't answer, striding across the suite like she knew the layout by heart.

The thought made Tom's blood boil.

The suite held a massive bedroom, a sitting area, a couple of side doors, and a bar. He could picture the sort of things that happened here. If he didn't want details about the killing, he wanted even less about her life with Marshall.

"We don't have much time, Tom."

He nodded and pushed the cart into position, following the simple plan. Hafni would make sure Randall had to return to his room; then Jess would do the rest.

"Will Hafni be all right?" he asked.

"If Randall wins this, no one will be all right."

"I know, but she could get killed."

Shouts erupted in the corridor and heavy footsteps approached. Jess slipped behind the door, a bottle she'd lifted from the bar in her hand.

"That bitch!" Randall barked as he shoved the door open and stomped inside. "I'll make her pay for insubordination!"

Jess kicked the door shut, and Tom rolled the cart to block both doors so the bodyguards couldn't force their way in.

"What the—"

Jess cracked the bottle over Randall's head. He dropped with a heavy thump onto the carpet.

Outside, footsteps pounded; kicks and shoulders hit the wood.

"Help me," she said, grabbing Randall's legs. "We have to get him into the closet."

Tom jammed the cart tight against the door, then sprinted to the couch and rammed it into place for extra weight.

"Are you sure they won't shoot us?" he asked, taking Randall's arms and dragging fast toward the closet.

"They won't risk hitting him."

She swung the closet door open; lights flared, reflecting off hundreds of mirrors that made the room look bigger. The space was large enough to hold another full bedroom, but instead thousands of hangers displayed clothes of every color and style.

"See that door at the end?" she said.

"An elevator?"

Jess nodded and hurried toward it. "I need his hand to call it," she said, hauling Randall's arm up, not caring that he wasn't tall enough to reach.

"What is—" Randall groaned, coming to, but Jess grabbed his hair and slammed his head against the wall.

"Tom, the button!" she snapped, propping him into a seated slump.

Tom lifted Randall so his hand hit the button. The doors slid open immediately.

Jess slipped inside. Tom vaulted over Randall's legs and joined her.

The suite door cracked under an ax-head as the elevator closed.

"I hope you've got another way out," Tom said.

"Listen, Tom." She met his eyes. "We're looking for a dark block—smooth, hard edges, a faint shine. It won't look like it opens."

"All right. Very clear description."

The doors opened as strip lights flickered on—and Tom's heart sank.

The storage room was huge and filthy, like no one had cleaned it in years. Tables, shelves, and teetering stacks of boxes filled the dim space. Jess didn't hesitate; she shoved packages aside, sending things crashing, and dug in.

"What size?" Tom asked, kicking himself for not inspecting the relic when she hid it behind the cabinet board.

"Um... glasses-case size? Maybe smaller."

"Great. We're looking for a small thing in a mountain of junk."

She hurled a box aside and swept clutter off a table. "It has to be close. He hasn't had it long."

The elevator light came on and the doors began to close.

"Holy photons!" Tom said. He shoved a heavy bench in front of the elevator and stacked two massive boxes on top.

"That won't hold," Jess said, still searching. "They'll shoot this time."

"Awesome." He pawed through debris. "Why hide something important in all this... garbage?" He lifted a fishing pole and a broken compass.

"This is the ship's vault. All Corrupt airships have one." She knocked aside an old, expensive-looking lamp that shattered at her feet. "This one's just messier than Marshall's."

"What if it isn't here?"

Jess froze, fear flashing in her eyes. "Then Marshall will take revenge on his family—and you—me... It has to be here."

Tom moved to another table, scanning dusty valuables: gems, gold, trinkets. He pushed a vase aside and picked up a book. Next to it lay a dusty frame with an old photo inside. The blurred woman's face made him grab it.

The glass was cracked, and the photo slid out onto the table. His head spun as he picked it up with shaking hands. It was the same photo his grandfather kept by his reading chair—his mother smiling down at baby Tom by the woods behind their house.

The elevator bell chimed, snapping him back. He shoved the photo deep into his pocket.

The door hadn't fully opened when a wedged box toppled free. Tom lunged and shoved Jess aside as gunfire ripped through the room.

"We have to go!" he shouted.

Jess's eyes widened. She reached under a desk and pulled out a black box. She hesitated, fingertips hovering, then lifted it. The lid was open.

"It's not possible," she breathed, as footsteps flooded the room and another volley burst their way.

"I'm going to find you, bitch!" Randall roared from the far side.

"Jess?" Tom said, crouching beside her.

Randall wasn't hiding his fury. He kicked debris aside, a rag pressed to his head. A guard leveled a shotgun at Tom.

Tom dropped flat as the blast thundered past.

"We have to get out!" he yelled, but Jess didn't answer or move. Pain crushed his chest as he kneeled in front of her. "Did you get hit? Jess?"

She shook her head, cradling the box like it might shatter. "It can't be... No one can open this." She looked up, panic in her eyes—more questions than will to act.

Another barrage struck closer. Tom covered her as glass and plaster rained down.

"Jess!" He gripped her shoulders. "We need to move. Now!"

She exhaled but remained frozen.

He'd feared this moment over the last two days as she'd frayed before his eyes. Giving up made sense—even if he couldn't picture her defeated—but this wasn't the time. Holm's words echoed: it was his turn to save her.

He'd never used a gun, which he proved by fumbling his holster and falling on his back.

"Oh, Jessica!" Randall crowed. "Did you find it already? Or would it surprise you if I told you I only have an empty box?"

Tom raised the pistol and pulled the trigger. Nothing.

He drew it closer—careful to keep the barrel away from their faces—and spotted a small button near the trigger.

"You see, bitch," Randall went on, too close for comfort. "We planned this before you were even in the picture. My loser father never understood, but I did. To survive, we had to evolve—make new partnerships. Too bad Dad won't see me thrive."

Tom flicked the safety off. "Photons," he muttered, and aimed toward the elevator.

"I've got an idea!" Randall said, closer. "I'll tell Marshall you killed Dad after he found out you were cheating—"

Tom fired. The recoil launched him onto his back.

He was certain he'd only shot once—but the room roared like more rounds followed. Something exploded. Glass and concrete blasted through the air, and Jess threw herself over him just as the lights died.

"You all right?" she whispered, so close he could smell the floral note in her hair.

"I'm fine," he murmured. "What happened?"

"I'll explain later." She helped him upright.

Randall cursed and shouted orders, but Tom couldn't see them. Jess was only a shape against the dark.

"The darkness won't last," she said as a yellowish glow seeped from the edges of the walls. Footsteps quickened; more debris clattered down.

"Tom," Jess said beside him, "do you see the laundry line?"

He scanned while she fired back. The chaos grew—Randall's men swore louder. At the far end Tom spotted a square opening in the wall.

"I see it," he said, drawing her attention.

"All right. I'll follow you."

He started forward, but Jess grabbed his arm. "Make sure the carrier isn't blocking the vent. When you signal, we jump. Don't let go of me and—" she hesitated—"whatever you do, don't swim up. We have to swim toward the bottom. Got it?"

Tom crawled, laughing at himself. This time he didn't even care what they were getting into.

The vent was only across the room, but Randall's men were closing fast, and they were furious. Crossing that distance felt like a lifetime. Tom forced himself not to look back every time Jess stopped shooting.

At the chute, he guessed Randall had figured out their plan; the stampede of boots and falling boxes shifted toward them. Jess kept firing and, without pausing, grabbed Tom's pistol and used it instead of her own.

Opening a laundry chute wasn't hard—he'd installed several in his builds. He just hadn't used one personally, and certainly not while being shot at. Of course the carrier was at the bottom. He hauled on the cable, dragging it up and leaving enough space for them to jump.

The tube wasn't wide, and judging by the weight, it was a long drop. He was about to tell Jess it was ready, but remembering her fear of heights, he simply wrapped an arm around her waist and pulled her back.

"Close your eyes," he said, and without another thought, dove headfirst into the vent.

25

CHAOS REALM

188Ch22 Year Week 17,
Seventh day, Night

J ESS COUGHED AGAIN, HER throat burning as she crawled
up the beach and away from the sea. Beside her, Tom collapsed onto the wet sand, staring at the sky above them.

Part of her wanted to punch him for what he'd done—jumping headfirst into a long, dark, narrow tunnel was insane. Just
remembering the drop in her stomach and the pull of gravity
made her nerves jolt again. The other part of her wanted to hug
him.

Her plan had been to get Tom out, not to follow him through
that nightmare of an exit. If he hadn't pulled her down, she
never would've jumped.

"How... What..." Tom managed between coughs.

"A peculiar set of portals," Jess said, still breathless.

She'd had an escape plan. Marshall once told her how unique
Randall's airship was—the only one with a portal built into it.
His father wanted his baby extra safe. She knew they'd land in
the middle of the Axiom Sea and then be sucked through another portal back to Chaos. She also knew the realms switched
gravity planes when crossing through water.

Tom had gotten only her brief warning to swim against all logic—toward the bottom. He hadn't even known they'd cross realms.

"We need to start a fire," she said, standing on shaky legs. "It'll get too cold. And there are predators out here."

She climbed to the higher part of the beach, where the dense forest swallowed the moonlight. It had been a long time since she'd visited this sector of Chaos. The cloudless sky by the sea always amazed her, even here.

As she gathered sticks, each step grew heavier. The ache in her muscles and numbness in her fingers weren't the only reason—her mind was stuck on the open box. After an agent's death, their keys became relics, sealed in epoxy cases that only the Welder could open. No one but him knew how to unlock them.

Finding one already open—and the relic gone—meant their enemy knew more than she'd ever imagined. Nothing was safe now. She needed to tell Holm, but doubted there was anything he could do. They'd have to wait and see what the Corrupts planned to do with it. Maybe she should warn Marshall.

"Jess?" Tom called from the pile of sticks. "You have something to light it?"

"Sure." She sat on a small rock and rolled up her pant leg to expose her boot. From the heel, she twisted out a hidden lighter.

"Nice! Do I get one too?"

She shrugged with a tired smile. "Who knows." She handed it to him and hugged her knees.

Tom watched her for a moment before sparking the flame. Once the fire caught and steadied, he gazed out at the sea. The water stretched endlessly until it met the horizon.

Jess let herself enjoy the view, too. It looked almost the same as the Axiom seas, except Chaos's moons blocked out the countless stars from her home realm. She'd lived by the ocean until her father died and her mother moved them away.

"Which do you like more?" she asked.

"I've never been by the sea in Axiom," he said, eyes still distant.

"What? You always talked about going."

"Life happens, right?" He looked at her, his soaked hair clinging to his forehead. "Usually not the way we want it to."

She stared into the fire. "Next time you shoot a gun, unless you're aiming for it, don't hit an electrical box. The bullet bounces and the system—" She stopped. "What am I talking about?" She shook her head. "I'll take you back to Axiom. Once you're there, please be careful. Things are going to get bad."

"Jess," he said, kneeling in front of her. "I get that whatever you were after—"

"The relic."

"Yes, that thing—is gone. But..." He brushed his hair back. "You can't give up. What about Arlett? I thought we were also looking for her."

Jess leaned back. "Arlett? She's probably the one who set up the robbery in the Village."

"You have to be joking," he said, standing and crossing his arms. "You don't really know her. How can you be so sure she's involved?"

"The light, remember? When Arlett disappeared, you said you saw a white light. That only happens with natives of each realm. When we cross into Chaos, the foreign particles we carry tint our light. Going back to Axiom, it's white. Unless you take something to adjust for the foreign realm—which is rare—you can always tell who's from where when they cross."

"What? No, Jess. Even if she's from here, she didn't leave willingly. Remember?"

"How do you explain—" She sighed. "Never mind."

"I can't believe you only care about your job. This is a person's life we're talking about. I never believed Bill, but maybe he's right about your priorities."

"My priorities? What are you talking about?"

"You needed to find the relic to keep your position at the Agency. That's it, right?"

"Honestly, Tom?" She stood, arms crossed. "How can you think I'd risk your life for a job?"

"Why not? Being an agent is all you've ever wanted. It's the most important thing in your life."

"No!" Her voice wavered despite her effort to hold it steady. "You have no right to judge me." She turned away but stopped and faced him again. "I lost my position—the entire career—the moment that relic was stolen from your room. It was never about a job. That 'thing,' as you call it, holds energy beyond your understanding. They can use it to manipulate the energy wave and blow up entire sectors." She shook her head. "People are in danger, Tom. Here and in Axiom. That's why I needed to find it. Thousands, maybe millions, of lives are at risk. I'd never have asked for your help, or put you in danger, for a job."

Her throat tightened as tears streaked her cheeks. She turned and walked toward the trees.

"Jess, wait!" Tom called, chasing her voice into the dark. "I didn't mean... I wasn't trying to hurt you..."

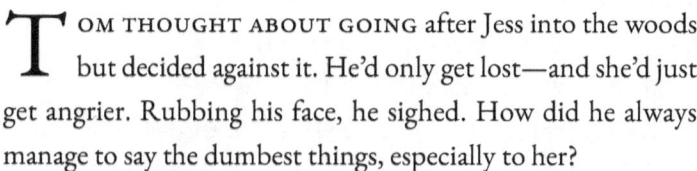

TOM THOUGHT ABOUT GOING after Jess into the woods but decided against it. He'd only get lost—and she'd just get angrier. Rubbing his face, he sighed. How did he always manage to say the dumbest things, especially to her?

He sat by the fire, trying to calm his thoughts. He hadn't meant to insult her; he'd only wanted to give her another reason to keep going. Resting his head in his hands, he started counting slowly. Maybe if he kept track of how long she'd been gone, he'd know when to worry—or when to wait.

He lost count several times before Jess finally returned. His clothes were dry, and he'd stopped shivering. Hers were soaked at the hems, and her expression was like stone.

He stood, ready to apologize, but her look froze him in place.

"How long have you known Arlett?" Jess asked, holding her hands to the fire without meeting his eyes.

"Jess, that's not—"

"How long?" Her tone was flat, calm—and far more terrifying than if she'd shouted.

"Uh... let me think... three or four years?" He rubbed the back of his neck. "But I can't be sure."

"Where did you meet her?"

"Jess, come on. I'm sorry about what I said, but if you don't explain things, how am I supposed to understand any of this?" He raked his hair back and sighed. "I didn't mean to insult you. I was trying to get you back on track. Please, let me—"

He took a hesitant step toward her, but she stepped back, arms crossed.

"Where and how did you meet her? You helped me find the relic. I owe you. You're worried about her, right?"

"Well, yes, but you don't owe me anything."

"Just answer the questions. It'll save us time."

Tom groaned and looked heavenward, throwing his hands up. "Fine. I think Charlotte introduced us at a party a few years ago."

Jess nodded, the firelight catching the hard lines of her face.

"So she's Charlotte's friend? Or did she meet Bill before you?"

"Kind of both." He shoved his hands in his pockets. "Charlotte knew her first, but I can't remember where. After I met Arlett, she started dating Bill. Charlotte told me Arlett wanted to meet me."

Jess frowned. "What do you mean?"

"Well, I guess Arlett was looking for a contractor and heard about me." Tom gave a small laugh. "Actually, your brother pretended to be me when Charlotte introduced them. I was working late that day. Guess he liked her."

Jess's eyes didn't soften. The warmth he knew in them was gone—replaced by the cold, analytical stare of the agent who had interrogated and shot without hesitation.

"I don't know, Jess. That's just what Charlotte told me. Maybe it's not true."

"Did you ask Bill about it?"

"No, why would I? Charlotte liked the outcome, and Arlett didn't seem to mind once she found out. We cleared it up that same night—no games, no drama."

Jess nodded once and kicked sand into the fire, scattering the embers. "I need to talk to Charlotte. Where is she?"

"Charlotte? I don't... know. And I'm not sure you *want* to talk to her."

She stamped out the last flames. The night grew darker, colder. Tom shivered.

"Here's the deal, Tom," Jess said. "If you want to find Arlett, I need details. Where can I find Charlotte?"

"I guess at her apartment—or the Village. I could call her, but we're... in the middle of ending things—"

"Great." Jess turned toward the woods, walking fast and sure. "We'll get your truck, and you'll drive me to her house."

"What if she's not there?"

"Her stuff will be. That's usually all I need." She half-turned, her voice firm. "We need to move quickly. I don't have a gun, and this is a dangerous sector."

Tom caught up and whispered, "Do you know all the portals in Chaos?"

"I can't answer that question."

And with that, he knew he'd lost her trust—and probably her friendship—for good.

26

Axiom Sea Periphery

188A23 Year Week 24,
Fifth day, Morning

J ESS HAD BEEN IN the Square for five days. She'd managed to place most of the spheres so their plan would work, but she still needed to find Tom. It was a crucial part of the operation—and time was running out. She blamed the Square's renaming system as much as her fear of facing him.

That morning she decided to finish setting the mechanisms.

The lower level of the Square was outside her authorized zone, but she had no trouble convincing a guard to let her take his shift. She was new and curious; he had no desire to work the turn.

As the elevator descended, the ocean rushed up so fast it felt like the metallic cage would land in the water. She gripped the railing until a few drops of blood welled at her palm. The elevator stopped only inches above the sea, and she still had two steps down to go.

It was darker here than on the upper levels, and the tide's roar echoed against rock. The corridor she followed ran above the water, but splashing waves had made the floor slick. The prisoners in their cells weren't so lucky.

Each cell sat a step lower, the water level ankle-high during the day. The bunks barely stayed dry. She tried not to think about the rising tides that must drown the prisoners overnight.

None of the inmates offered more than a cursory glance; most stared at the walls. They all seemed agitated, so Jess forced herself to look closer. She noticed small openings in their cells—tiny holes that connected them.

The deeper she walked, the dimmer the light became. Earlier she'd blamed the guard's laziness for leaving the level so poorly lit. Now she suspected neglect for a more sinister reason.

Alert wasn't strong enough a word. Patches of pitch black kept her nerves taut; she trusted the floor only because she had to.

She stopped at a lamp and reached up—but changed her mind. Plunging the corridor into darkness wasn't appealing. Instead, she stood on tiptoe and checked behind the socket. Her fingertips brushed something soft and sticky. She recoiled and bit her lip to stop a sound when she saw a pale thread of web clinging to her skin—the thick, orblike silk of a large aracnpoda.[1]

A cold shiver crawled down her spine. She wasn't afraid of spiders, but anything could be a bigger threat here. For a moment she steadied her breathing and summoned the courage to finish the task. The mechanism had to be close to the circuit and aligned between levels; otherwise their energy wouldn't flow as planned.

Her hand trembled as she pulled her sleeve over it and stood on tiptoe again. Against better judgment, she pressed the dark device into the web, twisting it so the original structure stayed intact—hoping the web's maker wouldn't notice.

She worked quickly. Convinced the circle held, she moved away and scrubbed her sleeve in a puddle.

A dim light fell on the wall of the nearest cell. Numbers, formulas, and misspelled place names in chalk covered three consecutive walls. A faint greenish glow haloed the scrawl, making it hard to read—but the handwriting she recognized. And her perfectly clear name erased her doubt.

"I'm going to kill you, bastard," a prisoner shouted farther down, and Jess jumped, splashing water.

The two inmates nearest the shaft paid no mind; they stared into the small holes. All the convicts she could see were focused in the same direction.

"Why don't you try?" another taunted.

It wasn't the approaching footsteps or the tone of hatred that made Jess hold her breath and clamp her hands over her mouth.

"Son of the void," Tom sneered. "Why don't you probe it?"

It didn't matter that she hadn't heard his voice for months, or that the cadence sounded different. It was him.

Footsteps multiplied. The prisoners yelled, pushing their hands and whatever they had through the small openings toward Tom's voice. Cheers and clatters echoed around her.

"Your mother was a photonic bastard!" one voice spat, but Jess couldn't see the speaker. "And your father—"

A crash reverberated off the wet walls, and she heard Tom again.

"I'd rather talk about your mother."

More crashes, more screams—bodies and items thudded against metal. The commotion swelled as more prisoners surged toward the noise.

Jess had no way to help. She didn't know exactly where Tom was, and even if she did, she couldn't open these cells. The lower level's gates were sealed; access was impossible from her side.

She ran.

The rising tide made the bridge slick; she slipped twice before reaching the elevator. Her pulse pounded as she hit the alarm.

A red light stabbed the corridor. Spotlights snapped on inside the cells; the sudden glare burned her eyes. A horn shrieked, forcing her hands to cover her ears.

Gears and chains hummed, then hundreds of sprinkler heads opened. Water spouted into the cells. The prisoners' screams shifted from fury to fear as the tide rose, drowning their rage.

The elevator engine spun. Guards climbed down from above. Another gate clanged and descended, sealing the cells. Jess raced for a gear or stop button, but the gate slammed to the floor before she could reach it.

On the other side, the water poured in. The metal gate blocked sound but not the rising flood.

The elevator opened and five guards stepped out, unhurried.

"You okay, newbie?" one asked.

Jess stared at him. "The prisoners—the tank's flooding! We have to get them out!"

"Oh. They'll be fine," he said.

"What? They're going to drown!"

The guard cocked his head. "Why'd you turn the alarm off? You just wanted to see what would happen?"

"No!" Jess said. "Someone started a fight. I needed help!"

"There you go!" a guard said, smiling. "Their fault for fighting. They know it'll happened, and they still tested it."

"Every time!" another guard, who was holding a large sack, said.

"But the water—" Jess tried to protest.

The first guard put a hand on her shoulder. "The water only reaches the necks of the shorter ones. Then it drains out. Once it's safe for us to walk in, we'll check the damage."

"How many would you guess will visit the infirmary?" he said, looking at Jess.

She had no words as she tried to assimilate what they were saying.

"It's all right. You'll get used to it. The last time, we had to bring up nine. Hopefully, it'll be less today. I'm kind of ready for dinner."

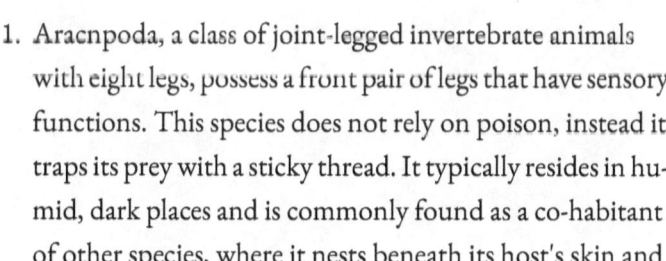

1. Aracnpoda, a class of joint-legged invertebrate animals with eight legs, possess a front pair of legs that have sensory functions. This species does not rely on poison, instead it traps its prey with a sticky thread. It typically resides in humid, dark places and is commonly found as a co-habitant of other species, where it nests beneath its host's skin and

nourishes itself with its host's blood. If signs of infection are present, medical attention should be sought out immediately. Aggression level: 2 out 5

27

Axiom Realm

Peter sat in the car while Millie walked into the Village hotel one more time. Pressure in his skull made him feel like it could explode any second. His body trembled so badly he doubted Millie would drive him anywhere but the hospital.

She stepped out of the lobby, and for the hundredth time Peter noticed how her eyes shone beneath long eyelashes and how her braided hair bounced on her shoulder. He felt foolish for paying attention to such things now.

After today, Millie would be out of his reach forever. He didn't know how anyone could forgive him for falling again. Worse—this time he might have gotten Jess killed.

"She isn't here," Millie said as she slid into the driver's seat. "The manager says the only ones who haven't checked out are Bill's parents."

"Makes sense," Peter muttered, holding his head. "I'm sure they're still at the hospital. Their bags aren't that important."

Millie turned the key and exhaled. "Now what?"

He stared at the window. "Maybe Arlett's father?"

"We can't talk to him. His status bars us from even getting close to his gate."

"We should—" He stopped, a raw pain twisting in his stomach.

"You need medicine," Millie said.

"No." He leaned back and closed his eyes. "Jess is in danger."

"She may already be dead. But you're not. That's the fact. I will take you—"

He grabbed her hand. He'd imagined this moment before, but not like this. "Arlett's friend."

"What? No, Peter—"

"I can't live with doing nothing, Millie." He met her eyes. "If you were in her position, you'd expect me to try. I may look like an idiot, and it's my fault, but I'm still her captain. It's my job to keep you all safe—or die trying."

Millie stared at him for a long moment, then sighed. "All right. We can find Arlett's friend, but after, I'm taking you in. I won't live with your life on my conscience. Agreed?"

Peter nodded and leaned back, trying to hide how his body trembled harder.

"What's her name?" Millie asked, pulling out her transmitter.

"Charlotte Leph-Anim."

28

Axiom Realm

188A22 Year Week 17,
Seventh day, Night

Tom parked outside the familiar building and sighed. Jess hadn't looked at him during the entire drive from Center District, and she'd barely spoken since they'd left Chaos. He'd even joked that his old truck had a new scratch, but if she heard him, she said nothing. Now he remembered how their years of silence had started. After she told him she'd been accepted by the Agency—and he made her cry—she just stopped talking to him.

Her mom's or Bill's criticism and demands didn't help, but even when she did visit, she never stopped by Tom's home. If he was at her house with Bill, she stayed in her room or left when he arrived. Then she took off for real when the Agency offered her a position and she moved farther away. He'd never gathered the courage to say goodbye.

Now, as they reached the glass entrance to the apartment building, Tom had the feeling their past was about to take over their future, and he had no idea how to stop it. He'd tried to apologize, but Jess wouldn't listen. Tom ran to catch up before she reached the glass entrance. "She lives on the top floor," he said, and his heart skipped a beat when Jess actually replied.

"How many apartments are on that level?"

"We built four on most floors, but the owner decided to reduce the last two. Most are still empty." He cleared his throat when he noticed Jess's expression. "There are two apartments, one on each end. Charlotte has the one that looks out over the city."

"Of course she has the best one." Jess stopped and turned to him. "Wait. Didn't you live here? Never mind."

"Yes. That used to be my apartment. We gave it to Charlotte when she left our company, for her years of hard work and investment."

Jess frowned and pressed her lips together.

"It was an excellent decision. She worked for it," Tom said. Jess rolled her eyes. "Hey, no. It was just business. Plus, I usually work out of the city, and driving here is a nightmare."

"Driving is a nightmare? You, who would love to live in that truck and drove two extra hours to the airport?" She faced him. "Since when is it company policy to give away prime real estate to former employees?"

"She was a cofounder and—" Tom rubbed his face and groaned. "What do you want to hear, Jess? That she was my girlfriend, that we were living together, and things didn't work out, so I took the easy way out? Are you happy now? You proved how stupid I am because I didn't fight for my property. Does that sound better?"

Jess's features darkened. "My happiness has nothing to do with your decisions. Your life, your problem."

He crossed his arms. "Then why did you ask?"

"It's my job. I need to know as much as possible about the person I'm going to interrogate."

"Oh? And that's all?" He held her gaze. "You don't care about me?"

She walked toward the main doors, and he threw his hands up in the air.

Jess was showing her official insignia to the new custodian when Tom stepped inside the building. The guy looked pale and concerned, and Tom couldn't blame him. Jess was a dangerous agent and didn't lack authority.

Tom let her push the elevator button and followed her. He was about to comment that at least no one was shooting at them but reconsidered and shoved his hands into his pockets.

To his surprise, when the doors opened, Jess didn't just stomp out. Instead, she signaled him to walk in front of her. His nerves spiked, and each step made him more aware of his surroundings: the smell of new paint, the echo of the empty floor, the polished wood under his feet, and the silent presence behind him.

Charlotte's door came into view, and he sped up and knocked.

"The custodian told me she's not here," Jess said, but Tom knocked again.

She moved him aside and used a key he recognized as one of the master ones—he'd installed them a few years ago.

"How did you get that?"

"This is an Agency investigation. Anyone in my way is obstructing justice. A penalizable offense, in case you have any ideas." She pushed the door open. "Isn't this why you hate us so much? Too much power and dominance?"

The comment turned Tom's nerves to anger, but she didn't wait for an answer and just walked inside without turning on the lights.

Tom stood by the door.

The double-story windows allowed the city lights to illuminate the living room. He half-smiled at the sight. Although the decoration was different—messier—the design was one of his favorites. Clean lines, open views, simple but with enough details to make a home. If he could name one of his constructions as real architecture, this building—and especially these two top apartments—would be the ones.

Jess didn't waste time with the view and kept opening the drawers of Charlotte's desk. As he watched her, he couldn't bring himself to walk inside. He was familiar with the place; it had been his for more than a year. But he wanted nothing to do with invading Charlotte's privacy. It felt like betraying a friend, even when they weren't anything anymore.

Jess said, "Do you know where she keeps—"

Suddenly, a voice called out. "Tom?" Charlotte said as she walked down the corridor.

"Hey!" he said a little too loudly. "You're here."

Charlotte raised an eyebrow and approached him. Her thick, long hair bounced against her shoulders, following the rhythm of her hips and emphasizing her narrow figure.

"I live here." She put a hand on his chest and leaned closer. "But I can't say I'm surprised. I was sure you'd come back."

"You suck as a lookout," Jess said, making Tom jump.

Charlotte opened the door wider and stepped inside. "What the hell are you doing?"

"So, you are surprised to see me?" Jess said.

"Did you let her in?" Charlotte pointed at Jess without taking her eyes off Tom.

He cleared his throat but didn't answer.

"Why not?" Jess said. "After all, this is his place."

The change in Charlotte's attitude didn't surprise Tom. Since school, she'd hated Jess, and at every chance she got, Tom's ex-girlfriend would annoy or insult her. He knew it came from jealousy—Jess was everything Charlotte wanted to be: smart and confident. Jess also held his heart, and he was certain Charlotte had figured that out long ago.

Charlotte stomped in, threw her purse on the couch, and shook a finger at Jess. "You bitch! This is my house, and I want you out right now!"

Jess smiled, crossing her arms. "Great! Give me a reason to treat you like a hostile witness, and I promise I'll enjoy every second of it."

"A hostile witness?" Charlotte looked at Tom, half accusing him and half pleading for help. "I already answered the police officer at the hospital. I have nothing else to say—especially not to you."

"We'll see," Jess said, picking up a piece of paper from the desk. "This is Marshall Neon-10's signature, correct?"

Charlotte crossed her arms and lifted her chin. "I can't break client confidentiality."

Jess laughed. "So, you agree that Marshall, one of the Corrupts' leaders, is your client? I could arrest you right now."

Charlotte's eyes went wide. "No, I—I'm not saying—"

"You knew who he was?" Tom said, this time stepping inside.

Charlotte shook her head. "It isn't that simple. Arlett is my friend, and I had—"

"Yes, let's talk about your friend," Jess said, walking around the desk to sit on it. "Where and when did you meet her?"

"That's none of your business."

"I won't ask nicely a third time. Where and when?"

Charlotte cleared her throat, wrapping her arms around herself. "It was at a party years ago."

"Be more precise," Jess said.

"What? Why?" Charlotte raised her voice. "Forget it. I'm done with this. I can't remember."

Jess pulled her sleeves up and leaned forward.

"It was in the city," Charlotte said quickly, "at one of those places you have no idea exist, and we just bumped into each other and started talking."

Jess nodded. "If it was such a privileged party, I'm sure you remember exactly when and where.

How did you get in?"

Charlotte exhaled. "Unbelievable! Are you questioning my—"

"Of course I am! You're a liar."

"A liar? I don't lie. I don't need to, I am—"

Jess slowly shook her head. "Do not change the topic. And without any exaggeration. Understood?"

Charlotte's cheeks turned red. "Fine. It was five years ago at a designers' convention in Main City. Arlett has always been involved in fashion, and I was starting my interior design line. Like I said, we bumped into each other and started exchanging ideas."

Jess narrowed her eyes but remained silent.

"I can prove it!" Charlotte walked over to the pillar next to the kitchen counter and grabbed a frame. "Here. We took this picture because we met Lady K-Axon that night."

"Who?" Jess stood up and took a slow step closer.

"Lady K-Axon! Oh, dear Maker, you have no idea who she is." Charlotte put her hands on her hips when Jess snatched the frame from her. "She's the best designer in Axiom—hence her last name, Axon, as in Axiom's best—which she totally earned."

Jess stared at the photo, which started to tremble in her hands.

"She works for the most prestigious homes and families here," Charlotte continued. "Arlett was so excited that Lady K-Axon was at the party, so she walked up to her, introduced us, and guess what? She was super nice."

Tom took a step toward Jess when she started to shake her head and the color drained from her face. "Jess?"

"It can't be..." Jess mumbled so low that Tom wasn't sure he heard her or read her lips. "I don't—I can't remember..." She stepped back until she hit the couch and closed her eyes.

"There was blood. So much blood, but—no holes... She could have planned—She said she was sorry... Holm said it looked staged, but—it explains the clumsy extraction, finding her key... the epoxy—she must have the Welder."

Jess covered her face with one hand, still clutching the photo with the other.

"Jess," Tom said, unsure of what to do. "What is it? Talk to me."

"She's lost it!" Charlotte said, touching Tom's arm. "Or maybe she just realized who Lady K-Axon really is—and how important her designs—"

"Who?" Tom said, but his attention stayed on Jess's shaking hands.

"Come on, Tom. I told you a million times about this! But no wonder—you never listened to me.

That's why we broke up."

"Arlett just walked up to Lady K-Axon and talked to her?" Jess asked without looking at her, gripping the frame so tightly her knuckles turned white.

"Yes, she spoke to me, too." Charlotte turned back to Tom. "Remember when I quit TowerUp? I left because Lady K-Axon offered me a job at her firm." Charlotte's eyes lit with excitement.

"She's the reason my dream as a designer worked out!"

"Your dream as a—" Jess exhaled and paced between the large window and the kitchen. "Tom said Arlett was looking for him. Why?"

Charlotte rolled her eyes. "That was after we met. Arlett wanted to build something, so she asked me if I knew anyone."

"She asked you for a contractor—or specifically for Tom?" Jess said, her tone tightening.

Charlotte looked at Tom and then back at Jess. "Well, she asked for Tom. But I guess she heard I worked with—"

"You didn't find that suspicious?" Jess raised her brows. "Such an important designer randomly wants to check out your designs? Then your new friend Arlett asks for Tom by name—not a contractor? Do you even know what she wanted to build? Did you even ask?"

Charlotte stepped back, closer to Tom. "No, I didn't ask. Why would I? But you're an agent. Everyone's a criminal to you. In the real world, things work like this—we meet people, talk, make connections."

"Very convenient connections. Why did she ask for Tom specifically? Why not Bill?"

"I guess she knew Tom's the one who does the manual part."

"Oh, really? Why not you? Wouldn't she ask for a design first? You're the exceptional designer, right?"

"I am!" Charlotte huffed. "I'm the best designer of the three of us. I think she saw Tom and liked him, so she wanted an excuse to meet him. I'm sure you understand that very well."

Jess looked at the ceiling and sighed. "Where did she see him? Before or after she noticed you? You don't get how dangerous this is! You're so stupid."

"Excuse me!" Charlotte tried to take a step closer, but Tom held her arm. "What are you doing? She's just jealous—"

"Stop lying!" Jess shouted. "If you were telling the truth, you wouldn't have become friends with Arlett, because you'd never have introduced her to Tom. You've always acted like he's your property and got jealous. Or you suggested Tom's work, which is how she would have found out about him. But you'd never do that."

"And why is that?" Charlotte said. "He was my boyfriend. I had no reason to be jealous of her. And why wouldn't I talk about his work?"

"You never talked about his work!" Jess yelled, making Charlotte step back. "You're ashamed of him because he's only a contractor. Nothing to brag about."

"That's not—"

"It is the truth." Jess held the frame close to Charlotte's face. "Don't you see the resemblance?"

Jess stared at the picture again, shaking her head, and for a second Tom thought tears were filling her eyes. "I should have listened... I should have noticed it when I met Arlett," she said softly.

"The same hair and complexion, exactly the same eye color. They even have identical smiles."

She glanced at both of them. "Didn't you notice? You don't just hug and lean into someone's shoulder with that smile. Obviously, they knew each other—and they were targeting you."

"What are you talking about?" Charlotte grabbed Tom's arm as if for protection.

He took the photo and really looked at it. He'd walked by it countless times and ignored it, as well as the story behind it. The three women—Charlotte, Arlett, and Lady K-Axon—were standing side by side, smiling in what clearly looked like a crowded party. Jess was right. It was obvious Arlett and Lady K-Axon were related.

"That's Arlett's mother?" Tom asked.

Jess nodded, pressing her lips together.

"Impossible!" Charlotte said, not letting go of Tom. "We met her that night. Wouldn't Arlett have recognized her mother?"

"See?!" Jess tossed her arms in the air. "You're so stupid!"

"I'm not! Arlett isn't the daughter of Lady—"

"Lady K-Axon?" Jess's tone was mocking and sharp. "The best designer in Axiom, who liked your designs and gave you a job after just meeting you?"

"I'm a brilliant designer! I have—"

"A brilliant designer?" Jess laughed. "Why? What did you design here? This is all Tom."

"Tom?" Charlotte grabbed the back of the couch. "He doesn't even understand how—"

"He knows exactly how to build and design. This apartment is full of his ideas. Nothing from you. Oh wait—I see! There it is! The hanging pot ready to hit anyone walking by!"

"For your information, Tom loves that plant. He even has one in his new place. A tasteful present from Lady K-Axon!"

Suddenly, Jess stomped down the hall and threw down the plant. Then she kneeled and dug through the dirt.

"Are you crazy?" Charlotte yelled, following her. "That's a very expensive—"

"Oh, I know! This is expensive, that's for sure." Jess held up a tiny piece of brass that looked like a clock gear.

"What the void is that?" Charlotte said.

Jess tossed it to Tom, who easily caught it. "Remember He-li-3 in Chaos? This is the kind of thing he monitors—Agency trackers."

"The Agency?" Charlotte turned to Tom. "What do they have to do with—"

"Everything, Charlotte!" Jess stormed toward her, making Charlotte back up into Tom. "Your famous designer is an agent. Chief Karen Falc-Axon."

"Karen?" Tom said. "As in your Karen?"

Jess nodded and lowered her voice. "Yes. My partner. And she's been tracking you two. How many years ago did you meet her?"

Tom pushed his hair back, but Charlotte was the one to ask, "What? No! Why would an agent be following—"

"You. Following you, Charlotte." Jess crossed her arms. "Obviously because you're the idiot of the group."

Tom stepped in front of Charlotte and put a hand on her arm.

"I'm not an idiot! You're making this up!" Charlotte said, her voice breaking.

"You put everyone's lives in danger because you're an overconfident, selfish woman who can't see beyond her own benefit."

"Jess, she isn't who you're angry at," Tom said, but she ignored him—or didn't hear him.

"You think you're superior to everyone, but you're nothing. You lack intellect and talent, and the only thing that works for you is your loose mouth and absurdity. No real professional will ever consider you a designer because you aren't one."

"Come on, Jess, that's harsh," Tom said.

"You're a fraud. For years you've been sucking up Tom's ideas, pretending to like him only to leave the moment a stranger—a total stranger—handed you an impossibly good job. How anyone with a little self-respect and ethical values could have fallen—"

"Jessica!" Tom yelled, finally getting her attention. "She got it," he said while Charlotte cried on his shoulder.

"Oh, I see," Jess said. "Only one of us is allowed to insult the other. Perfect."

"Jess, it's not the same. She isn't you, and this isn't about us. I get you're mad and worried, but—"

Jess put her hands up and closed her eyes. "I don't have time for this. Since you clearly care so much about this... woman, I'll suggest that you find Peter. Dear Maker, if he's still alive." She sighed and walked past them.

"Jess, come on. You can't—"

Jess pushed his hand away when he tried to grab her arm and stopped by the doorframe.

"Go to the Agency and look for Captain Peter Dulc-KaK. Show him the picture and the tracker mechanism. He'll set up protection surveillance for you two. Probably Bill will need one as well."

"Listen, I won't leave you alone." Tom took a step forward, but Jess walked out, slamming the door behind her

"Tom," Charlotte said, "I didn't... I had no idea—I promise—"

"Sure," he said, opening the door.

He looked down the hallway, and Jess was already pushing the elevator button.

"Jess! Wait! I can't let you go like this. You're in danger, too. I didn't mean—" He sighed when Charlotte barely touched his arm, her eyes full of tears—and fear.

The elevator bell rang, and by the time he turned back, Jess was gone.

T OM KNEW CHARLOTTE WAS talking at his side. He could feel her hand tighten around his arm since they left the building, and for the last few minutes, while they crossed the lawn and walked into the parking lot, he had been forcing her to walk faster. Still, he had no idea what she was saying. His mind was stuck on Jess.

He had never asked about the photo or about Arlett asking to meet him. In fact, not for the first time, he ignored Charlotte's stories. She wasn't a liar, but his ex-girlfriend did like to beautify her anecdotes. Because of that, Jess had gotten the impression that he and Charlotte were together at his grandpa's funeral—something he didn't clarify then and now wished he had. For almost two whole days, she had been with him, and for the love of the Maker, he couldn't figure out a way to talk to her.

"Are you listening?" Charlotte's tone was high and accusatory.

He had had enough. "No, Charlotte. I am not listening."

"Excuse me?"

"I need—" He stopped and rubbed the back of his neck. "I'm not sure if you would have been able to find out what Arlett and her mother were planning, but you had to know Marshall meant trouble, and even—"

"I had no choice." She held his hand. "I'm not stupid, but Arlett said she was in danger. Her father is so powerful here, and Bill told me that Marshall didn't care about the company. The deal was to protect Arlett while they got married. Things changed right before the wedding."

"What do you mean before the wedding?"

"I know little. I honestly didn't want to know more. After all, I didn't work for your company—"

"Charlotte! What about the wedding?"

She turned, forcing Tom to move closer to hear her. "It was a last-minute change. Jess was coming to the ceremony now, and Marshall wanted something from her. Arlett didn't like it and freaked out, and she went behind Bill and canceled the room he just got for Jess. You know the rest."

Charlotte lowered her voice. "I guess... I think Marshall took Arlett in revenge."

"Wait. Are you saying that Bill set up Jess?" Tom stepped back and paced around. "That can't be right. Randall is the one who took—"

"There she is," a woman in the parking lot said as she walked toward them.

She wore a black protective vest underneath the black jacket with the typical puffy pants of the Agency uniform. Tom thought he had seen her in the hospital before, but his attention shifted when the light from the building illuminated the guy behind her.

He was wearing the same uniform, but he didn't look like an agent. His skin was too pale. He stumbled in his steps, and once he got closer, Tom noticed the darkness underneath his eyes and the blood around his irises.

"Charlotte Leph-Anim," the woman said, "we have some questions for you."

"I have nothing to say." Charlotte crossed her arms and tried to stand taller. "I have had enough interrogations for the rest of my life."

"If you want to save your friend," the woman said, "you'd better answer me."

"Who the hell are you?" Tom put himself between the agents and Charlotte. She may have made many mistakes, but he was the one getting the answers.

"Excuse me," the guy said in a surprisingly firm voice. "This is an Agency investigation."

"Oh, I get it." Tom took a step toward him. "You can demand all the answers you want. But guess what? I don't believe you're an agent. You look more like someone who needs to be a recruiter in a recovery center."

"What the photons did you just say to me?!" the man shouted.

"Peter," the woman said, putting a hand on the man's chest. "He has the right to ask for our identification."

"You are Peter?" Tom asked in disbelief. "The Peter that people think so highly of?"

"Captain Peter Dulc-KaK. And if you have a problem—"

"Jess said you will help—" Tom started.

"Jess?" Peter said.

A burning sensation grew in Tom's stomach when he recognized the tone of fear and defensiveness in the man's voice—the same one he used every time he thought about Jess's safety.

"When did you see her? Where is she?" Peter kept asking.

Tom shook his head and took a deep breath before answering. "She was here. You should have crossed paths with her on your way in."

"Jess!" Peter yelled, looking behind Tom.

Tom turned.

He didn't expect to see Jess emerge from the shadows. He also wasn't expecting to hear the building's fire alarm—or Jess running toward them, waving her arms and yelling something he couldn't quite understand.

"Tom, no! Where are you going?" Charlotte tried to hold him, but he pulled away and ran toward Jess.

People started to run out through the glass doors.

Tom only stopped because a line seemed to have opened in the sky above the building. Then a heat wave flew over him at the same time Jess slammed into him, sending him backward a few feet before falling to the ground.

All the air was knocked out of his lungs. He had been in fights before, where someone had punched him like that, but the pain was different now as he gasped for air. His inhalation felt hot, burning his throat and scratching it at the same time. He pulled himself up on his elbows and looked back.

The last thing he saw was the building turning from white to orange and then to a red so bright he had to close his eyes. A heavy force pushed him down against the ground, and then the heat changed into a freezing breeze right before a loud explosion deafened him.

29

CHAOS REALM

188Ch22 YEAR WEEK 17, SEVENTH DAY, LATE NIGHT

J ESS FELT A SOFT touch on her neck and forehead, and a distant voice said her name. A sharp pain in her back and side became vivid as the sound of voices, the air, and a constant buzz grew louder.

"Jess? Please, Sunshine, wake up."

Strong but gentle hands moved around her face and held her up. She opened her eyes, and for a moment, she didn't understand why Tom was kneeling in front of her. Then her mind sped up, and everything that had happened came rushing back.

"Tom," her voice was barely above a whisper, and it burned her throat. "You are—"

"Thanks to the Maker." He rested his forehead on hers. "Don't move. I have to check on the others."

He helped her lie down and moved out of her sight.

Although she wished with all her soul she could stay there, she pushed herself up, and her body screamed at her, forcing her to hold her side. It wasn't the first time she had been hurt on a mission. She was certain she had at least one broken rib, and something was wrong with her back, but since she was sitting up—and her legs were a painful reminder of their existence—she knew she hadn't broken her spine.

Nausea rose in her throat when she tried to stand, so she settled for watching.

Around her, nothing made sense.

Tom's building wasn't there anymore. Instead, a mansion with thousands of lights rested on top of a rock formation. She had seen a picture of that place before, and it wasn't a good sign.

The sound of running water reached her, but it didn't smell bad. The cold was bitter, but she was sitting on a beautifully cared-for lawn, green and tender.

"What happened?" Jess followed the voice and saw Tom helping Charlotte not too far from her.

"Tom, I don't understand…"

"Jess," Peter's voice woke the last part of her brain, and all her nerves became aware of their surroundings. "What happened? I saw you running and then… where is Millie?"

"Millie?" Jess said a little louder, but her throat still hurt. She tried to stand, but once again, the whole world spun around. If it weren't for Tom, she would have hit the ground.

"I told you not to move," he said in a very serious tone. "You cut your forehead, and I'm sure you have a concussion."

"Help me find Millie," Peter said to Tom. "She can't be too far from here. She was standing right by me when—"

A loud scream reached them, and both men ran toward it.

Jess tried to turn, but the nausea and dizziness were too strong, so she touched her forehead. Her fingers were wet, and the warmth of the liquid told her it was blood. The sudden pressure in her head confirmed the concussion.

"I don't think you should touch it," Charlotte said. "You'll infect it or make it worse."

Jess looked at her, and another realization dawned on her. "Are you feeling sick?"

Charlotte covered her face, but she didn't need to answer. Her skin was pale, her hands trembled, and although it could be the shock, Jess knew Chaos. Those were the first symptoms of the poisonous atmosphere. They needed to take her back to Axiom.

Peter walked behind Tom, who was carrying Millie in his arms. Once they were close enough, Jess noticed Millie's leg—her knee was twisted at an odd angle. The fabric of her pants had ripped, exposing a sizeable chunk of missing skin.

Tom helped her down, and although he was careful, she bit back a scream as tears rolled down her face.

Peter kneeled by Millie and covered her wound with a piece of fabric. He spoke to her while working quickly, his words low—too soft for Jess to hear—so she turned away.

"Tom?" Charlotte said in a weak voice. "Where are we? Was that a bomb? Where are all those people?"

A knot grew in Jess's throat. She had forgotten the people in the building. If she'd barely made it out alive, she doubted many—if any—had survived. She covered her face and closed her eyes. A hand rested on her shoulder, and for the first time in her life, she truly didn't want to look at Tom.

"Jess," he whispered. "Did that Lady Karen—your partner—I don't know—Arlett's mom—did she just try to kill Charlotte?"

Jess shook her head. Although it had only happened a few minutes ago, it felt like a lifetime had passed since she walked out onto the top roof patio of the building. She'd first noticed the buzzing noise growing. As she stepped out, she found a set of small metal pieces placed all over the roof. It wasn't until the first one lit up, sending a light stream to the next, that she realized it had to be some kind of energy generator. Nothing good could come out of it.

"I don't think so. It wasn't to murder Charlotte. Karen wouldn't have used such an enormous explosion just to kill—I don't know, Tom. It looks like a statement to me. She's showing how much damage she can cause."

He nodded. "So, she opened a huge portal to Chaos?"

She stared at him.

"I was hoping it had been a mistake, you know? Just trying to kill a specific person and making a huge mess." He chuckled weakly. "Not a good kind of hope, of course. More like the desperate kind."

A buzz started to approach them. The familiar sound forced a shiver down her spine, and the signature colors of the airship confirmed her concern.

"We have to hide," she said, taking a couple of deep breaths before standing up. She wouldn't have made it without Tom's support, but once on her feet, she regained her balance. He helped Charlotte stand after that. His lack of questions made Jess more conscious of how many lives were in her hands.

"There's nowhere to go," Peter said, trying to help Millie.

"This is Chaos." Jess looked at the mansion. "There's always somewhere to hide. Let's just avoid the woods."

Chaos

188A22 Year

Week 17, Seventh day, Late night

ALL ALARMS BLARED, JOLTING Holm out of bed. He hit the floor hard. "What in the photons—?"

He sprinted from the bedroom toward his office but froze at the sight through the living-room windows.

Airships. Hundreds of them.

"Oh, sweet Maker," Phoebe whispered behind him. His wife—usually calm, formidable—stood pale, arms wrapped around herself, eyes reflecting the glow outside. "Holm, what is that?"

He shook his head and shoved open his office door. The alarms vibrated through the house, but it wasn't the sound that made him shiver—it was the light.

As the Chaos safe-house operator, he alone maintained contact with Axiom. It was no easy task: communication had to cross the energy wave between realms. The only thing that half-worked was the morse-light system, and even then, decoding could take hours. Messages were rarely accurate.

This one was crystal clear—and he wished to every power it wasn't.

"Holm?" Phoebe asked from the doorway.

He looked from her to the panel, where the message blinked again and again.

"The Barrier... a sector of Chaos collapsed into Axiom."

Phoebe gasped, hand flying to her mouth. Tears welled instantly. "What does that mean?"

Holm darted to his desk, fingers flying over the controls. "It happened near the Barrier—east of here. The palace by the waterfall. Maybe Jess didn't recover the relic."

"Jess? No! Dear Maker—my poor Jess!"

The thought of losing her twisted his stomach. He'd met Jess when Karen first dragged her into Chaos, and from that moment he and Phoebe had quietly adopted her as the daughter they never had—though Phoebe would never admit it out loud.

"We have to find her," he said.

Phoebe nodded and, after a steadying breath, sat opposite him. Decades ago she'd sworn never to work with Axiom again. She was a retired agent from Chaos—one of those the Agency used for impossible missions. Holm understood her bitterness, but they both knew cooperation was the only reason either realm still stood.

"You don't have to do this," he said, grasping her hands.

She smiled sadly, tears glinting. "The East Sector isn't friendly territory. Those poor Axiom people will face horrors they've never imagined. You need to help them." She raised a hand to silence him. "Jess isn't a priority for the Agency, Holm. You know that. But she is for us. I'll find her."

Holm kissed her hand. She squeezed his in return, then turned to her old equipment, the professional calm returning to her face.

Finding Jess wouldn't be difficult; she'd only just come out of undercover status, so her emergency tracker would still be active. Holm just prayed they wouldn't be retrieving a body this time.

30

CHAOS REALM

JESS HAD BEEN RIGHT, Peter thought, trying to ignore his nausea and trembling limbs as he helped Charlotte walk. Chaos had no shortage of hiding places. They hadn't gone far before reaching the base of the rock formation, where Jess found the service entrance with unsettling ease.

It amazed him how quickly she'd adapted to surviving in this realm. Then again, between her training and her undercover mission, she'd lived here for over a year. He wondered if that had been part of Karen's plan—but he still struggled to comprehend it all.

He believed Jess about Karen's betrayal. It sounded impossible, and there was no way to prove it, but Jess was right: he'd never checked for wounds when Karen lay bleeding, unmoving. Holm's report said there were no signs of an ambush—no Corrupt presence, no bodies, no blood. Yet there had been an emergency call from Karen asking for help extracting Jess. He had arrived in the middle of a shooting. And then the order to wait until the First to deliver the relic. All of it was too suspicious.

Karen's involvement seemed unthinkable—but it made sense.

A sharp crack drew Peter's attention as Tom broke the lock. Like Jess predicted, no alarms went off, no guards came running. A chill passed through him as he remembered why. No one dared invade the Corrupts' territory. They didn't need protection.

"Wait here," Jess said, heading down the corridor.

Tom held Millie, who had fallen into shock, unresponsive. Charlotte—Tom's ex, Peter had just learned—looked pale and feverish. Jess didn't look much better: exhausted, bleeding from a gash on her forehead, limping slightly, one arm pressed to her side. Likely a fractured rib. Pain that wouldn't let her rest.

"Charlotte, don't take deep breaths," Tom said.

Peter watched him. The man felt vaguely familiar, but he couldn't place him. He only recalled Tom's name from Jess's file—Bill's best man.

"It's still there," Jess said.

"What is?" Peter asked.

Jess touched Charlotte's forehead, who flinched and pushed her hand away.

"The portal," Jess said.

"What portal? What are you thinking?"

"Millie needs a doctor. I don't think it's just her leg, and Charlotte's burning up. The poison will—"

"Poison?" Charlotte's voice broke, and she slid down the wall.

Tom helped Millie down and kneeled by Charlotte.

Jess looked at those two for a second, and then, too fast, she turned to put extreme attention on the hallway behind her. If Peter didn't know her, the sign would have escaped his attention. He finally understood Jess's apprehension of being at the wedding. It wasn't only her family she was trying to avoid.

"If the portal opens," Jess said, "it should take you near the plaza in Main City. Find Holm. Tell him what happened."

"Wait—what? I'm not leaving you here," Peter said. "You've lost your mind. I'm your captain—you're my responsibility."

"Peter, there's no other option." Jess's tone went flat. "We lost the photo proving Karen is behind this. We don't know who else in the Agency is compromised. This is our best chance to stop her."

He shook his head. "I get that. But what are you planning to do?"

Jess's eyes turned cold.

"No! I believe you, but Jess—you can't kill her." He dropped his voice, gripping her arm. "If you do this—if you hurt her before a trial—you'll be a murderer. I can't let you do that."

"How many people have already died, Peter? Those buildings weren't empty during the ambush. And she isn't done—you know her." Her eyes glinted, but her voice stayed firm. "She's been planning this for over a year."

"Which is *exactly* why you can't kill her!" He guided her a few steps away. "We need to find Arlett and figure out what they're planning." He lowered his tone. "You said she was looking for Tom—and then tricked your brother into marrying her. Don't you want to know why?"

"Of course I do." Jess tilted her head. "But if we wait for an investigation, it'll be my word—the agent who lost the Corrupts' son—against the prodigy agent. They'll never believe me."

Peter held her hands. "I'll back you."

"I'm not asking. But Peter..." She gave a small, sad smile. "I know why you're sick right now. No one would believe you either. I need to stop her before more people die."

Peter rubbed his neck. "He broke me," he muttered.

"Who?"

"Marshall. He was after your relic and I... I'm sorry." He looked away.

"That's strange," Jess said softly.

When Peter turned, she was already helping Tom with Millie.

He followed them through the hall, nearly carrying Charlotte. Soon Jess stopped at a metal shelf stacked with cleaning supplies.

"How do you know this is a portal?" Peter asked.

"Holm made me memorize them."

"There are thousands of portals."

"Not all work for humans," she said. "Maybe a couple hundred."

She didn't let him ask more. "After you get help—for them, and for yourself—talk to Holm. He tried to warn me about Karen's involvement. I should've listened. He'll believe you."

"Jess, I—" Peter sighed. "I hate this."

"Me too."

She didn't look back at the others as she walked down the corridor. He waited until she vanished around the corner.

"I'll open the portal," Peter said. "Millie has a key—if you're touching her, you'll cross. The light will—"

"I got it," Tom said. "Just open it."

Peter clenched his jaw but nodded. He braced Charlotte by the waist and reached for his key. The moment his fingers brushed it, a white flash filled the hall. Relief washed over him—the portals still worked.

"Let's get help," he said. But before he could move, Tom shouted.

"Peter! Don't let go of Charlotte!"

"What—"

Peter barely reacted before Millie collapsed against him, shoving him into the light. He understood too late—he nearly lost his grip on Charlotte. The portal's brilliance swallowed them. Heat from Axiom wrapped around him as they fell hard onto cobblestones beside a fountain.

"Tom!" Charlotte screamed, crawling toward where the corridor had been. "No—Tom!"

Peter groaned and checked Millie—still breathing.

"We have to go back for him," Charlotte said, clutching his arm. "We have to—"

"We need a hospital."

That was when he noticed the surrounding sirens, the agency cars flying past, and the unnatural glow on the horizon.

Jess had been right. They were all in danger—and this time, he wasn't sure they could fix it.

31

CHAOS REALM

188Ch22 Year Week 18,
First day, One hour before
sunshine

J ESS WALKED DOWN THE hallway, leaning against the wall.
She didn't have much time.

The airship she'd seen earlier was Randall's. It could mean
nothing—or it could mean she may bump into Marshall's
brother. Either way, she had to find Karen before something else
went wrong.

The ground shuddered, nearly throwing her off balance. Her
back and side had become a constant cramp that weakened
her legs. Gritting her teeth, she pushed off the wall and forced
herself onward. The corridor's incline burned her muscles. At
least there were no stairs—these service halls were built for
carts—but the uphill stretch was agony.

For the first time, she heard voices before reaching a turn.
Her heart raced, her body protesting the rush of adrenaline. She
pressed herself flat against the wall, breathing slow and shallow.
Nausea twisted through her gut, and her mind prickled with a
thousand stinging needles.

She waited in silence, gripping her head until the dizziness
ebbed. When her pulse steadied, she crept forward. No one
noticed her. If they had, she'd already be dead.

Light spilled from a larger chamber ahead. Voices grew clearer. She slipped into shadow and listened.

"We got the first image, boss," a man said.

From her vantage point, Jess spotted several figures crossing a
wide vestibule. She ducked behind a niche that held a decorative
table and an oversized vase—perfect for hiding food trays from
guests' view.

When no one was looking her way, she darted across the hall.
That was when the voice froze her in place.

Karen.

Jess's vision blurred; her hands trembled so violently she had
to clasp them together. Memories crashed through her—the
partner she trusted, the woman she'd admired, lying in a pool
of blood as a building exploded. Her breathing turned ragged,
bile rising in her throat. For years, Karen had been her family,
her mentor, her confidante. The one person who knew about
Tom.

And she'd been using Jess all along.

"Exactly what we wanted," Karen said, her voice calm and
commanding. "Now, we send our demands to the government and the Agency—with specifics on what happens if they
refuse."

Jess moved closer. Hatred and grief fueled her steps. There
she was—Karen—hands on her hips, posture confident and
sharp, barking orders at criminals like she once led agents. Rage
burned away Jess's weakness.

Before she could reveal herself, another voice cut in.

"What is that? You said you wouldn't hurt anyone. How
could you kill so many innocent people?"

"Arlett," Karen sighed. "I never said I wouldn't hurt anyone. I said I'd *contain* the destruction. Collateral damage is life."

"What?" Arlett stepped into view, still wearing her tattered, mud-stained wedding dress. "Charlotte lives there! She's my friend—you liked her!"

Karen touched Arlett's arms, but the younger woman jerked away. "If you'd done what I told you, Charlotte might still be alive. You acted on your own—and tried to betray me. Their deaths are on *you*, my child."

Arlett's sobs echoed. "I didn't betray you! I just fell in love with Bill. I thought you'd understand."

"I know about Marshall," Karen said coldly. "You thought he could save you from me? After you lied to him? What kind of fool are you?"

Two men grabbed Arlett's arms as she struggled. "Now I have no choice," Karen murmured, stroking her cheek. "When Marshall finds out, he'll want revenge—but I won't let him hurt you. You shouldn't mix with those criminals."

"What about Bill? He—"

"I don't give a photon about Bill!" Karen's voice cracked like a whip. "He's a failure and deserves what's coming. Betraying his sister! He should burn in the void!"

"And you didn't?" Arlett shouted back.

Karen slapped her so hard the sound echoed. "That was your fault! Jess should've never been part of this. If you'd stuck to the plan—made Tom fall for you—none of this would've happened. But you had to love that pathetic man, Bill, and get mixed up with that Corrupt Marshall. What were you thinking?"

"I don't know what you're talking—"

"Sure you do! That ridiculous deal? Building that mansion in weeks? You forced me to pull Jess out of Chaos. Do you think I enjoyed faking my death? Taking sedatives and pretending to bleed out? My Jess deserved better!"

Arlett's voice cracked. "Jess will hate you for this! She's nothing like you!"

Karen stepped closer. "She might hate me, but that won't change how I feel. She'll always be the daughter I never had—and I'll protect her from her idiotic family and your fool of a friend, Tom."

"You have to stop! You can't kill for revenge. Your husband wouldn't want—"

Karen punched her. Arlett crumpled between the guards, limp. "Get her out of my sight," Karen snarled. "Put her in one of Randall's cells. Let her beg him for mercy."

A shove from behind sent Jess stumbling forward. She turned to find a yellow-toothed grin behind a shotgun aimed at her head.

"But what do we have—"

He never finished. A blade burst through his gut. Jess flinched as blood splattered the wall.

"You okay?" Tom asked, yanking the knife free.

"How—? I thought..." Jess gasped.

Tom kicked the body aside and offered his hand. "You didn't think I'd just leave, did you?"

Jess threw her arms around him, trembling as her eyes landed on the corpse. She started crying when she understood what this would do to Tom.

"Hey," he whispered, holding her. "I won't let anyone hurt you."

She looked up at him, then back at the fallen man.

"Don't think about it now," Tom said gently. "You can yell at me all you want once we're out of here. Okay?"

For a heartbeat, Jess considered retreating through the portal—leaving everything behind. But Tom had been right. She'd lost sight of her purpose. The relic had blinded her. Her duty was to protect lives—and she'd failed. Tom had killed a man because of her mistakes.

"You were right," she said quietly. "Arlett isn't part of this. We need to save her."

"What about what you told Peter? You're letting Karen go?"

Jess brushed her hair back, pressing a hand to her side. "Arlett's the only life I *know* I can save. That's more important than revenge."

Tom smiled faintly and touched her arm. "Where to, Sunshine?"

32

Axiom Realm

188A22 Year Week 18,
First day, Dawn

Amelia crossed her arms, her eyes brimming with tears. The confusion on her face was mirrored in her boyfriend Dan, who held her close.

"What do you mean she's still in Chaos?"

Peter rubbed his face and exhaled.

He hadn't meant to speak to Jess's family. When he'd arrived at the hospital, his only concern had been Millie. On the way there, she had lost consciousness, seizing violently. The last thing he'd thought about was keeping Charlotte from contacting Bill—or worse, Jess's mother.

"She's working on an important mission," Peter said.

"She's *what?*" Amelia burst into tears.

"A mission?" Dan echoed. "She wasn't working. And where's Tom?"

A doctor stepped out of Bill's room, and Amelia rushed inside.

Jess's brother was still in recovery. Apparently, he had been attacked, but the security footage showed nothing. No witnesses, no alarms. The doctors, nurses, and police had seen and heard nothing either. Peter didn't question it. The man's injuries spoke for themselves, but there were pieces missing from the story.

"Captain Dulc-KaK," a nurse called as she approached. Peter seized the chance to escape Dan's questions.

"How is she?" he asked, noting the way the nurse eyed him. Jess had been right—no one would believe him in his condition. His throat was raw, his hands trembled. He probably looked like a wreck.

"She'll need time to wake after surgery, but she's stable. You brought her just in time. The internal bleeding would've killed her." The nurse folded her arms over her clipboard. "There's an old guy looking for you. Doesn't look like he's from around here, if you catch my meaning."

"Thank you."

Peter walked to the lobby.

Holm was impossible to miss. His clothes were out of place amid Axiom's sleek fashion, his weapons gleamed openly, and his grim expression warned everyone away.

"Holm," Peter said, quickening his pace. "Jess told me to—"

"Jess? Is she all right? What did she find out?"

Peter gestured toward the exit, and they stepped outside into the hospital gardens.

The chaos outside matched the one in his mind. Ambulances screamed toward the hospital. Sirens echoed across the city. The crimson glow of the Barrier pulsed on the horizon, ready to erupt. Jess had been right again. People were dead—many more wounded—and the Barrier was breaking.

"Jess is in Chaos," Peter said. "She's going after Karen. She's—"

"Oh no." Holm pressed a hand to his forehead. "I wanted to be wrong. I *knew* Karen was part of this, but... How is Jess planning to stop her?"

Peter's jaw tightened. Jess's words—her promise to kill Karen—haunted him.

"No. That will destroy her," Holm muttered, pacing. "She can't come back from that."

Peter studied him. They'd worked together before, but Holm remained a mystery. A Chaos operative through and through—hard to read, harder to trust.

Finally Holm stopped. "We have to move fast. We're going back to Chaos. Phoebe should have Jess's tracker by now. We'll find her."

Peter frowned. "I can't. They attacked Axiom. Millie's in the hospital. I have to report to the Agency—"

"To tell them you're using?" Holm snapped. "That you dragged Millie into it? So they can throw you into rehab and put her in a cell?"

"That's not—"

"Oh, Peter." Holm sighed, shaking his head. "The Agency can't control this. They'll blame Jess, that girl, and you. Karen's dead to them, and the Welder—well, they have no idea how to explain *that, so* you'll take the fall."

"They won't do that."

Holm crossed his arms, frowning. "You're still green. I've spent years dealing with the Agency. Do what you want—but if you really want to help, save Jess. Protect your Millie. That's what matters now."

He turned and strode away.

Peter glanced back at the hospital, where Millie lay unconscious inside. He promised himself he'd make things right with her one day—somehow. Then he jogged after Holm, hating how right the old agent probably was.

Chaos

188A22 Year

Week 18, First day, Dawn

T OM FOLLOWED JESS, FORCING his focus to stay on her and not on the ghosts chasing him. From her clenched jaw and flinches, he knew she blamed herself for what he'd done. The last thing he wanted was to talk about killing the brute in the hall—or the one before that whose knife he'd taken. He didn't want to tell her he'd do it again to protect her. He just worried about her staying upright.

She moved fast but not straight, one arm clamped to her side. The bleeding at her temple had stopped, but it had to be throbbing. He had only wanted to get her home—drag her there if he had to—but he couldn't leave Arlett.

"Wait." Jess pressed to the wall. Ahead, a man crossed the corridor and disappeared around a bend.

"Here," Tom said, handing her a shotgun.

Her eyes narrowed, her mouth parted—but she said nothing.

"The dead bastard didn't need it anymore," he said.

She shut her eyes for a beat, then checked the hall.

"Do you know where we're going?" he asked. "Back down to the entrance?"

Jess shrugged. "We need the cells. I've never been here. My guess is lower levels."

He glanced at the ceiling, then down the passage. "I'm not sure this building—never mind. Let's move."

She touched his arm. "What do you think? You know construction better than me."

"Yes, but this is Chaos."

"Chaos or not, what do you think?"

Tom sighed. "When we came in, it took a long time to find another corridor. As we went up, cross-halls got more frequent."

Jess nodded.

"My guess: the rock formation carries the structure. Probably no basement—earthquakes. The Barrier's wave means you don't dig deep here."

"Right. Holm says the wave moves randomly."

"So we're close to it. That explains the blast—and how we crossed back." He pointed up. "See the lights? Less industrial as we go—more... elegant."

"Elegant?"

"Irrelevant. Point is: service runs low for food and waste. Cells and machinery? Up top."

"Wouldn't you save the view for residents?"

"Sure. But how do you escape from the top? Unless you fly."

"The airship port is above," she said. "You're right. If they keep hostages aboard, they wouldn't march them down through the house. All right—lead."

"I don't know, Jess. You're better—"

"I won't let you get hurt." She grinned. "Besides, I don't know where to go."

"What if I'm wrong?"

She tilted her head, suddenly the playful girl he'd fallen for. "Then we try again."

He read the piping lines as they went, grateful to be on the service side where no one had bothered to hide them. After fifteen minutes, they reached a metal gate and a staircase beyond. Unlocked. He exhaled. No steps down; that meant he was probably right.

He paused.

"What is it?" Jess asked, gripping the rail, breathing hard.

"The risers won't help us anymore." He pointed to a chase where multiple pipe runs turned upward and vanished into the wall.

"You said the top floor," Jess said and blew out a breath. "Let's go."

She wouldn't let him steady her and kept a relentless pace. He hovered close anyway.

The staircase wasn't accessible to the first three levels. As far as Tom could see, the next two floors had a nice finish, a carpeted hallway, and hanging lights. It had a hotel style, with white doors and tables with flowers.

It was different on the next floor.

The door was metal with three heavy deadbolts. The adjacent wall was steel, cold under his palm—thicker than standard.

"This one?" Jess asked, winded.

"Wait here." He jogged up another flight. The upper landing had a metal gate, but concrete walls and a low engine hum.

"That's my bet," he said, dropping back.

Jess rose and headed for the first door. "Great."

Tom spotted a supplemental fuse box on a far wall and a dark cable up to the ceiling, then down to the latch. "Jess, wait!" He vaulted two steps, shoving her back before her hand reached the knob.

She hit the wall and caught herself.

"Sorry," he said, moving back. "Did I hurt you? I'm so sorry."

She shook her head, eyes closed a moment. "I'm fine but what happened?"

"You see that wire? Hot door." He pointed. "They electrified it."

"Well... not ideal."

He checked the fuse box. "The security here isn't very high but for those locks. Should this be a concern?"

Jess lifted a shoulder.

He killed the breaker. Red emergency lights flooded the stair and sirens erupted.

Jess pulled a thin brass pick from her boot and popped the three bolts. Tom didn't know anything about picking locks, but he made a mental note to use better locks in the future.

"Stay back," she said and kicked the gate open, keeping her back by the wall. Loud yells and metal banging filled the staircase from the first level and the hallway ahead.

"Keep your back to the wall," Jess yelled above the alarms. Carefully, she peeked into the room twice before motioning him to follow her.

Tom didn't know what he was expecting but it wasn't what he found.

All the walls were made of thick steel and brass, and small cages formed some sort of maze. The first two spaces were empty, but after Tom's senses sharpened, he realized they were cells—human confines. A bunch of people were crowded against the bars, hitting them with objects: pans, silverware, the legs of broken chairs or cots. Even after the horrors he experienced in Chaos, he wasn't ready for the smell: human waste, sweat, and rotting organic matter. He had to swallow down bile as they walked down the corridor.

"Just see if you find Arlett," Jess yelled above the noise. "She is wearing a wedding gown. It should be easy to spot her."

Tom nodded and focused his attention on the cells. The people confined within them were certainly not friendly, and they were all in rough shape. He wondered how long they had been trapped in here.

Suddenly, a hand clutched his arm and dragged him so hard his vision blurred for a second when he hit the bars with the back of his head. Before he could move, another arm crossed in front of his face and pulled against his neck. Tom grabbed the arm, trying to push it down so he could breathe again.

"Let him go!" Jess said, pointing at the cell with the shotgun.

"You are Marshall's girl," a raspy voice said behind Tom. "Is he with you?"

"Let him go!" Jess said, but the arm against Tom's neck just pushed harder, making him gasp.

Tom heard the bolt of the shotgun engaging and a loud laugh right by his ear. "You can't shoot me without hitting him, honey. So, open the cell or I'll kill him."

Jess didn't lower the gun, and she said nothing. The raspy voice laughed, and that was enough for Tom to let his anger take over his reasoning.

He moved one hand down, letting go of the arm that was wrapped around his neck. The force pulled him against the bars, but he ignored the pain in his back. He had little time before the lack of air knocked him out or the bastard behind him broke his neck.

He took the knife out of his belt and grabbed the guy's arm tighter. Instead of moving away, Tom pushed the blade into the arm, slicing it from the elbow to the wrist. A metallic essence filled Tom's nostrils as a loud squeal buzzed in his ear and the force against him released.

Now it was Tom's turn.

He moved forward, pulling the arm with him. Behind him, he heard a loud crash, and the weight on the arm became heavier. He twisted the arm until the man shouted. Sure, he was taller than Tom and probably stronger, but the growing bruise around his eyes and the bleeding nose gave Tom a win.

He pulled the guy up by his shirt. "You are lucky there are bars between us," he said, forcing the guy's face against the bars. "Otherwise, we'll figure how fast you bleed out."

"Tom," Jess said behind him.

Her voice reminded him of the reason they were here. He released the bastard and watched him fall, weightless, to the floor.

"Let us out and we'll fight with you," another voice said from the cell.

Tom turned, and to his surprise, he wasn't talking to Jess, but to him.

The prisoner stared into Tom's eyes, incapable of moving away and certain of his words, reminding Tom what Jess had told him about the color of his eyes, a very peculiar one.

"Let's go," Jess said, touching his arm.

Although he walked behind her, he didn't stop glaring at the guy in the cell until the corridor blocked his view.

He shook his head and rubbed his neck, but he had trouble concentrating. It wasn't until Jess pulled his hand that his attention came back to the present.

The hallway became wider, and the design of the confines changed. On the right side of the corridor, instead of bars, a clear window allowed them to look into the cells. From the oblivious expressions of the prisoners, Tom figured the cells were soundproof and mirrored on the inside. There were no doors evident, but a panel at the bottom that would have given him trouble to use as access.

The sirens blared louder, and the lights flickered and switched from white to red.

"There," Jess said and rushed toward the last cell in that row.

In one corner, he saw a bunch of white fabric with some dark stains on it. Arlett was lying on the floor. Her wrists had been handcuffed so tight that he could see the cut lines on her skin. Her breathing seemed uneven, and from time to time, her body shook. He was certain that she was groaning, either from pain or delusion.

"Hey!" Jess pounded on the glass, but if Arlett heard anything, she didn't move. "Photons!" She pushed her hair back and looked around.

"Look who showed up here!" a whiny voice said from the cell behind them.

Tom turned and saw He-li-3, the Tracker they met in Chaos, in handcuffs, with bruises on his face and a few more missing teeth.

"I would never forget that hair!" a robust guy in ripped and bloody clothes said, pointing at Jess. "Look at her! It's Marshall's wife!"

"Fiancée," He-li-3 said, shaking his head. "I'm sure her new boyfriend won't like the mistake."

Tom rolled his eyes but secretly appreciated the correction.

"Where is Marshall?" a woman said, walking behind the other two. She wasn't any smaller than the robust guy, but she had significantly more tattoos than he did. Some of them even covered her eyelids. "Did he figure out it was Randall who kidnapped the Chief?"

Jess shook her head and groaned, turning back to Arlett.

"Dear Agent," He-li-3 said. "You won't be getting any of us out of here without—"

"Shut up!" Jess said and walked away, probably looking for something to open the cell.

"These are blood DNA locks," the woman said above the alarms. "Only the Chief or his sons can open them." She waved her hand and sat down again. "You two will get caught here."

"We knew she was just a pretty face," the burly guy said. "I'm sure Marshall didn't like her because of her brain. It has to be her outstanding performance in—"

Tom crossed the corridor and hit the bars. "Close your photonic mouth!"

"I told you," He-li-3 said, shaking his head. "That's the one to watch."

The brawny guy pretended to be scared, but the second he gave Tom a second look, his act fell. His eyes bulged, and there was no humor left on his features.

"I can't believe it." He patted the woman's head without taking his eyes off Tom. "She found the older one."

"What the—" The woman pushed the guy's hand away but glanced at Tom. "Holy Maker! You even look like the Chief when he was younger."

"Son of the void!" He-li-3 shouted. "You are right! How did I miss it? We are safe!"

Tom took a step back, holding a strong desire to close his eyes and run away from here. Once again, Jess's comment about his eyes came to mind, along with another detail of his life.

His grandfather barely talked about his father. The old man hated the Agency because Tom's dad had worked for them and had chosen them over his mom. Or that was what he'd told Tom.

Now other things started to hold more significance, like the portal by his home, or Arlett asking for him, probably under

Karen's orders. He put his hand into his pocket and touched the photo he took from Randall's storage room. At that time, he didn't comprehend, but now the photo felt burdened, as the puzzle pieces began to align.

"Photons!" Jess screamed from down the other corridor, and Tom ran toward her.

The second he turned the corner, he found her standing in front of a table in an area similar to a surgical room. Weapons hung around the tiled walls, and long chains dangled from the ceiling.

"What is—" Tom froze.

A body was lying on the table with a blanket covering most of it. Dry spots of blood and other liquids stained the blanket. A shiver ran down his spine when he recalled the image of his grandfather in the hospital, but he shook it off.

"This is—" Jess rubbed her face. "I can't believe how deep all of this goes."

"Jess, I don't understand. What am I looking at?"

She stared at him for a moment before pacing around. "This is Marshall's father. You see his—dear Maker, They drained his blood. I just... these monsters, they are sick."

Tom slowly lifted the blanket and had to step back to avoid throwing up. The face was beyond recognition—too many cuts and burns with open, rotting wounds. A carved sign on his forehead read: Chief. This was Marshall's father, and in that moment, it meant a lot more to him.

"See the engraving on the jacket?" Jess said. "That's the Welder's emblem." She leaned against the wall and kept her eyes on the ground. "You were always right, Tom. The Agency and the Corrupts, they are all—"

"Stop." Tom grabbed her shoulders, careful not to hurt her. "Don't think about it now. You don't know everything, and we need to get out of here. Now."

"Tom, I don't know how to open those cells. We can't use a regular key and we can't break the glass."

"Make sure this thing works," Tom said, pulling a gun off the wall and handing it to Jess. "I'll get Arlett. The door at the end of the corridor is the exit. Meet me there."

"But you heard them. It's impossible to open the locks without a blood DNA match. And the Chief's body is... For the Maker! That's why they took all his blood out." Jess closed her eyes, and Tom's world tumbled on him.

He grabbed the back of her neck and pulled her closer. Her lips felt as soft as he remembered them, but she tasted sweeter, much better than his memory. He pulled his lips away and rested his forehead on hers.

"Meet me there," he whispered.

Jess stared at him and slowly nodded.

He walked away, knowing after that moment everything Jess knew about him would change for the worst.

He stopped at Arlett's cell and wiped the knife on his pants. The blade was cold and easily slid down his palm. It wasn't until a line of blood showed on it that he felt an intense pain. He didn't mean to make such a deep cut, but he didn't expect the blade to be so sharp.

He scanned the glass and found a small indentation in the mirror panel at the bottom. It was ironic how such an insignificant element would mark his life. Part of him wanted to be wrong, but the second he rested his hand on the panel, the lock made a click and the entire window slid open.

Arlett was still lying down when he crouched beside her and moved her hair out of the way. She opened her eyes in alarm and pushed her hands up, but Tom stopped her from hitting him.

"It's me. It's Tom."

She stared at him a second before her eyes filled with tears. "How—no, you can't— Your life is in danger here. Tom, you have to go."

"I agree with all of that. And yes, we have to go."

He pulled her up, but when he set her down, her knees locked, and he had to catch her before she slumped over.

"I can't— I'm sorry... I'm so sorry!"

He sighed and put the knife back on his belt. He hated the idea of walking with both hands occupied, but what option did he have? "Just hold on tight," he said to Arlett and picked her up.

"You won't get far without help," the burly guy said. The woman was standing close to his side.

Tom gave a fast look down the corridor. Most prisoners were trying to look in his direction.

He let Arlett hold on to his shoulder for a moment while he ripped a thread from the bottom of her dress. He grabbed it with his open palm and squeezed as much blood as he could on it. Before he touched the panel, he made eye contact with the heavyset guy. "Randall and that photonic woman need to pay for this. Just make sure Marshall recognizes his brother's face." He turned to He-li-3. "The rest is all for you."

He-li-3's smile couldn't be brighter, but the hulking guy didn't stay too far behind. He showed Tom how many teeth he had lost as he chuckled, "Yes, sir."

Tom used the fabric on the panel to make sure it worked. As soon as his bloodstain touched it, the cell door opened. He cursed himself for putting his knife away before letting those people out, but the bulky guy only took the fabric and rushed to open the other panels.

He-li-3 bowed and bolted to follow the man. The woman barely looked at Tom.

He picked Arlett up and turned.

Jess stood in the middle of the corridor, watching him.

A shiver traveled down his body. Her head tilted to the side, and her eyes were full of questions. The last time he saw that expression was at his grandfather's funeral, and plenty of times he had wished not to see it again.

"Now where?" he said, ignoring the tightness in his chest.

Jess stared at the corridor, now crowded, but before she could answer, the entrance door blew open, pushing them backward down the corridor.

Smoke filled the area, turning the air thicker, but it was the surrounding screams that made everything confusing.

"Jess!" Tom yelled and crawled around. "Jess!"

Someone coughed by him, but his concern only grew when he only found Arlett. Steps and shots sounded around him, so he brought Arlett toward the wall and was about to leave her to find Jess when she slid next to him.

"Are you—" she was saying, but Tom hugged her.

"Thanks to the Maker," he whispered in her ear and kissed the side of her head.

Jess moved back, and he wished the smoke wasn't so thick so he could read her expression.

"I don't think we can reach the portal anymore," she said. "How is Arlett?"

Tom looked back, but Arlett was nothing more than a white blur. "Not good. She can't walk by herself."

"That's inconvenient," Jess said.

Tom heard her loading her gun. "We need another exit, something closer." She grabbed his arm and moved to his ear. "There is another portal on the roof, on the other side of the building. Any ideas on how to get there?"

Tom wanted to make a joke about just strolling through the palace. Then he remembered the last floor on the stairs.

"Yes! We have to go back to the staircase."

"Are you crazy?" Even without seeing Jess, he could easily imagine her expression. "That place is filled with guards."

"Exactly! That's why we are going to let all the prisoners out and ahead of us. Then we will climb up."

Jess exhaled. "You can't trust them."

"I don't trust them, Jess. I'm just using their thirst for revenge to open a path for us."

33

AXIOM SEA PERIPHERY

A FTER HOURS OF CLEANING and checking, the guards brought out seven prisoners and took them to the infirmary. Jess couldn't visit that area. Only the so-called nurses and the doctor were allowed behind the emergency doors. Rumor said only the personnel of the Square walked out of those doors alive.

Tom was among the convicts.

She only saw him when they dragged him down the corridor. He was unconscious when they put him on the elevator. His head was bathed in blood, and one of his hands was twice its normal size. The tone of his skin shocked her. As a fan of the sun, he always had a tan, healthy color that now looked ill and pale.

The guards moved faster—or that was how it seemed to Jess—when they pushed Tom on a squealing stretcher. The last thing she saw was his feet. Like the other prisoners, he bore deep open wounds. The worst was the skin at the bottom; peeling in an unhealthy reddish tone, probably because of the salt and humidity. An irritating line on his leg marked his waterline, just above his ankles. She doubted it would ever go away.

It had been the longest day of her mission and probably of her life. She couldn't bring attention to herself by asking a lot of questions about the prisoners, especially about Tom, but she needed to know. The unreliable guards' gossip kept her informed. By the time her shift was over, two prisoners in the infirmary had already died. Tom was alive because the bets about his death were still up.

The Square was the last stop on Axiom's peripheral train line. Most trains didn't travel that far. Between the prison and the closest town, there were at least a hundred miles of woods filled with detonators and traps. If someone ventured into that massive wilderness, no one would risk their life to look for their remains.

Jess took the half-hour ride back to the poor village where the Square staff lived in silence. Her mind stuck on images of Tom being rolled out on a stretcher and the way he looked. Her fear of confronting him turned into guilt and anxiety. Maybe she should have found him before. Maybe now she would never have the chance.

As she walked toward her small shelter, only a shy streetlamp illuminated the post office and the general store, both already closed. The only place that remained open was a filthy pub, where she'd bet all the off-duty guards spent most of their free time. She envied the ease of the laughs inside and their oblivious concern with the state of the world, but especially their lack of guilt.

"Oh, dear Maker! You found him," Phoebe said the moment Jess stepped into the one-bedroom shelter that had served as her house for the last week.

"You are here," Jess said, trying to avoid the topic. "Did you encounter anyone?"

"All went as planned. No one cares about me visiting my baby sister." Phoebe crossed her arms and stood in front of her.

For the first time, Jess became upset by the size of the shelter. In that position, Phoebe was blocking her way to move any-where.

"So?" Phoebe said.

Jess rested her head in her hands as she sat by the door. "He is in the infirmary."

"Did you put him there?"

Jess frowned and swallowed a knot before speaking. She couldn't let herself fall apart, not yet. "I was placing the last mechanism on the lower level. He got into a fight and... It's horrible!"

"The lower level, huh?" Phoebe shook her head. "That's the worst one. Well, aside from the cages."

"I just can't believe how it is possible to survive that place. I don't know how Holm survived there, and he was inside for less than half the time Tom has been in there."

A warm hand rested on Jess's shoulders. "It wasn't Holm. I was the one who was working in there those three months."

Jess looked up at Phoebe and, for the first time in her life, saw that strong woman from Chaos with tears in her eyes.

"We were married already, and he was very patient with me when I made it out." Phoebe walked back to the counter and leaned against it. "Why do you think I stopped working for the Agency?"

"They sent you there?"

"They left me there, Jess. It was supposed to be one week." She lifted her shoulders and smirked. "Chaos people have always been disposable to the Agency."

Jess couldn't argue. In the past she would have, but the Agency had failed her too, and she wasn't part of it anymore.

"How bad is he?" Phoebe asked.

Jess rubbed her face. "He is—he got…" She sighed. "No idea."

Phoebe reached for her transmitter in her pocket. "Let's ask Holm. If they cancel your appointment, we'll know for sure. Just rest now."

Jess walked into the other room and followed Phoebe's instructions. The bed increased her remorse, though, and her mind couldn't stop the images of Tom unconscious; her imagination only created worse ones.

If Tom was too sick, their plan would have to change or be delayed. Neither option was good. If he was dead, there would be no reason to attack the Square, but they would lose all hope of fixing everything.

Jess closed her eyes and bit her lip. If there was no reason to strike the Square, she had no reason to keep fighting.

After a couple of very long minutes, Phoebe poked her head into the bedroom. "We'll keep the plan since there is no news," she said. "Tomorrow you'll see Tom."

34

CHAOS REALM

188Ch22 Year Week 18, First day, Early morning

H OLM PUSHED THE DOOR open and stomped into the living room of his apartment. He had never used the stairs outside, and he wouldn't start now. Behind him, Peter crawled into the apartment and sat on the floor, resting his head against a wall.

"Phoebe!" Holm yelled without looking back at the agent with him. "He should take some of our stew, and, dear Maker, he needs something else."

However, Phoebe wasn't the one who rushed to help him.

"Peter!" Gall-I said as she emerged from Holm's office. She helped Peter up and supported him until they reached the kitchen table. "What happened to you?"

Peter collapsed into his chair with a loud groan.

Phoebe walked out of the bedroom with a few rolls in her hands. She gave one look at Peter in her kitchen and shook her head. "There's some stew left from Jess's visitor." She slammed the roll on the table in front of Peter. "How could you fall again? And now?"

"I wasn't trying to," Peter mumbled as he rested his elbows on the table to support his head. "Marshall was—"

"Marshall?" Gall-I said, placing a bowl by her brother and gently brushing his back. "Where is he? I thought Randall was behind it all."

"That's not important now," Phoebe said, turning to Holm. "My sources helped check her tracker and we found her. "

He glanced at his wife. The wrinkles around her eyes and the deep sadness made him close his own. "Please don't tell me she is..."

She touched his arm. "I don't have a way to confirm if she's alive, but she's by the East Mansion."

"I know." Holm rubbed his neck. "Peter told me how he left her there."

"I had no option!" Peter said. "We had two injured people with us. Neither would have survived in Chaos, and I'm not—"

"Of course, you are in no condition to help anyone," Phoebe said, raising a hand to stop Peter from interrupting again. "Like I was saying, the Barrier broke right there. I can't get enough information to track her movements... if she's moving." She took a deep breath and lifted her shoulders. "I'm going."

Holm took a step back. "You can't go! It's suicidal. Unless we have proof Jess is still alive, you can't—"

"I'll go with you," Peter said, trying to stand, but Gall-I placed a hand on his shoulder. "Listen, Holm. We just showed up there after the explosion, and she guided us to the portal in the hallway. I'm sure she's alive. We need to help her and Tom."

"You were inside the mansion?" Phoebe was by the table in two steps and slammed it so hard some of the stew spilled over the sides. "Have you lost your mind? Aren't you a captain from Axiom? Don't you know who owns that place?"

"I had no idea we were there. It's not like I took a tourist tour and memorized the houses of the famous criminals in Chaos. Besides, we had no choice." Peter rubbed his face. "Believe me, I hated leaving her there. But like I said, we were in Axiom when the Barrier cracked, and we got dragged back there. You know how rough it is outside that area. What did you expect Jess to do? Wait for the takuosums to attack us?"

The house fell into silence, allowing the cacophony from Chaos to reach them. It was a rare cloudless morning in the realm, but impossible to enjoy. The extra movement and buzz from sirens and airship engines were a bad omen.

"We can't just leave her," Gall-I said, not surprising Holm.

Years ago, Peter had brought his sister to Holm and asked him to help her. Holm hadn't asked for details. He only knew that Gall-I's husband wasn't the nice man she thought he was, and she needed a hideout. She had thanked him ever since and become an asset in Chaos.

"She wouldn't have left me," Gall-I added.

"All right," he said without taking his eyes from the window. "But we can't all go." His shoulders dropped, and this time Phoebe's hand on them didn't make him feel any better.

"I'll bring her back," Phoebe said.

"I'll go with—" Peter began, but Holm shook his head.

"You have to help me here. We need to figure out how to protect Axiom. And there is not much time."

Holm grabbed his wife's hand. "Come back home, all right?"

Phoebe kissed his forehead and walked out of the window onto the balcony. If anyone could get inside that fortress, it was his wife. He just hoped the next time he saw her, a smile lifted her eyes.

35

Chaos Realm

R EACHING THE ENGINE'S LEVEL was difficult. The prisoners ahead of them were eager to leave in either direction, and gunshots were flying from all sides. The staircase was the worst part—such a narrow space full of people trying to go down while guards kept shooting up. It wasn't something Tom would want to try again.

It had been worth it, though, and after they reached the top floor, Tom made sure to block the access door by throwing down an extra-large vent shaft and a fan from the ventilation system. Then, only the sound of the engines surrounded them.

Although this level was open, the machines and massive air vents didn't leave much space to walk, and carrying a person didn't make it any easier—especially someone wearing such a big dress. The fabric was too smooth, and the many layers made it difficult to adjust his grip. He also disliked how he could barely distinguish Jess in front of him.

Arlett kept going in and out of consciousness. She mumbled a lot, but the most he understood were "sorry" and "Bill." He wished he had a way to get rid of the handcuffs. It worried him that her circulation was constricted, as evidenced by the blue color of her hands, but there was no time to stop and take them off.

After a while of walking and not hearing anyone chasing them, Tom dared to stop.

"Jess, wait." He let Arlett down, resting her by one of the water tanks. "Why do wedding dresses have to be so big?" he said, touching Arlett's forehead.

"I don't know," Jess said, not too far ahead. "Is she all right?"

"No fever." Tom stood up and found Jess leaning against a wall. "You never thought about your wedding?"

"My wedding?" She rested her head against the wall and closed her eyes. "What? Why would I care about that?"

Tom's muscles tensed when he noticed she was holding her gun with her left hand—something off for a right-handed person. "Marshall? You were supposed to marry him, correct?"

She pushed herself up, shaking her head. "I don't know, Tom. Maybe. It was just a mission. And the point was to protect him, not to pick a gown."

Tom realized Jess was covering her left upper arm with her right hand. "Jess!" He stepped forward, but she took a step back.

"I'm fine. It's just a scratch."

"Just a scratch? Jess, you're bleeding."

The floor near her feet had a dark stain, and the corridor they'd come from had a clear path of blood drops. "How did—let me—"

"No," she said. "I'm okay. We just have to find the portal."

Tom looked up and groaned. The ceiling caught his attention. It was full of pipes, as it was supposed to be, but they were all turning at a forty-five-degree angle.

"I'll be fine," Jess said, taking another step back. "I promise you. We just need to get going."

Tom's mind worked a second too slow. The aggressive turn in the plumbing had to be expensive—and for a special reason. The clear glass of the mansion's dome was straight ahead. It had to be early morning because not much light came through. The room underneath them must have had an amazing view of the sky.

"Jess, stop!"

"No, Tom, this is—"

Behind her, she reached the opening for the dome above. She tried to grab the electrical box beside her, but it broke open, and her heel slipped.

"Jess!" Tom shouted. He missed her hand but caught the thick cable of the box. He heard the wire rip, and the weight loosened, causing Jess to fall down the ledge a few more feet.

"Hold on!" Tom yelled, lying down on his stomach and grasping the cable. He slid to the edge, where Jess was hanging. Her eyes were closed, and she was grabbing the open door of the box with one hand. Her other arm hung loose at her side.

Tom made a quick loop around his arm with the cable. "I'm going to slide you down, Jess."

He didn't wait for an answer and slid the cable between his hands. The wire was thick and difficult to grab, so it moved fast, making Jess scream.

"Just hold on."

Tom groaned when the cable burned his palms, but he didn't let go until the weight suddenly vanished. He was propelled backward with the wire in his hand. Jess screamed again, and a second later, a loud crash echoed around him.

"No!"

He crawled to the edge and saw Jess lying below, not moving. "Photons! I'm coming, Jess!"

Tom couldn't find anything to help him climb down. At that point, the worst he could do was jump, leaving Arlett up there. His chances of getting back up from the hole were close to impossible.

"Arlett," he said, picking her up. "Come on."

She started to mumble.

"Listen," Tom said, walking toward the edge. "I'm going to lower you down."

Arlett's eyes widened when he set her by the ledge. The second her legs were dangling off, she gave a shy scream, and her nails dug into Tom's arm.

"I won't let you go."

He kept sliding her down until he was holding her by the armpits.

"Now listen, you'll fall for a second, but the floor is right there."

Arlett shook her head, but Tom ignored her. He held her until he only had a grip on her hands. Unlike Jess, she fell less than five feet, and although she screamed and there was a crash, this one wasn't that loud.

He didn't wait and let himself down the edge, then jumped. As soon as he touched the floor, he rushed over to Jess. Thankfully, she was sitting up, holding her head.

"Sunshine," he said, grabbing her cheeks and making her look at him. "Let me see."

"I'm—"

"You're not fine, Jess."

He checked her arm, and although he wasn't a doctor, it didn't look like a scratch to him. He opened her jacket, and the little her corset allowed him to see was scary enough.

"Holy Maker, Jess!"

The skin by her hip and under her armpit had a deep purple and green color, and it had started to swell.

"How did you—" He exhaled. "You need a hospital."

She smiled at him, but it wasn't reassuring—quite the opposite. And when she didn't fight him, the urge to save her grew even bigger inside him.

"What is this place?" he asked, standing up to check it.

He would have assumed it was a fancy meeting spot because of the clear dome above. Instead, they were surrounded by huge steam engines, gear mechanisms, and massive reflectors.

"A generator?" he said, trying to find a door.

"Tom," Jess said, and he rushed back, kneeling in front of her. "Look." She pointed behind him.

On the other side of the room was a grand window. It took him a second to comprehend that the parking lot with sirens, lights, and debris was in Axiom. He was looking at his now-destroyed building, even though he was in a mansion in Chaos.

"What is this?" He looked at Jess. "Karen managed to create a portal? Why is no one here?"

"I guess the small war on the other end is keeping them busy." She had to take short breaths, and her voice was faint. "Do you see that?" She pointed to the wall next to her.

A larger engine that almost touched the floor above them covered the entire wall. For a moment, Tom thought she was thinking about climbing up, but then he spotted the blue light and the glass box underneath it.

"The skeleton key?" he said. "Is that the relic? Not very creative."

"It usually isn't the obvious item."

He looked again and noticed a metallic ring at the top of the elegant copper key.

Jess tried to stand, but he easily held her down, careful with her arm. "You shouldn't move."

She stared into his eyes, and he felt as if the surrounding temperature dropped. "Tom, I have to—"

"No." He tried to get up to reach the relic, but Jess grabbed his sleeve.

"Don't touch it... not yet. The moment we remove it, all the people you think should be here will get here."

"So, let's go." He turned toward the newly opened portal, but Jess didn't move. "I'll bring Arlett, and—you can walk by me."

"You saw Chaos, Tom. You saw its predators and how dangerous it is. I can't let those things into Axiom."

He shook his head and swallowed a knot. "All right, I'll leave you and Arlett safe in Axiom, then I'll come back."

Jess bit her lip. "Can you guess what will happen the second one of us crosses this portal?"

Tom rubbed his face. "And what do you want? To stay here, shooting at them? I don't even know where your gun is!"

"You take Arlett and the relic—"

"No." He folded his arms, but she kept going.

"You can run to the portal—"

"No, Jess."

"Once you cross, I'll wreck the—"

"Jessica! No!" He grabbed her healthy arm and gently held the back of her neck. "I'm not leaving you."

She put her hand on his and sighed. "I will destroy the portal."

"You don't know how to do that."

"You taught me how." She smiled. "The tunnel? Close to your grandpa's house?"

"Please, don't ask me to... Jess, you're hurt—no, injured. I can't abandon you. I won't." His eyes felt wet, and his throat ached, so he rubbed his face again. "Don't ask me to leave you."

"Tom, I can't live knowing I could have stopped this." She glanced down and winced. "And I won't stay here," she said. "Phoebe will find me."

"How do you know that?"

"Her job used to be locating lost agents."

He pushed his hair back and groaned. "There has to be another way."

"There isn't, and you know it." Jess wiped his face. "Take Arlett to the hospital. Your truck is still over there."

He stared at her.

"No one else drives such an old car."

He turned to the portal, and to his surprise, he saw his truck surrounded by debris and dust.

Tom grabbed Jess's hand and touched her cheek. "Promise me. No, swear to me that you won't go looking for Karen. That you'll stay here and hide and wait for Phoebe to come find you."

Jess nodded, but it wasn't enough.

"Promise me, Jess," he said, and a few tears threatened to escape his eyes again.

She inhaled and cleared her throat. "I swear it. I won't look for her, and as soon as I can, I'll find you."

Tom kissed Jess, and this time it tasted of sand and finality. He pressed his lips against her forehead and then quickly retreated without glancing at her. Otherwise, he would have lost his courage to leave. He wiped his eyes while walking toward Arlett and helped her by his side. This time, he would need his hands.

When he turned, Jess was supporting herself by the wall closer to the relic, waiting for him. She smiled at him when he stopped in front of her, but her face was far from happy.

"Here." Carefully, she took her necklace off and placed it in Tom's hand.

"I don't understand... why?"

"Remember what I told you about the relic? Crossing over and living in different realms increases their power."

He looked at the small cuckoo clock necklace in his palm. She didn't have to say anything more. Jess's realm key had to be more powerful than Karen's. Now he understood Marshall's reason for making a deal with Bill—he wanted Jess's key, not Karen's relic.

Jess closed his fist, and his eyes met hers. "It isn't the obvious thing, although it may be hard for you to figure it out." She tilted her head. "I love the little clock, but you handmade the chain."

He didn't have time to reply.

She reached up and took the glass box with Karen's key inside. A red light illuminated the place, and the portal flickered for a second. Around them, sirens went off while Jess handed the skeleton key to Tom.

"Once you get back, find a way to toss it into the Barrier."

"Jess..."

"Go, Tom." With great effort, she moved to the middle of the room, where he could now see her gun.

Something smashed through the doors. He put Jess's necklace into his pocket and rushed toward the window looking at the parking lot in Axiom. Behind the metal entrance, people's shouts started to reach them, and a second later, he heard the first shot.

Arlett jumped at his side and pulled herself closer to him. The quick movement launched her dress in front of Tom's feet. He got stuck in the fabric and tumbled forward, barely having time to hold on to Arlett and the key, unable to see if Jess was still there.

A bright light blinded him at the same moment a loud explosion propelled him forward. A sudden cold turned into intense heat right before he hit the asphalt of the parking lot, knocking the air out of his lungs.

Karen's key landed a few feet away from him, and Arlett tumbled at his side.

Tom coughed and, half crawling, half running, reached the space where the portal had been just a second ago. Similar to what had happened back at the lake, a bunch of rocks and metal pieces covered the opening, camouflaged by the surrounding debris.

He stepped back.

The sunlight shone, allowing him to see the new landscape. Instead of a green lawn with perfect landscaping and a glass building with balconies, rubble and dust filled the place. Ambulances, patrols, and firetrucks were parked all over the destroyed yard, along with police officers and agents in uniform. No one seemed to have noticed them.

He covered his face and fell to his knees. Carefully, he took off Jess's necklace and stared at it.

"Tom," Arlett said behind him, and the fabric of her dress shuffled toward him. "I'm—I don't know what—"

"No," he said, moving toward the skeleton key—a meaningless object with a silly ring around it. His entire life had changed for such an inconspicuous thing.

He picked the key up, and an electric shock almost made him throw it away.

"Let's get out of here," he said as he shoved the key into his pocket.

36

Axiom Realm

188A22 Year Week 18,
First day, Midmorning

Tom felt slightly hopeful when he found his truck keys inside the pocket of the jacket he had borrowed from Gall-I. If he could recover such an insignificant item after all the mayhem, he'd have better chances of finding Jess again.

He grabbed his steel tweezers and, being careful not to cut Arlett's skin, broke the handcuffs off her wrists. It hadn't been easy, but he couldn't imagine the hospital not asking questions if he arrived with her in chains.

The drive to the hospital was thankfully short. At his side, Arlett kept rambling, and from time to time, she sobbed and apologized.

Tom didn't ask questions and did his best to check on her when she was quiet, making sure she was still breathing. However, he just wanted her to shut up.

He wasn't ready for the chaos in the emergency room.

Dozens of ambulances were parked at the front entrance. People kept coming in and out of the building, pushing beds or bringing bags, blocking the entrance. A very different sight from only two days ago.

He decided to avoid the main door. Although it would have been the fastest way to find help, he had no desire to fight his way inside that place. His hands continued to shake, and his jaw hurt as he fought to contain his anger.

He used the garden gate. People also blocked that exit, but he only had to push four or five concerned visitors who weren't shy about expressing their complaints about his manners.

"Bill?" Arlett said when he sat her on a bench.

"You need to see a doctor."

"Please, Tom..."

He didn't have the heart to stop her. If they had switched places, no one would have been able to take him anywhere but to see Jess.

He made his way to the nurses' station, but it was empty. Waiting for someone to help them was a waste of time, so he jumped to the other side of the counter to look for Bill's room number. No one cared to check on him, not even the guard by the entrance, who seemed more concerned with moving out of the path.

The desk was a mess of papers that sat randomly everywhere. Tom opened the cabinet under the counter. From it, two lines of metallic file hangers hung from each door. He figured each line belonged to one of the hospital's floors, but he didn't understand how they arranged the patients.

Jess's memory came to him. She had sat for hours with him, trying to help him study, and never once doubted him. Even in that stupid mansion, she trusted he would figure out where to go.

Tom sighed and stared at the files. He was certain the main floor was for emergencies, and he knew Jess and her mom had

been on the second floor for intensive therapy. Feeling confident, he grabbed the papers for the third level.

The typing font looked so small that Tom felt a headache
coming on, but he had no choice except to read. After a deep
exhale, he rubbed his face. The letters seemed to become smaller,
so he used his finger as a guide to get through the names.

He finished all of that level and half of the fourth before he
found Bill's last name, Hiem-Sagac, highlighted and attached to
something that looked a lot like a police report. There was no
way he would read all of that, so he overlooked it and focused
on finding the room number.

As soon as he got it, he jumped out of the station. He had
lost enough time. However, when he was going to get Arlett, he
noticed an empty wheelchair in a corner.

"This should be better," he said, pushing the chair.

She grunted when he sat her in it, but Tom ignored her and,
at a fast pace, walked to the elevators.

When the elevator opened on the fourth level, he was half
expecting to be shot. Instead, considerably fewer people wel-
comed him. By the window, he recognized Amelia and Dan. She
was looking outside, and he was resting his head on the back of
a chair.

Tom didn't feel like talking to anyone, especially Jess's mom,
so he just pushed the wheelchair down the hallway.

The shades were closed in Bill's room, and a lot of machines
kept a steady beeping. For a second, Tom wondered if he had
made a mistake, but he didn't have time to check, because Arlett
grabbed the sheet on the bed and was trying to pull herself up.

"Bill..." Her voice was barely above a whisper, but Bill woke up.

He pushed himself up on his elbows and looked at Tom first, then he stared at Arlett, and the signal sped up.

"Arlett?" Bill sat up.

Tom noticed a small box that fell open from Bill's hands, but Arlett's dress blocked it before he could realize what it was.

She quickly leaned over and hugged him while he kissed her head.

"What happened? Dear Maker, you need a doctor!" He glanced at Tom. "You should have taken her to the emergency room. She needs medical attention!"

Tom rolled his eyes and crossed his arms. "Did you sell your sister to a Corrupt?"

Bill's eyes widened, and he looked away, keeping Arlett in his arms. "Not now."

Tom chuckled and walked closer to the bed. "Not now? Really? What were you thinking?"

"I was thinking about saving my fiancée!"

"By setting a trap for Jess! Photons, Bill! What's wrong with you?"

Bill shook his head. "She messed it up. All right?"

"Who messed it up? Jess?"

"Yes, Jess! Always Jess!" Bill gently moved Arlett and worked his way to sit at the edge of the bed. "She wasn't supposed to be at the wedding. That's when Marshall changed the plans. I didn't think he would hurt her. The deal with Marshall was to finish his house. I figured he was passing resources and using the construction project to cover it all, but he only wanted a stupid thing from Jess."

Tom paced around the room. "You have to be kidding! She is your sister! You knew exactly who Marshall was. It never occurred to you that he could hurt her?"

"She is an agent, Tom!" Bill raised his tone, standing up. "She is as corrupt as them!"

"Don't you dare—" Tom tried to jump the bed, but something grabbed the back of his jacket and pushed him face-first against the wall.

"Well, look who we have here."

Tom couldn't see his assailant, but the voice made his blood boil, and he closed his fists so tight that his nails dug into his palms.

Steps filled the room, and his captor forced Tom to turn and look at the room. Another three guys had walked in. Two of them stood by Bill and Arlett, and the last one grinned at Tom.

"Randall," Tom said, and in response, Randall punched him in the stomach.

The lack of air and intense pain forced Tom to bend down. The person holding him let him go, and Tom fell to his knees, gasping.

"Jess's lover," Randall said. "I wonder what Marshall will do if I just take you to him."

"What are you talking—?" Bill yelled, but a guy held his arm, and another guy pushed Arlett onto the bed.

"Oh no!" Randall covered his mouth, shaking his head. "You didn't know your sister is an easy slut? It hurt me too." He turned to Tom. "Speaking of, where is she?"

Tom's heart started racing, and his hands were shaking out of frustration.

"I see." Randall sighed, placing a hand on his heart. "That's too bad. I really was looking forward to teaching that bitch why she shouldn't cheat my family."

"Like you didn't betray your brother!" Tom yelled.

The person behind him hit the side of his head, causing the room to spin. Then Randall pulled him up by his hair until their eyes were at the same level.

"Hand it over," Randall growled.

"Hand you what?"

A guy grabbed Arlett's arm and yanked it back, making her scream.

"No!" Bill shouted, but the guy holding him grabbed his neck and pushed him against a wall.

"Jess's key," Randall said, getting Tom's attention. "Well, a relic now, I guess. Bonus points for me. Give it to me!"

Tom put his hands up when the machines attached to Bill turned their alarms on and Arlett's scream filled the room.

Randall nodded, and the guy behind Tom let him go.

"Does Karen know about this?" Tom didn't care for the answer, but he needed to gain a few seconds.

Randall grinned, fixing his suit.

"Interesting," Tom said, shoving his hand into his pants pocket. He pretended to look for the key, but instead he held Jess's chain between his fingers and broke the chain. As he pulled the cuckoo clock charm out, he let the chain slide back into his pocket. There was no way he would give the real key to those bastards.

"It's just fair," Randall said. "Now we both have one."

Tom opened his fist, and the little silver charm shone in his palm. Immediately, Randall held his hand out in front of Tom. "We have to keep the balance," he said.

"Let them go first," Tom dared to say, and to his surprise, Randall complied and waved at his men.

They released Bill and Arlett. Half coughing, and with the alarms still sounding, Bill climbed onto the bed and checked on Arlett, who was curled up and crying.

Tom's stomach twisted when he placed the cuckoo clock in Randall's greasy palm. Randall loudly kissed it and put it inside his pocket.

"You want to talk about betrayal?" Randall said, pushing the sheets and grabbing the small box. He closed it and tossed it to one of his guys. "Just as we talked, Billy, you and your girlfriend don't have to worry anymore. You did a great job."

Tom turned to Bill, hoping he'd misunderstood, but Randall's laugh confirmed his friend's betrayal.

The guy holding Tom dragged him back and slammed him against the wall one more time.

"Nothing good comes to those who cheat," Randall said. "Thanks for the assistance, though."

Randall's men followed him out of the room. The last guy took a moment to kick Tom before slamming the door.

Tom coughed as he pulled himself up. A rush of energy traveled through his veins, causing his muscles to numb and making the trembling of his arms impossible to contain.

Bill held his side, his face contorted in pain, glaring at Tom. "Why are you looking at me like that? I'll do anything to save—"

"Your sister saved her life," Tom said in a low tone. "Jess could have left Arlett with her mother, who, by the way, looked thrilled to lock her in one of Randall's cells. What do you think he would have done to her?"

"Exactly! What was I supposed to do?"

Tom shook his head and pushed his hair back. "Do you even care where—what she had to do to save Arlett?"

"No, Tom, I don't care."

"Bill," Arlett said, pulling herself up as she held onto Bill.

"No, Arlett." Bill gently forced her to sit down. "Stay out of this one." Then he looked at Tom with his chin up, crossing his arms. "Jessica is an arrogant, selfish, spoiled girl who always does what she wants and doesn't care who she hurts along the way."

Tom clenched his fists at his sides.

"Bill, stop!" Arlett said, holding on to his shirt. "Please, don't—"

"No. He needs to hear this." Bill pushed Arlett's hands away and took a tumbling step closer to Tom. "You are blind and stupid! I can't believe you even like her! She is nothing but—"

"Shut up," Tom said, controlling his tone. "You are the one who sold—"

Bill's jaw set. "I'll do anything to save Arlett. I love her."

"That's not a justification for what you did to your own sister—a sister who, despite everything, still cares for you."

"It's a solid reason in my book! It's not my fault you have never put those you love first."

"Bill, no!" Arlett launched herself up, blocking Bill. "He doesn't mean it, Tom. He is just—"

Tom jumped to the other side of the room and easily moved Arlett out of his way. In a quick movement, he punched Bill in the stomach so hard his hand hurt.

"Not your fault?" Tom kicked Bill's side and grabbed him by his shirt. "You are the photonic arrogant bastard who has been getting away with everything you want."

"Stop!" Arlett yelled, grabbing Tom's jacket, but he pushed her to the side and punched Bill's jaw. The sound of cracking bones made Tom shiver, but he just kicked Bill's side again.

"You are right, though. It's time for me to do anything for the one I love."

Tom pulled out the wires from Bill's arm and crouched in front of his face. "Your sister is worth everything. Not you. Never you."

He punched Bill's face, and blood covered his knuckles.

Tom let him go, shaking his hand while Bill hit the ground. He stared at his blood, and Jess's image came to his mind. She was bleeding, injured, and maybe she would be at his side if they hadn't gone back for Arlett. She shouldn't be dying alone to save these two pieces of the void.

Bill tried to get up while Arlett grabbed Tom's jacket, trying to pull him away. To her bad luck, the way Arlett was trying to save Bill reminded Tom of how Jess always looked out for him.

He couldn't help but think about Jess smiling at him in the Village, completely oblivious to the danger her brother had caused. He lifted his leg and launched it down against Bill's back with all his strength. Beneath his boot, he felt more than heard something crack, right before Bill's body went limp.

Arlett's scream was echoed by another one, and a pair of stronger arms shoved Tom to the side.

"Tom! Stop!"

The firm tone made him look up.

"Stop!" Dan said again, pushing him away from Bill. "What are you thinking?"

"Bill!" Amelia rushed over and kneeled by her son, who wasn't moving anymore. "You killed him!"

Arlett covered her mouth, falling to her knees. "Please, no…"

Tom lifted his arms, trying to control his breathing and his rage, so Dan let him go and went over to Bill.

Tom turned just in time to see doctors and nurses rushing into the room. He bumped into the bed as they pushed past him and rushed out of the room just before the mass of medics showed up.

He was about to go down the hall but stopped short and ran the other way. The emergency exit and the stairs to the parking lot would be a better escape route.

Bill was a son of the void and should pay for what he did to Jess, but the part that hurt him the most was that his best friend had been right. He should have put Jess first.

Tom took the steps two at a time. If he moved fast, he might have time to reach her.

The light of the sun blinded him for a second, but he didn't stop. He kept running around the corner until he bumped into an enormous man near the parking lot. The man grabbed Tom by his shirt and pulled him up so only his toes were touching the ground.

"Take it easy, Yttri," another person said. "He isn't our ene-my."

The big guy carefully set Tom down.

A peculiar view opened to Tom's eyes. Black cars were block-ing the entrance to the lot. Tom recognized Randall's guys. Some were kneeling, while others were lying down. A group surrounded them, pointing shotguns at them. None of the newcomers were wearing uniforms, and their humane protocol seemed to differ from the Agency's, as most had been badly beaten.

"It's never a good idea to try to play me," the man said.

When Tom glanced at him, he noticed the resemblance. He had the same eye color as Randall—callous and obscure. Their noses and hair looked similar, but this man seemed more com-posed, confident, and with no hate or guilt in his voice or ex-pression.

"Marshall?" Tom asked.

"Yes." Marshall stared at him for a second. "And you must be my older brother."

Marshall walked around Tom, examining him. "I can't be-lieve Randall didn't notice. Well, his brain stopped working long ago." He tapped his mouth with a finger, never taking his eyes off Tom. "What do you think, Yttri?"

Yttri didn't move or say a thing, but Marshall smiled wider. "Your eyes..."

Tom looked at Marshall, and if he hadn't opened those cells in the mansion with his blood, he would have never known they were related.

"What do you want?" Tom said.

Marshall turned to the big guy. "Yttri. Did you hear that? He is asking what I want. Isn't that the sign of a nice big brother?"

He moved closer to Tom and lowered his voice. "My father... is he... by any chance, could he be alive?"

Tom remained quiet. He had no idea how to answer. He had seen the body—his own father—and had no desire to think about it. To him, it was still just a gross image that one day might grow into meaning in his mind, but to Marshall, it was his family.

Marshall took a deep breath and patted Tom's arm. Yttri moved a step closer and crossed his arms, never taking his eyes off Tom.

"He—my father—he ordered us not to reach out to you," Marshall stated. "My mother, of course, hated you, but respected my dad's past. You and your mom were before her time... our time."

Marshall looked back at Yttri, and his joyful tone and smile returned. "I didn't expect to find so much of Dad in you, though. I mean, the order you gave to my guys; just to make sure I recognized it was Randall?" He huffed. "Brutal! I'm proud, and slightly jealous."

Tom followed Marshall's gaze. Sitting against one of the cars, he barely recognized the now-destroyed fancy suit and broken nose of Randall.

Tom shook his head. "I'm not like—"

"I know." Marshall waved his hand at him. "And you are in a hurry. We'll have time to talk... maybe." He reached into his pocket and pulled out the small cuckoo clock charm. "I'd offer you a car, but yours is way cooler."

Tom's eyes widened. "Why are you—" He stared at the silver charm but didn't dare take it. "What do you want? I won't betray Jess!"

Marshall tilted his head, grabbed Tom's hand, placed the charm on his palm, and closed it. "Good. She doesn't deserve any of this. She had nothing to do with it. Plus, I'm certain the chain is somewhere in your pocket? Useless without it, right?"

"You had a deal with Bill," Tom said, and Yttri took a step forward, but Marshall just nodded.

"To protect her from this, Tom!" He lifted his shoulders. "Sure, an agent and her key would have benefited the family business, but... well, I grew fond of her, and the safest place for her was with me. I mean, look at what her brother did to her. And her mother?" He rubbed his temples in a circular motion. "She isn't right. Protecting that jerk and pretending—anyway, now everything is different."

"You didn't want her key?" Tom asked. "You were going to kidnap her."

Marshall put his hands in the air. "Like I said, our families crossed paths, and Karen happened. Jess always looked out for me. She shouldn't have been in the middle. I'm sure we agree on that. I'm positive we also agree that now Karen will have to pay for it."

Tom looked from Marshall to Yttri, and then back to Marshall. He knew it couldn't be this simple, but he didn't want to figure it out. For a moment, he stared at Jess's charm in his hand, then he nodded at Marshall and walked away. He kept expecting that someone, anyone, would try to stop him, but he made it all the way to his truck, climbed in, and drove out of the parking lot unscathed.

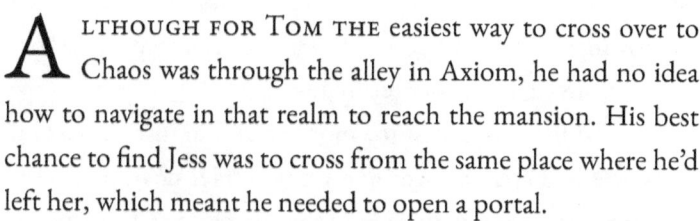

A LTHOUGH FOR TOM THE easiest way to cross over to Chaos was through the alley in Axiom, he had no idea how to navigate in that realm to reach the mansion. His best chance to find Jess was to cross from the same place where he'd left her, which meant he needed to open a portal.

The ambulances had already moved away from the collapsed structure, but the police patrols were still there. They were talking to drivers or passersby, but they didn't allow anyone near where he had to go.

"Photons!" He parked in front of the site.

Things looked worse in the sunlight. Chaos had cut his beloved construction into pieces. A bright light made it impossible to see behind the destruction, so Tom wasn't sure whether the concrete Barrier was still there or if the energy wave was floating out.

He removed the now-broken necklace from his pocket and held it in his hand. It had taken him a long time to put each small link of the chain together. He wanted it to be delicate, just like he used to perceive Jess. He had made nothing like it before, and when he finally gave up finishing it, he bought the charm. It was hard to believe it held that kind of power now.

Karen's key was still in his other pocket. He figured Randall didn't know they'd found it, because he never asked for it. He wondered if the airships they had seen flying over there weren't his, or if he'd sent them as a decoy so he could get Jess's key back in Axiom. Either way, it wasn't Tom's problem.

He stared at the keys in his hands, and realization dawned on him. Jess had told him these things gained power with the time their agents spent in the different realms and the number of crossings from realm to realm. He was now in possession of two very strong keys—especially Jess's.

She had lived in Chaos for months, and in just the last few days, she had crossed over many times. Her chain had to be one of the most powerful keys in the Agency, and he suspected Karen's was not far behind.

His engineering mind started to work. The Barrier was only a container for the energy wave, and he had never seen a container in Chaos. Like he told Jess, it probably meant the wave traveled underground in that realm, and he guessed the earthquakes had something to do with it, confirming the reason for the mansion not having a dungeon.

Things looked normal down the street. Not even a block away, he could see the top of the Barrier, still intact. The collapsed section had to have compromised the rest of the structure. All the energy behind that wall would react if he hit the right—or weakest—section, using the keys to push the particles between the realms.

Although he felt sick for doing it, he twisted Jess's beautiful chain into the rusted ring of the skeleton key and grabbed them with his left hand. He shoved the cuckoo clock deep into his pocket and turned on the truck's ignition.

As he pressed down on the accelerator, his truck responded just like it did on the third level of the highway. He gripped the wheel and kept his eyes on the tall concrete Barrier in the distance. He ignored the guards' signs to stop, and behind him, he overheard sirens but never looked back.

If the keys worked, he should be able to cross to Chaos to help Jess. If they didn't, he wasn't sure what would kill him first: the impact with the wall or the reaction of the energy wave to the keys in his hand. Either way, he just hoped the patrols following would find Jess and help her.

Jess hesitated, as her temperature seemed to drop, and the idea of hanging from a high wire again threatened to paralyze her. She tried to remember what Tom had told her about her fear of heights, and with that in mind, she broke the glass. After avoiding looking down, she forced herself to climb out.

Of course, her injured arm, back, and side didn't help. Thankfully, the window wasn't too high—she only fell a couple of feet—but rolled down the hillside of the rock formation until the shrubbery from the woods stopped her. Her nerves took over.

She ignored her pain and dizziness and pushed herself out of the grass. The blood on her shirt and her weak state were a beacon for predators.

All her energy vanished after climbing the hill by the mansion, and she felt stupid. She wasn't far from the house or the woods, and she didn't know where to go from here.

She kneeled and closed her eyes. Her body was in agony, but her mind was shutting down. She knew Phoebe would find her, but she doubted she would survive that long. As confirmation, a shadow covered her.

"Where do you think you're going?" a loud voice said, and a hand forced her to lie on her back. "You must be Karen's girl. I'm sure she'll love—"

The guy never finished his sentence.

The sound of a large explosion followed by a heat wave propelled him forward, headfirst into the rock a few feet ahead of them, turning his skull into a bloody blur.

Jess didn't dare to move. Above her, the color of the sky changed from grayish to green, orange, and then bright yellow, making her close her eyes. Her ears buzzed before she heard a second explosion—so loud that the rocks trembled.

She opened her eyes and watched a sort of bubble expanding from the woods toward her. A heavy pressure pushed her down the second it crossed over her and kept growing until it expanded over a mile or two. The ground vibrated underneath, and it felt different—like flooding in a pool. She looked down and, like a mirage, saw the houses of Main City through the rocks of Chaos. Everything stood still. Even the airflow stopped and became static.

A small dot moved up from the homes below. As it grew, Jess recognized Tom's truck speeding toward the mansion. Once it reached the edge of the bubble, its bumper, wheels, and hood smashed and pushed back, as if it had crashed into an invisible wall—but it went through.

She tried to stand up, but the ground dropped into a free fall, and the sudden drop pushed her upward. A few seconds later, she hit the ground, and the air was knocked out of her.

All around her, things changed. Instead of shooting, she heard screaming. The woodland now also had apartments among its trees. The mansion looked as if a sharp knife had cut it into pieces, and parts of a parking lot and houses grew in between them.

The buildings by the Barrier in Main City sat inside the woods and the mountains of Chaos. People were running out of the mansion, some holding guns and others holding kids. All of them were panicking and had no sense of direction.

Although her body screamed at her, she forced herself to her feet. The hill she stood on had been cut in half. Now, she was on top of a cliff above the streets, which was too high for her comfort.

Tom's truck had crashed in the middle of the mansion entrance and a bizarre water fountain.

"Tom..." she tried to yell, but her throat was dry, and her voice didn't seem to work.

The driver's door opened, and Jess sighed, holding her heart when she saw him. He tumbled out of the driver's seat and fell to the ground. Even from that distance, she could tell he was injured and confused.

She looked for a way down, but below, a well-known figure caught her attention.

Karen stomped out of the mansion and walked toward Tom's truck. She didn't seem hurt and knew exactly where she wanted to go.

Jess ran toward the shotgun of the guy who had just tried to kill her. She would have no trouble making a shot from this distance, but her left arm kept trembling, making it impossible even to rest the gun on her shoulder.

She lay on her stomach and pulled the barrel, using the ground to stabilize her aim. She took a few fast breaths and then dragged her arm forward. Tears blurred her vision, and she bit her lip so hard that a metallic taste filled her mouth. It wasn't only the excruciating pain but also her fear for Tom's life.

Not even a day ago, she had known Karen as her protector and mentor—the supportive mother she never had—and now she was about to kill Tom.

Axiom-Chaos Collision Realm

188A22 Year

Week 18, First day, Late morning

T OM PUSHED HIMSELF OUT of his truck, gasping for air. His head was spinning, his torso weighed a ton, and he couldn't move well, as if something had ripped it open.

"Jess!" he said as loud as he could, but it made him cough and spit blood. "Jess..."

He pulled himself up and rested against the back tire.

Everything smelled burned, and the surrounding smoke made his eyes watery and itchy, blocking his view. The only sign he had that his plan had worked was his being alive. No one could survive a frontal crash into a concrete wall.

Something kicked Tom in his side.

"Finally!" a woman's voice yelled in front of him.

He fell sideways and held his abdomen, struggling to breathe and cough at the same time. He tried to crawl or move, but he only managed a few inches.

Too close to his ear, he heard footsteps. A second later, some-one grabbed the back of his shirt and pushed him up against his truck. Through smoke and tears, he made out a woman's face level with his eyes. She pressed her fingers so hard against his cheeks that her nails dug into his skin.

Tom had a tough time focusing. His vision was a mix of blurs and light spots, and his mind refused to concentrate on what was happening.

"Arlett is so stupid. I told her you wouldn't be an awful husband." She moved his face from side to side without letting go. "Not so bad looking either—similar to your father. But of course, my foolish daughter had to fall for the wrong guy. Just like your mother."

Tom tried to grab her hand, but she released him.

The sudden movement made everything spin. His stomach turned, and a metallic taste filled his mouth. The effort of trying to throw up made his head pulse, so he ended up half spitting up and half choking.

"Jess..." he said.

The woman laughed. "Really? After years of playing and hurting her? You want to redeem yourself now?" She pressed something cold and metallic under his chin, forcing him to look up. "If it wasn't for her broken heart, she would have never left the labs." She pushed harder, forcing Tom's weak arms to try to hold her back, but his effort only made her laugh louder.

Tom finally recognized what was pressing against his throat after hearing the unmistakable click of a gun being cocked. "I'm sure your father would have—"

A shot rang out in the distance, startling him. Immediately after, a warm liquid splashed across his face, and the gun's barrel stopped choking him.

It took a second for Karen's body to drop to the ground.

38

CHAOS-AXIOM
COLLISION SECTOR

JESS WAS SITTING ON a bench inside the emergency room of Main City Hospital. She doubted these wards had ever been this full. There were beds and stretchers in the hallways. Doctors and nurses, along with agents and police officers, kept going up and down in a rush, as if moving fast would solve the problem outside.

It had been hours since Phoebe found her trying to get down the hill. She had wanted to take her away, but Jess had forced her to find Tom.

The image would never leave her mind.

He was lying on the ground, surrounded by blood. Too much blood. He was barely breathing, and she couldn't make him open his eyes. The only thing they could do was make sure the agents took him to the emergency room. She had asked Phoebe to go with him and made her promise she would force the doctors to check on him.

Since her wounds weren't as severe as many others, she waited to get a ride to the hospital. On the way there, what she saw broke her heart and dropped an immense weight on her shoulders. The city seemed to have been under attack.

In her home realm, some of Chaos's structures were visible and as damaged as the ones from Axiom. The sky was dark, and she could hear the rain hitting the windows. The worst was the sight of sneaky creatures lurking in the shadows of the streets. It was just a matter of time before those attacks started.

She sighed and struggled to stop thinking about the world outside. The surrounding view wasn't any better, though.

The tall figure of Yttri caught her attention as he easily made room to approach her. Part of her tried to become alert, but her body was in no condition to respond, so she just watched him until he stopped in front of her and handed her a folded paper.

"What is this?" Jess asked.

As usual, he didn't speak. Instead, he pointed at his eyes before moving to check on another patient on the other side of the hallway.

"There she is," a nurse exclaimed near Jess.

"Agent Hiem-Sagac?"

She looked at the pair of agents approaching her. The Agency was a large institution, so it wasn't surprising she didn't know them. "Yes?" Her heart sped up, and a knot grew in her throat, anticipating the worst.

"I'm sorry to bother you. We understand you aren't feeling well, but..." He shook his head and lowered his voice. "The system upstairs failed, and we can't identify two of our criminals."

"Criminals?" She looked at Yttri, who discreetly moved his hand up and pointed at his eyes.

"Yes. We have orders from the Agency's director to take them into custody—the guy in the truck and the man we found in the parking lot earlier today."

Jess held back her tears as her chest tightened. She was familiar with the Agency's protocol. They would blame Tom for everything: the Barrier failing, the explosions, the deaths—all of it. How could she be the one identifying him?

"I... umm... I'm not sure how—"

Yttri moved a wheelchair beside them and smiled at the agents. One of them took a step back, and the other had trouble taking his eyes off Yttri. Jess just inhaled and slid down onto the chair. He handed her the paper again and gestured for the agents to walk ahead.

As he pushed the wheelchair behind them, Jess unfolded the sheet.

She had seen it before—when Marshall was completing the paperwork for the next part of the undercover job. He had explained to her that their marriage paperwork had to be prepared in Chaos; otherwise, his people would never believe it. Like everything in that realm, it differed from any marriage certificate in Axiom.

The one in Jess's hands had names, witnesses, the place of the wedding, and the physical description of the couple. According to Marshall, it wasn't strange in Chaos for individuals to impersonate others and have fake marriages. Holm had confirmed it and made her sign the paper before handing it back to Marshall.

As the elevator went up, Jess read the first lines, and her heart skipped a beat at what she saw. Instead of Marshall, Tom's full name—Tom Umbrar-Ment—appeared on the certificate.

Marshall's description had been replaced by Tom's, and even his signature seemed legitimate. She read every paragraph twice, remembering how Yttri had pointed at his eyes.

Jess felt her hands trembling as she started to understand Marshall's plan. The Agency would take Tom prisoner and, without a doubt, send him to the Square. However, he wouldn't go as the driver who destroyed the Barrier and caused a section of the realms to collapse. She still needed to figure out why Marshall wanted to save him—and who the man in the parking lot was—but it didn't matter. No other crime could compare with genocide.

In the Square, only family or lawyers could have access to the prisoners. Obviously, Marshall wasn't going to step in there, even if he was Tom's brother, but she would be able to do it as his wife. Jess realized, not for the first time, how assertive Marshall could be, and why the Agency hadn't caught him yet.

"We thought we had the prisoners identified by the Chaos agent," one agent said, "but a woman came and, in her statement, made it sound like we had switched them."

The elevator stopped and opened on a floor full of agents and only a few doctors. Phoebe was standing in front of Charlotte in a corner. Neither of them looked happy, but Yttri kept pushing the chair toward the other area, and Jess lost sight of them.

She recognized the extra machines, the wider halls, and the enclosed doors of the surgery and intensive therapy level of the hospital. It seemed like a lifetime had passed since the last time she had been there. A nurse stopped them and directed them into one of those windowed rooms she hated so much.

She bit her lip, hoping her cruel imagination was worse than whatever she was about to witness.

"Who are you trying to identify?" Jess said before she looked down.

Yttri patted her shoulder, and although strange, she felt a sense of support that almost brought her to tears.

"Well, we have the truck driver who was with you at the impact zone. We also got a tip that Marshall Neon-10 had been beaten up in the hospital's parking lot, so we arrested him before the—you know—the event."

Jess nodded and stood up. Her body trembled, reminding her of the broken ribs and torn muscles on her side. Careful not to bump her right arm cast, she held on to the edge of the window and looked down.

A man was lying on the bed. He had a tube in his mouth and a few in each arm. The CLEO system kept a slow but steady beep, and the serum drip followed its rhythm.

His face was swollen, some of his hair had been pulled out, and for what Jess could see of his legs and arms, someone had beaten him badly. A wave of rage traveled up her spine. It didn't matter his physical state—she immediately recognized the face of the other traitor, Randall.

"We think this is—"

"The truck driver," she said flatly.

"Ah... well, that's what the Chaos agent said, but the—"

She turned, frowning, and raised her voice. "Are you telling me you'd rather believe a confused civilian than a professional?"

"No, of course not, but the system—"

"I don't know what happened to the system, but that man isn't the one I was supposed to marry while undercover."

The agent shuffled his feet and looked down. "Understood. We just needed to be certain."

"You want to be certain? Check the color of their eyes. Marshall had a very peculiar eye color. This guy here? Nothing out of the ordinary—just cold and hostile."

Jess sat back in the chair, and her body thanked her for it. "Where is the other one?"

"He's in surgery. We can't access him yet."

Jess's heart sank. She didn't know if she would be able to see Tom before the Agency took him, and the idea of losing him was unbearable. Still, she kept a poker face when looking at the agents. "In that case, is there anything else you need, or can I rest now?"

One of them shook his head while the other opened the door. "No, Agent Hiem-Sagac. That'll be all. Thank you for your help, but please stay close. We may require more information later."

She nodded and let Yttri wheel her out of the room.

Randall came to her mind, and this time she shivered. Now she understood—the other part of Marshall's plan was to punish his brother for what he had done to their father, and she had just facilitated his success to the new chiefs of the Corrupts.

Yttri pushed the wheelchair over to Phoebe and Charlotte.

"Jess," Phoebe said when she was almost beside them, and walked toward her. "I'll take care of her now."

Yttri stopped pushing and was about to leave, but Jess touched his hand. She had done nothing like that before, and it felt intimidating and familiar at the same time. He looked back at her.

"Please, tell Marshall I'm very sorry for his loss." Then she lowered her voice to a whisper. "I'll be in touch."

Yttri nodded and walked away.

"He's quite a sight," Phoebe said, pushing Jess's chair down the hallway. "But like Holm said: desperate times bring desperate solutions."

"What do you mean?" Jess asked, though she feared the answer. "Does Holm know about Marshall changing the marriage certificate?"

Phoebe raised her index finger to her lips and lowered her voice. "Things are getting ugly for both realms. We need to find who's behind all of it. Marshall has a theory and will work with us. At least for now, it seems like the smart thing to do." She huffed. "We don't think it was just Karen behind all of this. The damage is immeasurable."

Jess stared out the window in the distance. Nothing looked like the realms she knew—the mix of buildings, the strange weather, the constant sirens, the airships in Axiom, the highway in Chaos, and above all, the screams.

From there, she could see a huge section of the Barrier missing, but that wasn't the problem. Just as Tom had imagined for years, the Barrier wasn't a division but a holder of the energy wave. Now the energy wandered free, destroying everything in its path, and it was impossible to contain or predict its movements. Worse, the realms had always been on top of each other, and now part of one had collapsed into the other.

"Is Holm working with the Agency?"

Phoebe crouched down and whispered in her ear, "Not really. He doesn't trust them anymore, but he needs eyes on it. Perhaps Peter... maybe you."

Jess stared at her for a moment before turning back to the window. She trusted Holm and would continue serving as an agent. It was also her best chance to get answers—and more importantly, to save Tom.

39

Axiom Sea Periphery

A LTHOUGH JESS WAS RELIEVED no one recognized her, she missed the lack of interest from the guards when she walked as one of them. Now, every pair of eyes followed her as she made her way to the visitation center. She couldn't blame them, though. By experience, she knew how odd it was for prisoners to have visitors.

"Wait here, Mrs. Umbrar-Ment," the guard said, pointing to a door.

At the name, Jess's chest tightened.

After she misidentified Randall and Tom, the Agency processed them into the justice system. Marshall waited until the public statement to announce the mistake. In a big display of power and massive panic, he—the new Chief of the Corrupts—showed himself free and alive, explaining how the Agency had only caught his half-brother, Tom. No one asked about Randall, and nobody ever named the truck driver who destroyed the realms.

Jess walked into a small room with a table bolted to the concrete floor. In the middle, it had a steel chain attached to the top.

Each side had a chair. In front of her, a metal door connected the area to the inside corridor of the second level of the Square. She wasn't supposed to know the prison layout or how Tom would have to walk around the facility—by the bridge—bringing him closer to the exit for when Holm turned on all the mechanisms.

The door behind Jess opened, making her jump.

"Sorry, ma'am," another guard said. "I have to go over some rules with you."

"Rules?"

The guard half-smiled. "Well, yes. For your safety."

"All right," Jess said, unsure if he could hear her heartbeat.

"You can't address the prisoner until the guard has chained him to the table. Got it?"

Jess nodded.

"He'll be sitting in front of you, and you shouldn't stand until you're ready to leave. You can't have any physical contact with the convict, but since this is a marital visit, we're a little looser with the rules. Still, we have cameras in here." He gave her a knowing smile that left an unpleasant taste in her mouth.

It was strange hearing people refer to her and Tom as a married couple. Hopefully, he had followed the lie of being married to an unknown wife. The prison had strict rules—only family and authorized personnel were allowed to visit the inmates.

"The doorbell is on the handle," the guard said as he passed a metal detector along her sides. "It'll call us the moment you touch it. The visit is over when you do. No drama."

He took Tom's photo out of her jacket pocket. "What's this?"

"Just a family picture."

He looked at her before exclaiming, "Hey! You left your ring."

Jess's temperature seemed to drop. That detail had never crossed her mind, but the guard returned the photograph and continued the inspection.

"That's a good thing. You would have had to remove them, and those valuable things get lost here too often. Can I see your shoes?"

It took a second for Jess to understand the question. "Oh yes, of course," she said, taking them off and handing them to him. "Do you need to keep those too?"

The guard laughed, shaking his head. "No! I'm required to make sure there's nothing in them."

Jess had to agree with that inspection. She used her old boots to carry tools and weapons all the time.

It didn't take him long to inspect them, and then he handed them back to her. She felt relieved they didn't plan to have her pass Tom a note or a weapon.

"All right, ma'am. You're ready." The guard moved toward the door and stopped before leaving. "You should just leave him. The prisoners here..." He shook his head. "Just scum. Especially yours."

He didn't wait for an answer and left Jess shaking. For a long time, she had thought the same about them. Now she kept questioning everything, including her own actions as an agent.

The silence that followed weighed on her. She kept trying to stop remembering the past and focus on the present, but it was difficult.

After a while, footsteps echoed in the corridor. Her stomach turned into an empty void, and once the door opened, her body trembled as she watched Tom walk into the room.

He was looking at the ground. His hands hung in handcuffs in front of him. Behind him, the guard held a chain that was connected to his waist and to the shackles on his legs. His feet were still bare, and she could see on his face the pain that each step caused him.

"Hands," the guard said, breaking the heavy silence and making Jess's breathing speed up.

Tom lifted his hands, and the guard released one of them and guided him toward the table. That was when he saw her, and Jess's heart traveled to her throat.

He stared at her while the guard locked one end of the handcuffs to the table. The new chain connected both wrists, keeping him attached to the table but giving him more room to move. If he wanted, he could have reached for her. But he didn't.

"All right," the guard said, pulling the chains to check them before turning to her. "If the bastard misbehaves, we'll teach him how to treat a lady."

Jess watched him leave and close the door behind him.

She looked at Tom. He had bruises on his face and a deep cut on his head. She could see it because of the extremely short haircut. The worst were his eyes, darting over her so much it made her fear he hated her.

"Well." He rested his arms on the table, far from her. "I'm not sure how I feel about my wife having such dark hair."

By instinct, Jess reached for her hair but moved her hand down when she noticed how much it was shaking.

He tilted his head and examined her. "No. I don't think so. Looks fake to me, but I had no idea I was married until today, so what do I know!"

Jess cleared her throat. "It's easy to hide like this."

"What? Why? You didn't care when you were engaged to Marshall, right?"

She bit her lip and leaned forward.

"Tom, please. It's different with—"

"What do I care? I thought it was Marshall who sent someone to visit. But you. I never expected to see you again. Never."

Jess looked down at his hands and noticed the bandage, full of dust and dried blood. His wrists had marks from the chains—ones she had no doubt must hurt.

"What are you doing here?" Tom said, crossing his arms and hiding his hands underneath them.

"I..." She didn't dare look at him. "I need to ask you—"

"What, Jessica?" He raised his voice. "You, above all of them, should know what happened. How I didn't know what I was doing... why I had to help you—"

She placed the old photo on the table. "When did you figure it out?"

Tom slid his hands over and picked it up. His hard features softened as he passed his fingers across the woman's face, holding the baby at her side. The color of his eyes had never changed. His hair, when it was longer, curled at his neck the same way. She hoped the cheerful smile from that child was still somewhere inside him.

"Where did you find it?" he said in a tone that almost eased Jess's mind.

"Holm," she whispered. "He recovered all of your belongings after the—"

"Of course." Tom tossed the photo back at her. "He wants to figure out how I did it, right? How I destroyed the Barrier."

"Shh!" Jess looked around, holding her breath. "No one knows that you were driving the truck. Here, you're the Corrupts' son, not the guy who—"

"Oh, I get it!" He leaned forward and, mocking her, lowered his voice. "You should have warned me about it, though. My buddies here thought I was making things up, and they never let me forget it."

Jess didn't know if it was his voice or his smirk that set her off.

"Warn you?" She sat back. "Apparently, you knew very well who your father was and what to do." "Did you know all along? Did your grandfather tell you? Was that the reason you hated the Agency?"

"No. Of course not..." he said, crossing his arms again. "But so what if I had? What do you care? You're an agent. I bet you would've just turned me in. After all, it makes me a corrupt, right?"

"Really? I would've never... How can you say that?"

"Don't you see where I am?" He leaned closer. "Let me ask you this: When did you figure out I was here?"

She shook her head, and her throat seemed to close. "Tom, it's not that simple. We—I—I had to—"

"So, you knew all along." He lifted his hands. "You come here demanding answers. Why? What do you care? Why now?"

She took a deep breath, hoping her voice wouldn't break when she spoke, but Tom kept talking.

"Oh, let me guess. Your mom asked you to make sure I got what I deserved for killing Bill. I mean, how to deny anything to your poor mother, who always preferred that bastard above you? Or was it Arlett who—"

"Stop," Jess said, almost inaudibly, and she only knew he had heard her because he became quiet.

"I haven't seen my mother since that day. And you didn't kill Bill. He won't walk ever again, but he—"

"For the Maker's sake! I wish you hadn't told me that. Killing that son of the void made my days brighter in here." He looked at the table, and his tone darkened. "He deserves that and more."

Jess slid her hand closer, but he moved back, and when his eyes met hers, there was no compassion in them.

"More than a year, Jessica. I've been here more than a year. And you were aware of it all along. Me? I thought you were dead. I believed—no, I was certain you must be. Otherwise, you would've come here sooner. You would've never left me in here."

"Tom, I—"

"Now I know better. You put me in here."

Jess started to cry and wiped her eyes, but her throat was too constricted to talk.

"For days, I followed you, trying to help you." He leaned back. "I thought I owed you at least that. So stupid." He chuckled. "So, so stupid. I believed we could be together, but it was all business to you."

Jess shook her head. "That's not true. I mean, yes, you were helping me, and I shouldn't have let you. But it wasn't just business."

"Oh, Jessica, it was." His smile sent a shiver down her spine. Now his resemblance to Marshall was undeniable. "You dragged me all over Chaos—a place I had no idea how to handle—and you didn't even tell me the truth. How long did it take you to tell me about your photonic boss? You could've told me everything in the Village before anything happened, and I would still have gone with you and—no. You know what? It doesn't matter. I'm rotting in here, and thanks to who?"

It confirmed Jess's worst fear: Tom hated her. Her hopes to make things better, to fix the problem, died. He was right, though. Everything was her fault.

She nodded and put Tom's photo back in her pocket. The guards wouldn't allow him to have it, and she didn't want to lose it. She'd already taken so much from him.

The guard's warning came to her mind, so she remained sitting. She wiped the tears from her face. "The next time the alarms go off, hold your breath for a few seconds."

She got up and turned toward the door. Her body responded, but it was numb, so when a hand grabbed hers, instead of turning, she looked down at it.

It took her a second to comprehend the handcuff at her wrist wasn't hers but Tom's, who was stretching the chain between his wrists as far as he could to reach her. He pulled her closer and half wrapped his arm around her waist. Jess felt his breath behind her ear as footsteps from both doors rushed toward them.

"I didn't..." Tom's voice was nothing but a whisper as his hand gently brushed hers. "Never come back, Jessica."

The door behind him opened and a guard shouted and grabbed Tom, pushing him hard against the table.

"You've hurt enough people already, bastard!" The guard punched him and slammed him onto the table.

"No! Stop!" Jess shouted.

Another guard stopped Jess from moving closer. "He didn't hurt me. He isn't trying to—"

The first guard pulled Tom's head back and slammed it against the solid surface. Tom groaned as blood dripped from the side of his mouth.

"You can't do this!"

Jess took a step forward, but the guard beside her picked her up and carried her out, closing the door behind them.

"What are you doing? He wasn't doing anything wrong!"

The guard let her down, blocking the corridor. She could hear more voices entering the room and things crashing into the walls.

"I told you to stay sitting until you were done. Those are the rules. Now, get out of here. Your visit is over."

Jess groaned but turned and ran down the corridor.

Time was running out. Holm had warned her. The guards didn't like visitors, and they would do anything they could to avoid future encounters with them. Tom might get beaten to death that afternoon.

40

EPILOGUE

188CH23 YEAR WEEK 24, SEVENTH DAY, NIGHT

THE WARMTH OVER HIS arms, the surrounding silence, and the shy light against his eyelids woke Tom. He sat up quickly, ignoring the pain in his head and expecting to be attacked. However, the space wasn't a dark, wet cell with concrete walls, and he seemed to be alone.

After a few deep breaths, his mind started to remember.

Jess had visited him. She had been with him in the Square and warned him about the assault.

After the guards pulled her out of the visitation room, the bastard holding him called the others. They had attacked him before, but this time, they were more aggressive. They even unchained him from the table to improve their accuracy while beating him up. Right after someone hit the back of his head with a hard object, Tom understood—he had allegedly assaulted a visitor, giving them an excuse to kill him.

The alarm went off, and although he barely heard it between his buzzing ears and the guards' shouting, he took a deep breath and held it. Jess hadn't told him about the bright light, but the memory of crashing into the Barrier surfaced in his mind, and he closed his eyes, realizing what was about to happen. If it weren't for the guard holding his arms, he would have jumped down onto the floor and covered his head.

Around him, everything shattered. Pieces of concrete fell from the ceiling, making the guards panic, and in their hysteria, they kept blocking the doors. After that, their erratic behavior became their worst enemy.

Tom moved to a corner and waited for them to kill each other. That was when everything turned pitch black, and only screams reached him.

It was his opportunity.

Tom's eyes adjusted to the darkness faster—at least something good had come from being in that lower prison. He grabbed a guard and used him as a shield while he rushed forward, pushing anything in his way. On the other side of the visitor's door, he stumbled into a similar scene of panic and anarchy.

He hadn't moved more than a few feet when a bright light blinded him and forced him to step back. He would never know what hit his head, but he felt his mind flood with confusion as his body lost the rest of its strength.

"I can't believe you found him!" a male voice said while two enormous arms grabbed him.

He had tried his best not to pass out, but everything was blurry, and the lights were bright. Eventually, he surrendered.

He didn't know how long it had been when he woke up in a room full of mechanisms. His defenses forced him up, but his head wasn't ready, so he stopped moving, hoping no one was about to attack him.

"My dear brother, you're up!"

Tom opened one eye and glanced toward the voice. He would be lying if he denied how surprised he was to see Marshall standing there—grinning stupidly and with his arms wide open.

Marshall walked over to Tom and hugged him, then pushed back and stared straight into his eyes.

"You are finally safe," he said. "Right, Yttri? Welcome to the family."

Tom recognized the bald guy behind Marshall and figured he was Hafni's brother.

"You need a shower," a woman said to him.

Tom's mind raced, trying to piece things together, when he saw Phoebe standing beside her husband, Holm.

"Probably sleep too," she said. "That'll help... a little."

Tom looked around the room. Jess's friend Peter was sitting at the far end, looking at Holm and ignoring him. He recognized Gall-I, staring out the window in front of her, holding a wheel. Of course, she didn't care to look at him.

The outside view caught his attention, and a chill traveled down his spine. The landscape was nothing but a dreadful sky full of pieces of steel and concrete, loose wires, and metallic nets—most of them on fire—and all of it was on their path.

"Holm," Peter said. "We have to find—"

"Let it go," Holm said.

"We can't just leave her—"

"Yes, we can. We have hard work ahead of us."

Phoebe stood in front of Tom and offered him her hand. "Let's get you somewhere more comfortable."

"Why?" Peter said, but Yttri turned toward him, and Peter quickly raised his arms. "Whatever."

"Tom?" Phoebe said, waiting for him. "Let's go."

Marshall smiled at him but spoke to Yttri. "Let's go. The view will be better from up there. We can explain everything to him later."

Tom had tried to stand and walk without help, but his feet refused to hold him, sending sharp pain through his nerves. Phoebe slid under his arm and helped him in silence.

She walked at his slow pace but never complained about his weight, and Tom was certain she was holding most of it. After they crossed the mechanics room, the hallways made sense to him—he was in one of those airships, and judging by the décor, it was likely Marshall's.

Once she stopped in front of a nice wooden door, she helped him inside a bedroom, where she let him down on a bed. The soft surface felt strange, almost dangerous, and mesmerized, he brushed his fingers across the smooth sheet.

"Try to rest before you clean yourself," Phoebe said, and instead of closing the curtains, she opened them wide. It was dark outside. "You'll enjoy this later."

She was about to leave when he managed to recover his voice.

"Phoebe..." She looked back at him, and her sad eyes answered, but still, he needed to hear it. "Jess?"

She played with the doorknob. "She's alive."

Tom sighed, and a crushing weight lifted for a second.

"But she took off," Phoebe added, making Tom's world sink. "Time. We all need it, Tom."

She left him with his memories and regrets after that.

Phoebe had been right. Hours later, when he woke up again, he was thankful for the view of the sun on the horizon and took a moment to enjoy its warmth. He had missed it for too long.

Tom rubbed the back of his head, and a large lump made him grunt. He noticed then the clean new bandage around his hand and the ones covering his feet.

He would live in debt to these people. Jess must have convinced them to help him, and now she wasn't here.

With a groan, he stood up. She had been trying to save him, and he had just insulted her. He'd let his confusion and fear lead their conversation, letting her believe he blamed her for what had happened to him. In reality, if he could travel back in time, he would go through all of it—and more—for her.

He limped to the bathroom and stared at his reflection. His eyes, once again, accused him of breaking the heart of the girl he loved.

This time, without thinking twice, he punched the mirror, shattering it into hundreds of pieces.

I HOPE YOU ENJOY the first installment of Collision of Realms; Chaos and are excited to read the next book: Axiom.

Book 2 Excerpt:

The Square's darkness had a weight on all prisoners and made everything tougher. Tom had no idea if it had been days or weeks before he got a hold of a loose rock by his cell and realized he could write on the concrete walls. The small pebble left greenish marks on his fingers that burned at night, but he didn't mind. It was worth it to make sense of his time.

It was then that he figured out things about the energy wave and the Barrier. He understood how he crashed it and, from the little he heard of the world outside, he also figured out why he destroyed part of both realms. It all sounded perfectly rational until he talked to Holm after they rescued him.

In summary, the old man told him he was bluffing and should move to the void. He left them for that reason and began working with Marshall. Why tolerate pity and being treated like an idiot if Jess wasn't present?

Footsteps echoed in the hallway, but he didn't bother to look up. Heli-3's persistence was too much for Tom after his fifth visit of the day. However, when a shadow covered the tile, and he sensed a presence looking at him, he knew it wasn't Heli.

He lifted his eyes and lost his breath.

Jess stood across the bars, gazing down at him. Her expression was severe, and the dark hair just made her look angrier. He couldn't blame her, though. He deserved her hate and would gladly listen to whatever she had to say to him. At least she would be talking to him again.

He stood up but was afraid to move closer, so he remained farther inside the cell. Time had no effect on her beauty or the way she made his heart race.

"KG," the sheriff said from far away in the hallway. "Let me know if you need anything. I really appreciate you coming down here. You are very busy, and this goofball probably doesn't deserve it."

Tom pushed his mouth closed; he couldn't agree more with the sheriff.

"Thanks, sheriff," Jess's voice eased Tom's nerves, just like it always did. "I just need a word with my brother."

She turned to Tom again. "Right, Randall?"

Tom chuckled, daring to take one step forward. "Of course, Karen."

Jess kept her eyes on the hallway for a few seconds, probably making sure the sheriff left. Then she crossed her arms, staring at Tom for what felt like an eternity.

"Randall? Really?" she finally said, lowering her voice and taking a step closer. "Did you consider how worried I would be if I found out he was looking for me?"

Tom's head flinched back slightly. "He is dead. How could he—" he shook his head and softened his tone. "I'm sorry, but it's not like I can use my name, Karen."

Jess pushed her hair behind her ears and looked away. "Well, I'm here now. What do you want?"

E VERY STORY HAS A beginning. Discover this one through a bonus chapter and a confidential Secret Dossier—waiting for you here.

41

GLOSARY

Edward Lorenz, American mathematician and meteorologist best known as the founder of the chaos theory.

Ophidents; poisonous creeping reptiles. It inhabits the wooded regions of the Chaos and Axiom meadows, particularly near the Barrier. Poisoning by this creature ranges from severe to fatal. An annual protective antidote is required for those who work or live in these areas. Aggression level: 5 out 5.

Takuosums, native mammal with extremely strong front limbs and claws, which allow them to burrow quickly with great power. It has a fur coat and a toxic array of spines. Capable of surviving in subterranean areas and a remarkable resilience to high oxygen concentrations but a limited resistance to light. An encounter with these creatures can be deadly due to their behavioral pattern of hunting in large groups, isolating their target and using poison to subdue and finally immobilize it. It is mandatory to report them when found in cities or transportation systems. Aggression level: 4 out 5.

Portal, an induce opening into the realm's energy that pushes the particles from one realm into the other, allowing a person(s) to cross between realms.

Relic, the given name to a portal-key when its owner dies. The power obtained through years of service is retained within the object until it is reintegrated into the energy wave. It is required to release this energy without hesitation, since this power source is open for anyone's use.

The Village, luxury destination sector within Main City, Axiom. The northern ocean's proximity, as well as the exclusive restaurants, clubs, and casinos, make this a popular destination.

The Square, a high security prison, was authorized by the Parliament of Axiom in 104A22 Year, and it opened the year after. The area was proclaimed a danger zone and shut off from 110A22 to 115A22 due to the extreme flooding. Following a succession of assessments, it was granted permission to reopen in 116A22. Presently, it has a notorious reputation for its extreme sentences and is known for its dubious.

CLEO, centralized panel utilized to guide the mechanical bugs in employing supplemental drugs, medications and electrical treatments to those in critical condition.

Chaos S-Group, one of the funder groups of Chaos. Descendants now possess the wealth and privilege that was promised to them in former treaties and agreements. Continue to have a considerable influence in the ruling

Hyaerodea, a carnivorous mammal that relies on scavenging carrion, yet is extremely dangerous when it comes to protecting their territory. These creatures are characterized by long skulls, slender jaws, cone-shaped teeth, slim builds, and a plantigrade

CHAOS: COLLISION OF REALMS

stance. Posses little to no capability to adjust to any sources of light. They could be located in all parts of Chaos, especially in locations with poor hygiene in cities. Aggression level: 5 out 5.

Remedy, an archaic phrase used in Chaos to describe a concoction of antibiotics, probiotics, and antidotes to increase the tolerance to the high levels of oxygen and other toxins within the domain.

Ium's family, the original rulers from Chaos, separated their legacy into 15 different groups and became lost during the early 120A era. As dictated by their earlier statutes, each group within this family was expected to specialize in a fundamental service for their people, for instance, housing, exploration, heritage, resources, nourishment, transportation, etc.

Aracnpoda, a class of joint-legged invertebrate animals with eight legs, possesses a front pair of legs that have sensory functions. This species does not rely on poison, instead it traps its prey with a sticky thread. It typically resides in humid, dark places and is commonly found as a co-habitant of other species, where it nests beneath its host's skin and nourishes itself with its host's blood. If signs of infection are present, medical attention should be sought out immediately. Aggression level: 2 out 5.

For your patience, support, belief in the cause, staying with me and tolerating the time that I took away from all of you to sit down and write. During these years, I learned so much from all of you. For listening to my stories, complaints, and successes. For your help and critiques, for all of these and more.

To Each one of you, who loves to read mysteries and took the time to read my take on them. My amazing coaches; Scarlett and Bryan, my mystery group friends, Mom, Gloria, Teddy, Josephine, and You up there...

Thank you.

Hi, I'm Monica Red, and I have a passion for forging worlds where magic collides with destiny, and adventure is never far from danger—or from the heart. From sweeping romantasy to daring steampunk adventures, my stories are filled with peril, secrets, and bonds strong enough to change the course of kingdoms.

My greatest inspiration is my daughter, whose courage and imagination remind me why stories of love and resilience matter. At home, I live with two loyal dogs, five outspoken birds, and a husband who insists that golf and sports are the only safe escapes from the battles, quests, and rebellions unfolding in my head.

When I'm not writing fantasy, I step into another realm of storytelling under the name Montie Red, where cozy mysteries bring twists, secrets, and the occasional murder to small-town life. Whether the journey is through enchanted forests, skies filled with airships, or quiet streets hiding dangerous secrets, I'm always chasing the spark of a good story.

Thank you for traveling these worlds with me—arm yourself with courage (and maybe a little tea), and let's embark on the next great adventure together.